The Pull of the Earth

# The Pull of the Earth

## TEAGUE BOHLEN

GHOST ROAD PRESS

A version of the first chapter was initally printed in *Please Stay on the Trail: A Collection of Colorado Fiction.* (Black Ocean Press, 2006.)

Library of Congress Cataloging-in-Publication Data.
Ghost Road Press
*The Pull of the Earth*

ISBN 0977127273 (Trade Paperback)
Library of Congress Control Number: 2005937311

Book Design: Sonya Unrein
Author Photo: Jake Adam York
Cover Photo: Teague Bohlen

Ghost Road Press, Denver, Colorado
ghostroadpress.com

### ACKNOWLEDGMENTS

This book would not have been possible but for the support of the following people and institutions. My sincere thanks go out to:

The faculty and my peers at Arizona State University's Creative Writing program, who started me down this road, and the faculty and my students at the University of Colorado at Denver, who were there to walk with me to the end.

My wife Becca, who helped talk the book out, offered some great ideas, and loved me throughout this process.

Tom Legendre, Christopher Merkner, and Jake Adam York, all who lent me their support, their advice, and their friendship.

Matt Davis and Sonya Unrein at Ghost Road Press, who liked the book even in its rougher stages, and pushed me to make it better.

Tom and Judy Ward, who appreciate the history here, even if they've never been to Moweaqua (yet).

The Moweaqua Library and the Moweaqua Coal Mine Museum for their help in my research, and Gale Stewart, who gave me all the stories a guy could want while riding around in the Ford Galaxie 500 my grandfather had sold him.

And of course, Mom and Dad, who believed in me from the beginning.

*To the people of Moweaqua, past and present.*

*To my family and friends, living and gone, for their support and inspiration.*

*And to my Grandma Rita, who always makes me feel like I'm home.*

# What Can A Young Man Do?

In conversation with a number of our young men from the farm one day last week, the question was asked, what can a young man do? Our answer is to stay on the farm. While farming does not promise the largest rewards in the way of wealth or fame, it offers compensations that may be as attractive and satisfying. A competent farmer with a good farm is assured of a comfortable living and can win a moderate fortune. He has the privilege of constant association with his family. He enjoys the greatest degree of personal and business independence. His products are articles of universal use. If one market will not take them, another will. He has no occasion to fawn upon clients or cringe to magnates. Commercial panics rarely affect him. His goods are still necessary; and while their value may be less, the cost of production is often more than enough lower at such times to make up the difference. In fact, his margin of profit is often greatest in years of depression. While farm life is laborious, there is often a variety about it that contrasts pleasantly with the monotony of a life spent at a bench or desk. To the lover of home, a farm life is delightful, in that it is a constant process of home development. Each tree and vine acquires a personal value to him far greater than its worth in money. All the domestic animals are his pets and friends. A well kept farm is a bit of landscape gardening that helps to make home beautiful, and is a tribute to the character of its owner.

—*Moweaqua Call-Mail, 1898*

# Chapter One

*1932*

IT WAS FALL, AND FALL MEANT THRASHING. Traveling thrasher-crews appeared again like spring corn as farmers found themselves without money to purchase their own equipment or to repair what they already had. So the first thrashers, the tank-like monsters of old technology, were brought out again, repaired, greased, and put on the road and up for hire. They were huge, all gears and belts and teeth, manned by either boys or desperate men, both willing to work long hours for short pay. Reese Moss was the former, Tom Horseman the latter. On the thrasher together, they became friends that autumn, bound by common labor, and near the end of the fall, by common tragedy.

Reese was sixteen years old, and his father still worked the Moss family fields. Reese loved the smell of the place, especially in the autumn when everything finished its slow but certain arc toward use. Kernel to leaf to stalk to husk to plate—that was the way of things. He liked the idea the beans he walked became someone's noon soup, or the corn he detassled became someone's supper, roasted and slathered in butter and salt. He understood enough about crops to know these dinner-table visions were nothing but whimsy—the beans were processed into oil and the corn was mostly fit for feeding livestock, but the idea of it was what mattered. He was *doing* something, and the thrasher was the last part, the golden part, with the chaff floating in the air and the yellow blur of field after field after field. It smelled like life. Reese mentioned this once to Tom, who laughed at him. "Life?" he said. "Everything around you is dying." Tom cleared his throat and spat into the stalks.

Reese paid him no mind. Tom was like that. They'd moved in the same circles those past few months, looking for work and often finding it together, walking beans out near Taylorville, working a hay baler near Bethany, and most recently, manning the thrasher. They'd come to know each other as men who labor together often do—the rhythm of a pitchfork swing, the smell of a sweat-soaked shirt, the grunt of a back heaving.

They worked the thrasher all over Illinois, farm to farm, and the work had led them right back home to Moweaqua. They had both been born there and knew the town well—the streets, the stores, the ways of people, and the people themselves. Tom talked about their return as though it would be a sort of homecoming, a parade for Moweaqua's favorite sons home from the outlying fields, men who'd dared to brave the plains, to survive outside the comforts of home. People would give them free coffee with sugar cubes, offer them jobs working their farms. Like men coming home from war.

Reese let him talk as usual, but thought it would be enough to sit in the shade of the elm near his house, or go down to Stroh's Pool Room on Main just to hear the ivory balls clicking together sharply over the low murmur of the men who gathered there. The Pool Room was the most indecent place in town—even before Prohibition—and every Moweaqua man loved it for that. Stroh's was one of the few places in town that didn't cotton to the Volstead Act, having a supply of whiskey readily available upstairs where they set up the duck pins. It was almost always full. It was where Reese's father had brought him on his twelfth birthday, bought him licorice whips and root beer from Ben Hudson's Drugs across the street, and brought him into Stroh's. Reese sat in the line of chairs against the north wall, the ones raised up on a short step to better see the green felt of the tables and watch how the balls rolled across like water on greased metal. Reese's father winked at him while he worked the table, and right before they went home, taught him how to hold a cue. Reese remembered every second, the smell of cherry tobacco, the smooth wood of the chair, the gunshot of a good break, the promise not to tell his mother. Reese saw himself doing the same for his own boy someday. He thought of it whenever he went into Stroh's Pool Room, whenever he racked the perfect ivory balls, whenever he tasted licorice.

Tom had no family. The only son of immigrant parents, his mother had died in childbirth. His father supported them by working odd jobs around town until he finally landed permanent work in the Moweaqua coal mine. It was a deep mine with a coal house and tipple atop the shaft, and it employed nearly one hundred-and-fifty men. Tom's father was killed there, crushed under falling slate. Tom was sixteen. From then on, Tom lived alone in the shack his father had built, surviving by working odd jobs, stealing when he had to. He swore he would never set foot in the mine..

"Bad place, Reese," Tom told him one night while they were drunk on homemade whiskey. "Bad place."

"I don't see why," Reese said. "Doesn't seem like such a bad job."

"Let me tell you something about the mine," Tom slurred. "My father once told me about this block of almost pure coal they brought up outta there. Back in '24. And when they hoisted it out of that hole, they saw something scratched into one side. Four numbers. Six. Six. Six. Six."

"Wow," Reese said. It seemed like the thing to say. "What did that mean?"

"What it meant," Tom pointed, "was that it was one more six than the number of the beast."

"Oh," said Reese. And then, "But what does that mean?"

"Bad place," Tom shook his head and took another swig. "Bad place."

Reese was also alone, though his parents still lived. His father was a struggling farmer, working his land on the northeast side of Moweaqua, barely able to feed himself, Reese's mother, and their livestock. Reese felt an obligation to find his own way, even if he had no idea what that way might be.

Tom and Reese found work at the Stombaugh place to the southwest of town, out where Flatbranch Creek ran. Old Stombaugh's thrasher had quit on him, and hiring the team was cheaper than getting the old one fixed. It was a five-man team: Reese and Tom; a kid Reese's age named Wozniak who everyone called Woes because it seemed to fit his long, troubled face; a dull-headed boy of eighteen named Stupak with thick arms and tree-trunk legs; and Fiddler, the group elder at thirty-five, whose real name was Fiedler, but who didn't know one end of a fiddle from the other. Tom, Reese, Stupak, and Woes were the muscle of the team, the feeders working the forks, and Fiddler was the spoutman. Two worked on the ground, heaving the wheat by the forkfull onto a platform, and the two up top scraped the sheaves in a bunch at a time. Chaff filled the air and grain spilled out the other side like a shower of gold into a wagon minded by the spoutman. They worked from dawn till dusk, Sundays off. On their third day, Fiddler fell sick with the flu and couldn't work the wagon. So Old Jules called in another man to take his place. He was a stranger from St. Louis.

Tom wasn't much for strangers. Neither was anyone else on the crew. A new man disrupted the cadence of the job, threw everyone off in his attempt to fit in. Either his swing with the fork was too slow, his pace was too fast, he talked too much, or he tried to be too friendly. Anything new was a nuisance, possibly a danger. The men on the crew disliked strangers despite the fact they had all themselves been strangers at one time or another. So by custom, they disliked this new man before they even met him, simply because he wasn't Fiddler.

It was sunup when they met and the fields were quiet, aside from a cold wind coming up from the south. Tom and Reese stood closest to the road, while Woes and Stupak sat on the platform of the thrasher, talking quietly as the machine warmed up beneath them. The stranger walked up, slow and alone, wearing only a yellow rainslick. The coat was shining, dew-touched. It looked new.

Tom nodded to the stranger, but the man in the yellow coat said nothing, his face pointing toward the earth as though he were counting his every step.

"Morning," Reese said loudly. The stranger was still a few good strides away. It struck Reese that the man's face looked like a bird's: sharp, thin, perhaps weak. His nose was long and came to a crooked ball at its tip, and the man wore a few days worth of beard. His hair was sparse and dark, his manner the same. The man nodded.

"You in charge here?"

"No." Tom said, and crossed his arms over his chest. "I am."

"What's the job?"

"Didn't Jules tell you?"

"Mr. Jagerston?"

"That's right."

"Just that you needed a man to work for a day or two."

"You him?"

"Reckon I am."

There was a quiet, then, a tension hanging in the air like an icicle waiting to fall. Reese put out his hand. "I'm Reese. Good to have you here while Fiddler is down with flu. It's tough work with five, let alone four."

"Flu, huh?" the stranger said, taking Reese's outstretched hand weakly and shaking almost imperceptibly before letting loose. "What do you need done?"

"You ever worked a thrasher before?" Tom's arms were still across his broad chest.

"Been years, but yeah."

"How long?"

"Round eight. But it was one just like that one over there, what those two is sitting on."

"Done any farming in the meantime?"

"No."

"What you been doing since?"

The stranger paused. He started to speak, but caught himself. When he finally did answer, he spoke softly, scratching his head. "Mr. Jagerston already asked me all this."

"Mr. Jagerston ain't here right now. Hell, he ain't never here. We are. We work this thing. You don't know how to work a thrasher, then you got no business being here, I don't care what the hell Jules says." Tom took a few steps toward the stranger. "So I'm going to ask you once more. What you been doing since?"

The stranger paused again, and licked his front teeth. "I had some trouble with a man."

Tom cocked his head to one side and squinted.

"What kind of trouble?" Reese asked.

The stranger shook his head. "It's over now."

Reese looked at Tom. He was staring slit-eyed at the stranger. "What's your name, fella?" Tom asked one last time.

"Jacobs."

Tom nodded, as though that were all the information he needed, and turned to walk back to the thrasher without another word. Reese took one more look at Jacobs, and then followed. He could hear the stranger fall in step behind him.

The sun warmed the morning and the crows combed the fields, diving, snatching, and flying away again. Each man took a fork and they tried to explain the routine, but Jacobs was impatient, and seemed to know his way around. Reese took position up by the feeder. It was the best view the job offered. Down on the ground where Tom mostly worked, a man could see little but the wheat, a dizzying blur of yellow sheaf and black tine against the gunmetal backdrop of the thrasher. They were supposed to take turns, but Tom never wanted to switch, which meant Reese could stay up top for most of the day. It was up there where Reese felt most at home.

Jacobs fell into the team's rhythm, feeding the wheat into the ever-chewing maw of the thrasher with a steady pace. Since Fiddler ususally was the one who talked while they worked, his presence was missed. Instead of talk about Hoover's mistakes or how Roosevelt's New Deal was going to save the country, the conversation lagged until Stupak got on a roll about game three of the World Series. It had been over a month since the Babe had broken the tie in the fifth by pointing to the flagpole on the right of the scoreboard in center field, and then hit the next pitch into the Wrigley stands.

"The beginning of the end for the Cubs," Stupak lamented. He was a baseball fan like no other, having once made a trip up to Chicago just to see a double-header, sleeping in a city park and hitching a ride back the next day. Spent all the money he had doing it, too, but said it was worth it. Stupak had seen his team, and it was all he wanted.

Everyone but Jacobs had heard the story before, and none of them wanted to hear it again. But Stupak was on a roll. "But there's always next year, right? I mean, the Cubs, they were good this year, real good. If they can keep that play up, maybe they can put old Ruth down next fall. Right, Jacobs? What do you say, old man?" Stupak, who by this time was taking his turn working up top next to Jacobs, slapped him on the arm as he said it and Jacobs bridled like someone had just insulted his mother. He said nothing, but glared at Stupak for a long moment before returning to work.

Stupak flipped up the bill of his ball cap. "Oh, that's right, you're from St. Louis, ain't you? Probably a Cardinals fan. Hey you guys," he called down, laughing, "you hear this? We got ourselves a Cardinal fan!"

This time Jacobs fully ignored him, but Tom didn't. "Give it a rest, Stupak, and get back to work. We're losing sun," he shouted over the running grumble of the machine.

What happened next happened slowly, like time itself stretched out to allow it room. Or maybe it only seemed that way in retrospect, as they thought of it alone and spoke of it together, this small band of men, whispering over steaming cups of coffee. What happened next was this. Stupak, a strong boy but a boy nonetheless, began working with excessive force, with exaggerated movements. He was angry, and forked a load of wheat and threw it toward Jacobs' feet. Jacobs picked it up with his fork and fed it to the thrasher as Stupak turned to get more. The rhythm was off, the pattern disrupted. When Stupak came around with another forkfull of sheaves, Jacobs was just barely out of his way. Stupak was going too fast, or Jacobs too slow—there would be disagreement on this point later—but whatever the case, when Stupak came around to dump the wheat again, Jacobs' arm was still there.

Stupak reacted too late, tried to shift the pitchfork so as to miss

Jacobs, but still put the right tine fully through Jacobs' forearm. He jerked the fork back quickly, and Jacobs' blood followed, running down from wrist to hand to wheat. Stupak muttered something, maybe an apology, but no one could hear it. It was the last thing the boy would ever utter. Without a word, Jacobs pulled his fork up, some red, wet wheat still clinging at the end, and thrust its tines directly into Stupak's throat. The boy dropped his pitchfork. His hands fell to his sides and he shuddered, his body jerking violently. The stranger let go of the fork and Stupak crumpled off the side of the platform, falling like a shot duck, heavy and limp.

Reese and Tom looked at each other, stunned, each hoping to find some retraction of what had just happened in the face of the other. They both jumped for the platform at the same time, but Reese was faster. When he got up top, Reese saw Jacobs just standing there in the wheat and the blood, gazing down at Stupak's body. Jacobs looked up at Reese then, with dull eyes and slumped shoulders, like there was nothing left in him. His mouth was open slightly, his lips moving like he was trying to say some small thing, but no sound came. Reese lunged without knowing exactly what he was doing, throwing a clumsy punch. Jacobs brought his arm up to block the attack and used his other to push Reese hard. Reese teetered dangerously close to the wide, grinding mouth of the thrasher, but fell to the right and hit the wheel hard on the way down. He heard Tom bellow something guttural from above; from below, something in his knee snapped as Reese's leg struck the ground at an angle. The pain took the world away.

When Reese looked up, Tom was silhouetted, tall against the darkening sky, like an angry god. Reese held his knee, trying to catch his breath. Woes was nearby, rocking and moaning over Stupak, whose eyes were wide open, looking for all the world like he was following a well-hit ball up in Wrigley. But his neck was all wrong, torn and bloodied, unrecognizable as something that once held voice. Tom paused, and looked at Reese in a way that gave him chills. It was a look of decision—or was it opportunity? Tom charged at the stranger, who made no effort to defend himself as he stood there in his yellow rain-slick, spattered with blood. Tom picked him up as one would pick up a child and heaved him directly into the mouth of the feeder. Jacobs fell as though he were dead already. No clamoring for foothold. No flailing for his hands to find purchase. No last grasp for life. He simply fell back into the teeth and the gears and the blades, the way of the wheat.

Reese watched from where he lay in the blood and the broken dirt and the chaff. He saw Woes; his friend's head was buried in his hands. Tom looked down at Reese, sweat dripping from his hair like rainwater. He nodded, and then turned away.

"Shut it off, shut it off!" Woes screamed. The spout choked with human debris: the pink of flesh, the ochre of innard, the white of crushed bone. Brackish blood seeped down into the grain wagon, clumping. Tom moved slowly, but did as Woes asked. The thrasher slowly thrummed to a wet halt.

"It's all right now," Tom said.

Reese sat in the shadows of the hulking machine, now awash in wet crimson and dusty gold. He could hear the last sputters of the machine powering down, Woes crying, the sound of his own hard breath. He braced himself on the wet soil with one arm and cradled his knee with the other. It throbbed, and Reese's hand could do no good for it, but he kept it there anyway. Reese wanted to feel something else, anything else, but there was only the pain. The rest of him was numb and cold. Reese thought instead of licorice whips and the sound of ivory balls clicking together, how perfect that was, how wonderful, and how far from here it seemed.

# Chapter Two

THIS IS THE WAY HOME. A forgotten road, empty fields, old country music, a left into the gravel driveway. It's the way I remember it, coming back to Moweaqua. Getting there isn't so much about directions, about compass points or maps. It's about the experience, what you taste in the wind, what the truck sounds like ripping through morning air, how you wave to the guy on the tractor just because he's a guy on a tractor. Because you're here, and waving to everyone is just part of this place.

Central Illinois demands its own rules. Forget about Chicago and the cities to the north. This is the land of one-way bridges. You meet someone on the road, the only thing between you and disaster is good manners. It's always been this way, like everything else here. Things remain because they remain, because they're good enough. Because no one has the heart or the money to replace them, these obsolete bridges lined by the autumn with skeletal trees, dead men surrendering.

I hadn't set foot in Moweaqua for two years. I'd just turned thirty, and it was the first year Mom didn't send me a birthday card. I was surprised I even noticed—the cards, I'd come to believe, meant nothing. But I had noticed. I imagined her saying, "Well, James, you can't miss what you never appreciated."

Mom always called me James, even though I'd decided back in sixth grade to go by my middle name, Reese. After my father. It was important to me to carry something of his with me after he died: his pocketknife, his John Deere cap, his name. Mom would have none of it. She said she'd had one Reese in her life, and that was plenty, thank you kindly. Eventually, everyone in town called me Reese—all but Mom. I could never win her over.

I wasn't looking forward to seeing Mom. It was already cold, and she had the ability to lower the temperature in a room by ten degrees with a glance. But I had to go back. So there I was, on Highway 51, all pothole-riddled and patched up, with the fields to either side of me coming to a point on the flatland horizon so it looked like if I kept going, I'd drive straight into the earth. I took the driving slow. The sun peeked through high, thin clouds, glistened off the wet dirt like glass. The fields were all empty, and I found myself missing the blur of green, yellow, or tan. There was nothing to cradle me between the ditches.

Someone on the radio read the corn and bean prices. Being in a place where such information requires an hourly update felt like an invitation to me. There was this voice I would hear in my head I've often identified as my father's, even though over the years I've completely forgotten the sound of his voice. But it was strong and loud that morning: *you'll never be rich here, but you'll be comfortable. You'll never be happy here, but you'll be satisfied. You'll die young, but you'll never see it coming, and you won't argue when it does.* I know it doesn't sound alluring—my ex-wife Carrie thought I was crazy to think it was—but to me, yeah. It's why I was determined to get home, see Mom, set things right, and then leave it all behind again. I had to get away from that voice, that seduction. It's quiet, calm, and clear; it's shaded sunlight, black dirt, growth and death together. It's the threat and blessing inherent in all things at all times: wind, family, rain, and home.

This is a place where things happen slowly, without purpose. That's not to say things happen without meaning—but the seasons don't change because someone decides they should; they simply change. Rain doesn't fall because it's time; it simply falls. And crops, dogs, and people alike all die with no master plan. And that's why people here think the way they do. Why change happens slowly, when it happens at all. Because those who make a home here are used to change being made without their counsel or consent. It's the way of some things, and slowly, over time, it becomes the way of all things.

I never imagined Highway 51 would change. It was a dangerous road, a two-lane, undivided monster that claimed more lives than any other in the state, winding down from Bloomington- Normal, through the small communities of Heyworth, Wapella, into and out of Clinton, on through Maroa, skirting Emery, and into Decatur, the soybean capital of the world and home to just about every kind of factory a city can support. It came out on the other side of town, past the lumberyard and the smorgasbord restaurant, and led through some of the most fertile soil downstate. Through Elwin with its checkerboard Purina tower and its little motel; through Macon with the old red-brick high school, its own little motel, the old Amoco station, and Sweet's Bar and Grill; past the turnoff to Walker and into Moweaqua. That's the way it always had been, the way I knew it.

But things had changed. They'd widened the road, splitting the north and south bound lanes entirely in long stretches. New parts of the road now bypassed some of those tiny communities altogether, orphaning them out in the fields with the horse troughs and stable barns. Fifty-one still passed through Elwin and Macon, but they were different too. The Elwin Motel had become an antiques mall, and they had turned what had been the lobby into a little restaurant called the Raspberry Tea Room, all lace curtains and tablecloths. It occurred to me that Illinois wasn't big on tea unless was iced and sweetened, but then I saw their sign that mentioned pie. If you had pie, you could probably get most people to drink just about anything. Macon's Amoco station had boards nailed over the door and windows, and a pegasus-shaped ghost where the old logo once hung. Worst of all, Macon High was gone, renamed Meridian, become the Hawks. I wondered if Moweaqua had befallen the same fate. I didn't like the idea. It smacked of betrayal. All this change did.

I turned the radio off and rolled my window down. The air was cold, but the smell was good: corn dust, turned dirt, diesel engines, greased gears. My new Ford—an F-250—ran smooth. It felt right coming home in a truck.

My father made me a Ford man. It was all he ever drove, his gray 1954 F-250. He let me drive it when I was nine, as soon as my feet reached the pedals with the seat all the way forward. I sat behind that big grey steering wheel, feeling the pull of a sharp turn on the driveway dirt. I could still fit my head into the space above the horn. Dad always threatened to get a new truck, but I knew better than that. Dad lived for two things: farming and history, and believed the former was really a function of the latter. "What you leave behind is the only thing life's good for," he'd say. Mom nagged him, told him the past was better left alone, that he had a family to consider, a farm to keep his hands busy. Maybe he was guilty of living in the past a bit, but he knew what was important, and he stayed true to it until he died.

Dad's truck sat out in the garage for a few years, and I would climb into the front seat once in a while and pretend to drive. My head stopped fitting in the space above the horn, and I stopped going out there as much, and one day I noticed it was gone. Mom said she'd told my cousin Earl to sell it, that some farmer east of town had bought it for his son to drive. When I turned sixteen, she helped me buy an old Ford to replace it—a convertible Galaxie 500—but I missed that truck. I remember feeling like I would when one of the dogs would die. It was a gnawing inside me, a wish to do all the things I always meant to do, but never did. And it was exactly the way I felt that morning, coming home again.

Aunt Glorrie had died of a massive stroke brought on by some accident at Fathauer's Grocery. I wasn't sure of the details yet, but Doc Pistorius had called me at school, right in the middle of first period American History, and told me she was gone, that I needed to come home. But his news didn't end there—I don't think I'd have been driving home that morning if it had. I'd loved Glorrie, sure, but she was dead. I'd already missed my last chance to see her, and seeing her in a casket isn't really *seeing* her. But there was more—Doc said there was something wrong with Mom. Something he described as *untethered.*

I hate to admit this, but I *still* might not have come home. Earl was there, and gave Mom a little of his profits and a lot of his time to be able to work the fields that had passed to Mom when Dad died. That was the deal, and helping Glorrie was part of it, since she'd moved into the farmhouse with Mom years back. Earl could deal with Mom, I told Doc. He was around. The guy was always around. Doc got quiet for a moment, and then said five words that cut time like my father's sickle. "She's asking for you, Reese."

She was asking for me, her only son, her greatest disappointment. The sheer shock of it pushed me into blind action. I had to go, no choice. This morning was different. My mother was asking for me.

A crow flew across the road, and I found myself wanting company, wanting distraction. So my mind went, as it often did, to Carrie, even though it had been six months since our divorce was final, and over a year since we'd separated. But we'd been together for almost eight years before the breakup, and it's a tough thing to get used to, being alone, not having to consider how whatever you're doing might affect someone else. This was how Carrie crept into my thoughts most of the time, not so much for want of her, but for want of someone.

"My love for you is like shaving cream," I'd said to her, trying to be charming. This was my opening line. We'd met at a grocery store, in the toiletries aisle, and a can of shaving cream was what I happened to have in my hand at the time.

"What?" she said, raising an eyebrow. She had great eyebrows, and I never saw her pluck them. Born with them—those and her straight, straw-yellow hair.

"I love you like shaving cream," I said, holding up a striped can of Gillette.

"So, your love is cheap and utilitarian?"

"I was going for something along the lines of plentiful and expensive. But I like your answer better."

"Nice," she smiled, and I knew I had her. "I'm seeing someone."

"Ah," I said. I followed her into produce, and she seemed to enjoy the attention. She finally admitted the other guy she was seeing was, in actuality, her cat. By the time we were at checkout, I had her number, and we had plans to get together that Friday. We went to the White Horse Inn for dinner, and we talked about a lot, including our future plans. She said she was going to teach math. I said I was going to get a degree in history, and then go back and farm, most likely. She said I was an idiot. *What the hell are you going to do with a degree in history?* she'd asked. I smiled and told her to mind her own fucking business. That was our first date. I used the exact same phrase—*mind your own fucking business*—in our last big fight before we separated, though I wasn't smiling. I guess she finally took me up on my invitation.

Carrie did get me into teaching, and for that, I'll always owe her. She was wrong about a degree in history being useless, but teaching was the right thing for me. My fallback had always been farming—all I needed to do was say the word, and I could come back home and give the farm another go. Earl wouldn't much like it, but it was an option. That is, until Carrie and I got married during our senior year—she made it clear she had no intention of ever living on a farm. We worked hard to get offers from the same school, and succeeded at Normal Community High School. Teaching at the same school was great when we were married. After the separation, not so much.

I glanced at my rear view mirror and the tiny Spider-Man webswinging from it. It was one of those shrinky-dinks, a gift from Carrie for one of our anniversaries, sort of a joke about me watching *Spider-Man and His Amazing Friends* on Saturday mornings, maybe sort of a jab, too. One day, I realized something was wrong with our marriage—it was the day Carrie came home from working late, sat me down, and said, *Something's wrong with our marriage.* That was the beginning of us trying to fix it, but it ended up being the beginning of the end. By that point, there was nothing much left to fix. We were done, just run out of love. We'd gotten to the bottom of the can.

Carrie took most everything in the divorce, mainly because I gave it to her. The car, I didn't want—I'd never liked that Escort Wagon—so I just took my Spidey off the rear-view and handed her my set of keys. We didn't have a house, or much of anything else. We split our music, our books, and our debt, and went our separate ways. I heard she'd been dating someone pretty seriously for a few months by then. I told myself I was happy for her, even waved to her when I passed her in the hallway at school, which was mercifully rare.

I pulled my truck into the gravel lot of Sweet's, which sat just south of the Macon curve. Donnie's old yellow Jeep was parked there. The beer signs—Bud and Pabst—were the only things marking this as a bar at all.

Sweet's was the closest place to Moweaqua that served liquor since the town voted itself dry when Prohibition ended. Donnie Sweet ran the place with his wife Meg, who used to do the cooking back when it had a counter-service diner attached to it. Meg did a little cleaning and balanced the books, but no one was ever behind the bar except Donnie. When he needed a break, he'd just close up, put a note on the door, and assume his customers would come back when he did.

It took a moment for my eyes to adjust when I walked inside. Sweet's was lit like a tomb. Nothing much had changed here. There was still the long, room-length bar against the left wall, with the bottles stacked behind it, and the TV on a shelf right smack in the middle, always on ESPN unless a high-school team was playing on the local channel. There were a few tables in the center of the room, and booths lined the wall across from the door. To the far right was a big-screen television—that was new—but everything else was exactly the same.

"Well I'll be damned," Donnie called from the bar. His voice was as gravelly as his parking lot. "Reese Moss. What the hell are you doing back here?" Donnie had always been a stout guy, but he'd put on more than a few pounds since the last time I'd seen him. He still had a full head of hair, which he'd finally let go completely gray.

"Donnie," I said, taking a seat at the bar and shaking his outstretched hand firmly. "Hope you don't mind me dropping in. I know you're not open yet."

"Don't mind at all, son," he said. "What happened to your hair? You look like a banker."

My hand went instinctively to my hair, short-cropped and neatly trimmed now, in stark contrast to the long mess I'd sported back in my KISS days. "What can I say? If you want to teach, you can't look like a kid anymore. No one listens to you. I had to go respectable."

"Respectable Reese Moss. Never thought I'd see the day," Donnie laughed.

"You and my mother both," I said. "So you're in early today, aren't you?"

"Yeah, just doing some stocking. I had a boy from Meridian doing some work for me, but he had to quit last week. Interfering with his football practice."

"At least he has his priorities straight."

Donnie pointed at me and laughed like it was a better joke than it was. "Damn right."

"So what's all this Meridian crap? What happened to Macon High?"

"You know the story. Consolidation." Donnie shrugged. He was counting mugs as he spoke. "They've been singing the same song for a while, but they finally got enough people to join in the chorus. Happened last year."

"What about Moweaqua?"

"Consolidated with Assumption. Now they call it Central A&M."

"Central A&M?" I scowled.

"Yeah," Donnie grinned. "Central Assumption and Moweaqua. The joke going around was they should have called it Mo-Ass."

I laughed half-heartedly, shook my head. "Well that just plain sucks."

"Reckon it does," he said, "but suck or not, it's a done deal. You should have heard the guys bitching about it. Went on for months. I told them if I heard the old school song one more time I was closing the bar for good."

"Bet that shut them up."

"Nah," Donnie smiled. "They got over it. Got to bitching about things without songs attached to them, which is fine by me. How'd you miss hearing about it, anyway? It was big news around here for a good long time."

"I haven't been around here for a good long time."

"Guessed as much. So you're still teaching. Still up at Normal?"

"Yeah," I nodded. "NCHS has a good ball team this year, matter of fact. They have a chance at taking conference."

"Just like the old days."

"Not quite," I said, "but close."

Donnie nodded, put down his bar towel, and leaned over the counter. "So what brings you back, Reese?"

I took a deep breath, shrugged off the question. "Long story."

He gestured around the bar. "Hell, I got nothing better to do. Let me get you a drink, and you can tell it."

"I can't stay. Just came in to say hi. I have to get out to the farm."

"Something up with your mom?"

"Glorrie passed away this morning."

"Aw, Damn," Donnie said, lowering his chin. "I'm sorry, son. She was a good woman. I didn't know her well enough."

"I didn't either, Donnie," I said. "Did you know she sent me to college? She's the one who paid for it."

"I didn't know that."

"Yeah. She came in one night. We sat right there," I pointed down the bar, "and she more or less told me to get off my ass. Told me to do what I wanted—work the farm, or go to school and do something else—but to *do* something. It was good advice."

"Sounds like it," Donnie nodded. He slapped the bar twice,

stood back up, and reached down to pick up a cloth and a shot glass from a drying rack. "So you're going home to be with your mom?"

"Yeah."

"Good man," he said. "Take care of your own. You know when they're going to have the funeral?"

I shook my head. "Just got the call this morning."

"It's a shame," Donnie said. "Here I was thinking you were here to sign the papers for Earl."

"Papers?"

"Selling the acreage. It's all he's been talking about for months now, how he finally socked enough cash away to buy a good portion of it outright, how it took him twenty years, on and on like that. Nearly drove some of the regulars away with all his blathering." Donnie stopped talking when he saw the look on my face. "Oh, shit," he muttered. "Was I not supposed to say anything? You and Earl going at it again?"

"I don't have the slightest idea what you're talking about, Donnie."

"Damn, I'm sorry, Reese. It's just that Earl's been talking about nothing but for so long, it's like it's a done deal, all but the paperwork. You mean he didn't even talk to you yet?"

"I haven't heard anything at all."

"Well, I imagine you'll get an earful."

"So will Earl," I said, getting up from the stool.

"Hey, Reese," Donnie held out a hand to stop me, "I'm sorry. I didn't mean to upset you, today of all days."

"It's okay," I said. "Don't worry about it. I have more important things on my mind today than anything Earl's been planning. It's just so out of the blue, you know?"

"You just take it easy driving up to town. I want to see you back here in one piece. I'll buy you a beer next time you're in."

"And I'll drink that beer," I said, forcing a smile as I zipped up my jacket.

"You keep Meg and me posted about the visitation and all."

"I'll call you when I know. Take it easy, Donnie." And then, on a sudden whim, I added, "Hey Donnie, you ever see Amy Lakin around here?"

Donnie's smile returned. "Once in a while. More now since she got separated from her husband, and he moved down to St. Louis."

"Separated, huh?"

"Maybe a year now. Maybe more. You want me to say hi for you next time I see her?"

"You will anyway."

Donnie waved. "True enough."

# Chapter Three

*1932*

REESE WATCHED THEIR EYES. He, Tom, and Woes looked up
at Wayne and Mary Kinney, who were up on their porch listening to the tale Tom was spinning. It was a long story explaining
the blood on their clothes, why one was trembling, why another
couldn't stand of his own strength. Reese watched their eyes to see
if they believed.

They had limped in from the fields and found the nearest farm—
the Kinney place out by the old tile mill. They didn't know what
to do, but they were all sure they didn't want to stay with Stupak
and what was left of Jacobs. It would have been a while before Jules
would be back around with the truck, so they took to the road,
hoping to flag down a ride or at least make it someplace else. Woes
whimpered the whole way—he'd only stopped when Tom told him
to shut up so he could think. Reese had his arms around Tom's neck,
being carried like a sick calf. It was slow going, and dark. Only the
sliver of a moon lit their way.

Tom had concocted what was going to be the truth as they
walked. At first, he argued for saying it had all been an accident—
that the stranger had just slipped and fallen in, pushing Stupak
onto the tines of his own fork and Reese clean off the thrasher in
the process—but he soon dismissed it. Too unbelievable, Tom said
with a smile that shook Reese's stomach. By the time they had gotten to the Kinney farm, the story was complete.

The tale they told the Kinneys was the same one they would later
tell Jules, and later still Sheriff Dawes. It had been the stranger from
Missouri, Tom said, with Reese now leaning on his shoulder. Reese
noticed Tom refused to use the man's name, calling Jacobs only *the
stranger*, and described the scene as if it was a Flash Gordon serial
down at the Lyric Theater. *The stranger just went crazy all of a sudden, like he was possessed. He'd been acting up all morning, muttering about nothing, swearing and throwing his fork around like there*

*weren't three sharp tines at one end at all. And then when poor Stupak asked a question about baseball, well, his answer was a pitchfork in his throat. The boy was dead before he hit the ground,* Tom said, shaking his head, and it was then that Mary gasped, made the sign of the cross against her breast, and clutched her husband's arm.

"I still don't see how killing a boy gets you run through a thrasher," Wayne said. Tom shifted Reese's weight, and Reese winced. "It was Reese here who was up on the platform first," Tom said, "trying to get the fork away from him. None of us knew what to do, I reckon. Reese here, he was the first, and fast too, boy. But the stranger—he was faster. Knocked Reese to the ground like he had Stupak, only with the butt of the fork this time. Reese here bounced off the wheel on the way down, fell crooked on his leg. His knee is all busted up six ways to Sunday."

Wayne nodded, and looked at Reese for a moment, down to his leg and up again. "That right, son?"

Tom cut in sharply. "Course it is."

Wayne's gaze tightened. "So how'd he get in the thrasher?"

Tom shrugged, like he regretted it. "Fell in. Slipped on the blood, I reckon. There was a lot of it up there, after Stupak and everything. Reese can attest to that." Reese looked at Tom, suddenly aware that Tom was leaving himself out of the story altogether. This wasn't the story they had talked about on the road, the one where Tom tackled the stranger and nearly went into the thrasher himself. Suddenly, Tom was a bystander. And Reese had been the last up top. "Must have been swinging the fork at Reese here, what threw him off balance. Whatever it was, I'm glad for it, to be truthful."

Wayne raised an eyebrow. "That so?"

Tom nodded earnestly. "That's right. Cause if he hadn't slipped?" He paused here, his face taut and serious, his manner booming. "We might all be as dead as that boy back there."

"My lord in heaven, you boys," Mary said, stepping down from the porch and away from her husband. "You get yourselves inside here so we can clean you up and get you warm. You must be catching your death out here, what with the night air those wet clothes."

Their clothes weren't wet—the blood had long since dried—but Mary Kinney saw what she wanted to see. They all did. The Kinneys fed them stew, warmed them by the fire, and Mary brought them a basin of hot water, a cake of soap, and a towel apiece.

"With all this fuss, it's like we're staying at the Hotel Drew uptown," Tom joked, winking at Mary as she brought him his towel. She blushed a little, smiled, and went into the kitchen to heat up coffee.

Wayne had more questions, but Tom had an answer for everything, and not always the ones Reese or Woes expected. Reese tried to memorize everything Tom said, just in case someone asked him later, so they had the same story. But the pain in his knee was too much for him, and he found himself drifting in and out of the conversation. Woes wasn't paying attention at all; he held his unused towel in his lap, absently scratching the fabric like it was a cat. The only time he looked up was when Tom and Wayne both agreed they'd have to talk to Sheriff Dawes the next morning. Woes' eyes opened wide as saucers, and then he buried his head in his hands.

Two hours later, Wayne was out of questions, Tom was out of answers, and they talked like old friends. "One thing's for certain," Wayne said. "A farm is a dangerous place."

"That ain't no lie," Tom agreed. "Dangerous, dangerous." They toasted with their cups of coffee, drinking to it as though it were an occasion.

Later that night, Wayne Kinney drove them back to town in his truck, and Reese lay in the back and looked up at the sky. The world had changed suddenly, tipped over on one side, left everything off balance. The pain in his knee kept rhythm with a south-bound flock of geese overhead. The air was cold, but Reese barely noticed it, or the half-moldy straw beneath him, or the blood under his fingernails and on his clothes. And the moon—it had moved up into the sky since they walked in from the fields a few hours earlier, but it still looked for all the world like a closed eye.

Sheriff Jim Dawes examined the scene, along with Fred Howser, the new mortician who'd just opened in Moweaqua. Stupak's death was considered a murder, but with the killing already so well-avenged by God himself, as many in town claimed, there was little uproar. Stupak did have one of the largest turnouts for a man who was to be buried in a pauper's grave out in the Oddfellows Cemetery. Tom stole a baseball from the school gymnasium to bury in the ground right above him. It was a gesture that both surprised Reese and confirmed his faith in Tom. For a time, it made him forget his nagging doubts about their friendship.

The matter soon passed, or so it seemed, and Moweaqua returned to normal. Reese's mother begged him to come home and let her take care of him, but Reese didn't want to burden his parents. Tom had offered to let Reese stay with him for a while, and Reese thought this was the better idea—he was a man, after all. He had seen a man kill and then, in turn, be killed. He could no more go home than he could change the fact that Stupak was dead, that Tom had lied, or that he'd fallen to the ground with no more resistance than a stalk of corn offers a sickle.

But in December, talk of the thrasher began anew, at the pool room, in the mines, at the grocery, and at Snyder's Restaurant in the Hotel Drew downtown. People said the hired man from Missouri hadn't just fallen in by the will of God, but that a fight had broken out amongst the men, a fight that had ended badly. Folks traded the new story around town for a while, and the more it got traded, the more specific it became. By the time Reese first heard about it, it was weeks later, when he, Tom, and Woes met at Snyder's for coffee.

"You heard the latest story going around?" Woes asked. He was leaning forward at the table, looking from side to side as he spoke in a low, hushed voice. Woes was dressed, as always, in the blue wool coat that had been his father's before he died. It didn't fit him well, but on Woes, few things did.

"What is it now?" Tom asked, and turned to Reese, who sat

next to him. They both had on the same sort of heavy winter dusters the miners wore, dyed black to hide the coal marks. "You want something to eat? I'm half-starved."

Reese shook his head, but Tom ordered a plate of biscuits and coffee all around. "So what the hell is it? I'm getting sick of all your whining. Don't make me wish you'd been up on that platform instead of Stupak."

"Jesus, Tom, be quiet about it. Or I'm leaving." Woes glanced around like a wary rabbit.

"C'mon, Woes, everyone knows who we are and what we're talking about," Tom grinned. "Hell, we're the three survivors of the thrasher. What do you think people are expecting us to talk to each other about? You're the one making us look bad, always looking like you done something wrong."

"I am not," Woes said, too loudly. He glanced around the room, and then repeated himself, subdued. "I am not. Besides, it's easy for you to say. You're getting the best of it."

"What does that mean?" Reese asked, rubbing the cloth and splint he and Tom had fashioned from Doc Hudson's instructions. He had posed the question to Woes, but he remained silent, never taking his eyes off Tom. "What does he mean, Tom?"

"He don't mean nothing," Tom said.

"Like hell I don't." Woes said. "I was playing duck pins above the pool hall last night with a few fellas from the mine, and they was talking up a storm about us. Said some things I wished I hadn't heard, because I'm thinking they was true. The pure and simple truth. Nothing like what we fed the Kinneys, Jules, Sheriff Dawes, everyone around here. Makes me want to leave this town, I tell you that. Leave and start all over again."

The conversation paused when Glorrie Sanner brought the coffees and biscuits. Glorrie was a fiery, ample girl—everything about her, from her attitude to her curled hair to the curves that led the eye as she walked. "Here you are, boys," she said. "Butter and jam there on the table." She was Reese's age, and they had known each other since they were learning their letters. Glorrie winked once at Reese, then turned her attentions to Tom.

"Thank you, Glorrie," Reese said, trying to call up a twinkle in his eye like he saw the men in the movies do all the time when they tried to charm.

"Yeah, thanks," Tom said, grabbing her waist. "Hey, how about you blow on my coffee? I like it sweet."

Glorrie laughed—a breathy giggle she couldn't have done better had she practiced it for hours in front of a mirror—and bent over slowly, blowing softly into Tom's cup. Watching her lips purse, and the steam rippling up off the black coffee, made Reese's pants tight.

"Can I get you anything else?" she said, leaning into Tom's face.

Tom winked at her. "I'll let you know." As she walked away, Tom turned to Reese and shook his head. "You can breathe now," he said, cuffing the back of Reese's head.

Reese laughed, leaned back in his seat. "Want to trade coffees?"

"Not on your life," Tom said, taking a quick sip. He turned to Woes, and his grin faded. "Jesus, Woes, have a little fun. Or at least have a biscuit. I'm buying." Tom had taken some odd jobs around the Hotel Drew for food money.

"I don't want your damn biscuit," Woes said.

"Fine," Tom shrugged. "Reese and me'll eat them." He finished off the one in his hand and reached for another, dipping it into the small bowl of red jam. "These are pretty good," he said to Reese, who was breaking off crusty pieces of his biscuit and eating them slowly.

"I want you to stop talking, Tom," Woes said.

"You do, do you?" Tom's mouth was full of biscuit.

"That's right." Woes' voice was small, but firm. "I want you to stop telling the story."

Tom stopped in mid-chew. "What damn story?"

"The story of how you took out the man-killer from Missouri."

Reese laughed. "The what?"

Woes smiled despite himself. "That's what the Negri brothers called him last night, them and some of their pals from the mine. Sounds goofy, I know."

Tom laughed and shook his head. "I swear to you, Woes, I never said anything like that."

"Well, someone is saying it," Woes said.

"Whoever it is, they've seen too many boxing matches up in Decatur."

"Maybe," Woes said. "But the point is, people are talking, and you're not helping things any by bragging about it all over town."

"I haven't been bragging," Tom said, his voice flat.

"That's not what the Negris said."

"I don't care what the Negris said," Tom said. "Don't go believing everything you hear from a coal-jockey. I know the stuff those fellas talk about down there. It's dark, and there's nothing to do while you're working but talk about nothing, make up stories to pass the time. And then the dust gets into your head and clouds everything up, and you start believing your own lies. It's nothing, Woes. It's just miners talking."

Reese finished his biscuit, brushed the crumbs off the table. "So what's the story? What's going around?"

"You want to tell him?" Woes asked Tom.

"No," Tom said simply. "Nothing to tell."

Woes took a careful look at Tom before he began. "They're talking about us, about what happened. About the thrasher, about the stranger. Jacobs. Call him whatever you want. The Negris were talking about how he went all crazed and attacked Stupak with his fork and how Tom here dragged Jacobs up to the top of that thrasher, all kicking and screaming like the devil was in him, and Tom threw him plumb into the mouth of it, and how it was too late to save the boy, but Tom damn well sure got his eye for an eye."

Tom shrugged and the muscles in his shoulders made little popping sounds, like corn in a fire. "Close enough to the truth," he said.

"You think so?" Reese asked.

"Yeah, I think so. What does it matter, anyhow?"

Reese shook his head. "I don't know, Tom. Maybe it doesn't. Maybe it doesn't, Woes."

"Like hell," Woes said. "Stop watching your feet and look down the road a piece. What the Negris say today is what the guys at the filling station are talking about next week, and then it will at Ayar's Bank. Pretty soon, it'll get back to people who care about stuff like this."

"Like who?" Tom sneered.

"Like Jim Dawes," Woes said.

"The sheriff?" Reese said. "You think he'll do something?"

Tom put out his hands to stop the conversation. "That's enough," he said. "Woes, you're just scaring yourself, and now you're worrying Reese, too. Jim Dawes ain't going to care. No one cares. It's just a story."

"I think people will care more than you think," Woes said.

"I don't," Tom said.

"Well, I don't want to find out the hard way," Woes said. He took a sip of coffee.

Tom sighed. "How about the easy way then?" He called Glorrie back over to the table, and when she came, he pulled her onto his knee. "Hey, sweetie, I got a story for you. You got time?"

"Guess so," she smiled, "if it's quick."

"There's this stranger, see, and he kills a friend of mine in cold blood, just outright kills him."

"How awful," Glorrie said.

Tom looked at Woes. "What would you think if I up and threw that stranger into a thrasher? I mean just clean threw him in?"

Glorrie laughed. "I'd think you'd had too much whiskey in that coffee of yours, Tom Horseman. Everyone's heard that story, heard what happened. Everyone says you had no choice in the matter, that it was all a horrible thing. But everyone knows you weren't to blame. I know it, anyhow."

"You don't know nothing," Woes muttered.

"Shut your mouth," Reese snapped. "Don't talk to her like that."

Glorrie looked surprised at Reese, but pleasantly so. "Now boys, I don't want anyone fighting, especially over me." She got up from Tom's lap and cocked her hands on her hips. "If your story is done, can I get you anything else? More coffee?"

"Not yet, sweetheart. I'll let you know, though," Tom winked.

"I'll count the minutes," Glorrie said, and flounced off with a look back and a grin.

Woes shook his head. "Are you done with the flirting now?" he asked quietly.

Tom rolled his eyes. "Sure. I'd love to talk some more about how you're scared of your goddamned shadow. I'd much rather look at your ugly mug than to watch that pretty little girl walk away. By all means, you yellow god-damned bastard, let's keep talking about this. Let's keep talking."

"Quiet down, Tom," Woes said. "I just want—"

"Shut up, Wozniak," Tom said. "I've had it with you. I don't care what you think or what you want me to do. I'm going to do what I'm going to do, and if you don't like it, you can go to hell. And if you're not careful, maybe I'll be the one to send you there."

"Gonna murder me too, Tom?" Woes said.

"Murder?" Reese said. "Hey, c'mon now—"

"Forget it," Tom said, pulling on his coat. "Let's finish talking about this outside." He got up, tossed some coins onto the table, and winked at Glorrie from across the room. "C'mon fellas, let's go."

Tom led the men out to the back of the Hotel Drew. The shadows cast by the building were long and cold, but there were leaves burning in a barrel nearby, and Tom stepped over to it to warm his hands. Reese and Woes followed suit.

"Look, Tom, all I'm saying is that—"

Something flew through Reese's peripheral vision then, and it was only when he saw Woes drop that he realized what he'd seen was Tom's fist catching Woes squarely in the jaw. Woes spun and fell heavily to the ground, and he stayed there on the cold earth, holding up one hand to ward off any coming blows. When none came, he brought the hand down to gently lay against his chin. He spit blood and a piece of tooth out onto the frozen ground.

Tom stood over Woes, red-faced and pointing a trembling finger. When he spoke, he did so through clenched teeth. "You listen to me, Wozniak. That Jacobs guy was trouble, pure and simple, and I did him before he could do us. Some men are like dogs, just like dogs. They got to be put down before they can bite. It was no accident, you dumb polack son of a bitch. I threw him in there because he killed a friend of mine, and I'd do it again. I only wish I'd done it before Stupak got it in the neck. All that kid cared about was the ball scores, and he's dead now. And now Jacobs is, too. And I sleep fine with that. I sleep fine."

Reese rubbed his forehead. It was aching again, like it had for the last few weeks when he would re-live what happened on the thrasher. He wanted to kneel next to Woes, help him to his feet, get him cleaned up and back home, but he couldn't. Not with his leg. To his shame, Reese found himself glad for the excuse his knee offered him.

Tom offered Woes his hand. "Get up, you dumb kid," he said. "Get up and we'll get you home."

Woes looked up, took Tom's hand, and stood, still holding his jaw. When he spoke, his voice was thick and wet, and he paused intermittently to spit blood. "There's talk Dawes is into it again. That he's starting to ask more questions."

"Who said so?" Reese asked.

"Jules. I talked to him yesterday. He said the sheriff had come around, started up about the whole thrasher thing again, said there was talk that things weren't right."

"That so?" Tom asked. "What did Jules say?"

"He told the guy he'd heard the rumors, but that's all they were. Jules said this like he was asking me a question, but I didn't say anything back. I didn't know what to say. I think I may have nodded."

"Damn," Reese said.

"Yeah," Woes said. "If the sheriff gets to the Negri brothers, I don't know what will happen. And if the Negris know it, I'd bet a lot more miners have heard the story too."

Tom reached into his pocket, pulled out a red kerchief, and threw it to Woes. "Here," he said, "clean yourself up. We can't have you looking like you've just been in a fight."

Woes nodded, held the cloth up to his mouth, wiped off his tongue, and spit again.

"We're going to have to lay low for a while," Tom said. "Just act normal. But no one even mentions the thrasher again, all right? If Dawes wants to make a case of this, we ain't going to make it easy for him."

"Right," said Woes, nodding. Tom looked over to Reese, who nodded too.

"All right, then," Tom said. "I reckon we're settled. And don't worry, Woes," Tom said, putting his hand on his shoulder, "it's all going to be fine. None of us is going to jail."

"What are you going to do, Tom?" Reese asked.

"I'm going to have a talk with the Negri brothers." Tom smiled, clapped them both on the shoulders, and led them back into the Hotel Drew to buy them another cup of coffee.

A few nights later, Tom came home from the pool hall. He was whistling something tuneless, the happy, off-key sound of a man fully comfortable in his own shoes. Reese sat on the porch smoking.

"What are you so happy about?" he asked.

"Had a talk with the Negris," Tom said, sitting on the porch step and pulling off his boots. "They ain't saying nothing to nobody."

"How'd you get them to agree to that?" Reese asked.

"Simple," Tom said. "I made them see my side of things." He put his elbows on the porch and leaned back, grinning.

But the Negri's vow of silence didn't stop the rumors. That horse had already bolted. The thrasher was still the talk of the town, and the newest addition to the story was the part that worried Reese the most: Sheriff Dawes was going to start an official investigation come the New Year. He'd even contacted officials from Springfield to help conduct it.

Reese spent a lot of time thinking a lot during the daytime, when Tom was working at the Drew, imagining all the things that might happen. What the sheriff would do, what the police from the capital could do to discover the truth. He'd heard of some sort of serum they used in the Great War that would make you speak your mind, even if you didn't want to. He knew Tom would never tell—lying was like second nature to the man. Reese also knew he himself could keep quiet—so long as there were no war potions to loosen his tongue against his will. But he wondered about Woes. He was weak, and Reese wished more than once Woes would make good on his promise to leave town. Even then, though, Reese was afraid they'd find him, and Woes would tell all in a moment of panic. Reese considered all this from his chair on the porch, watching the coal mine and smoking what tobacco he could afford.

Reese wondered what jail would be like. He'd rub his still-swollen knee and look out on the streets he hadn't walked in days: Tom's shack sat on the corner of Cherry and Plum streets, though there was nary a fruit tree to be seen. The street was little but mud, with rotting planks set across for foothold. And the shack was wood plank and rusty nail, poorly insulated with newspaper. It sat on the north edge of what was considered the south end of town, made up of the ramshackle houses of miners and their families. Those who lived there were sometimes derogatorily called "Southenders," and were mostly immigrants. Few spoke English. Tom's shack was small: one room, one window. Reese laughed grimly. Jail would probably be a lot like this.

The only thing Reese had to look forward to was Christmas. He'd agreed to spend it with his parents, to have dinner after services at the Methodist church. His father would shoot a duck or two, and his mother would cook it in butter, mash some potatoes with salt and gravy, make up some bread stuffing and a corn casserole. She'd bring the jars of candied apples up from the cellar, then she'd set it all out in white dishes stenciled in blue, like she did for every occasion. They'd say grace over a spread of food and drink that would, on any other day, seem like sin. But even though this was their Christmas gift to themselves, still his father would pray and then turn to Reese and his mother and say, "God is sleeping, let's eat."

God is sleeping. That's what Reese's father said every Sunday before dinner. Reese supposed it came from the idea that Sunday was a day of rest, even for God himself. And so, as the Almighty slept, a man could get away with a bit more. Like eating too much, or bragging on himself, or sharing whiskey out in the barn with a neighbor. Reese had seen his father do all this. And each time, he'd say it: *God is sleeping.* Like it excused him. Like even God himself was in on the joke.

Reese was up early on Christmas Eve morning, smoking on the front porch, thinking about roast duck and candied apples. It remained unseasonably warm—had been all week—and was so foggy that Reese could barely make out the tipple of the mine. Neither Reese nor Tom had been able to sleep the night before. The air was heavy and dank, and it seemed like every dog in town was barking and howling. They'd stayed up all night drinking and playing cards on the porch, watching the goings-on of the mine like it was a feature at the picture show. They could see the tiny flickering lights of the candles mounted in the miners' helmets coming up out of the mine and going back down. This schedule wasn't unusual, but the job the miners were doing was. There had been a fire there the day before, and men had worked all night building stoppings to wall it off and smother it. They'd finished around dawn. Reese and Tom had seen the Inspector, Mr. Millhouse, who Tom recalled as being a small man with a rat's nose, leave at a little after seven that morning, and then, a few minutes later, the mine's whistle blew to call the miners back to work.

"Fire must be out," Reese said. He and Tom were drinking their coffee cold—it was water-thin, having made five pots now from a single scoop of ground beans. "Millhouse must have signaled the all-clear, or else they wouldn't be calling anyone in for work."

"Hell of a way to start a holiday," muttered Tom, sipping his coffee out of a chipped mug, and tipping his chair back, "Hell of a way. Still smells like smoke, all the way over here. I'd hate to think what it smells like down in that damned hole."

"Least they're working. I hear they're making seven-fifty a day. Some aren't so lucky."

"Lucky? Not to be working in that place. You couldn't pay me seven hundred and fifty to go down there." Reese didn't quite believe him—he'd once seen Tom drink from the horse trough in front of the livery on a penny bet—but he believed in Tom's aversion to the mine, which was, like most things concerning Tom, powerful. Reese admired Tom's resolve, and wondered whether he himself was as sure of anything as Tom seemed to be of everything.

The two men sat silently for a minute, and then Tom said. "You tired?"

"Not hardly."

"This coffee ain't very good."

"No."

Tom poured what was left of his cup out onto the ground. "You want to go down to the pool room?"

Reese shrugged. There was little else to do, and Dave Craven kept his place open all hours for the men who worked nights at the mines. "Sure, I guess."

"Let's go." Tom got up, slicked his thick hair back, stretched, and patted his stomach. "Might get us some eggs, too. Or maybe I'll have flapjacks."

"You have the money for that?"

"It's Christmas," Tom clapped Reese on the shoulder. "Loosen your belt a little."

Reese smiled. A little pool down at Dave Craven's, a plate of egg, a fresh cup of coffee at Snyder's, and then, tomorrow, a day at home with his mother and father and a fat, buttered duck. Sounded good. Reese rose slowly, leaning on his cane, and went inside to get his hat.

For a minute, Reese couldn't find the brown felt fedora his father had given him years before, but then he saw it beside the stack of tinder by the stove. He was just reaching down for it when a muffled sound seemed to come from all around him. It was a long, hollow rumble, like thunder, but coming from the ground instead of the sky. The wood shook a little; a few pieces clattered off and fell to the floor. Reese heard their coffee cups break against the floorboards of the porch. Had the ground moved? Reese wasn't sure if it was the earth or just his knee making him unsteady. He braced himself against the wall, and looked around.

"Jesus!" Tom swore.

Reese wondered if one of the boilers in the mine had blown—after the night they'd had, it wouldn't have been a surprise. He limped as quickly as he could out the front door to see what was going on. Tom stood there in the street, squinting up.

"What the hell was that?" Reese called from the porch, his eyes wide.

"Mine," Tom said, pointing. There, near the top of the tipple, Reese could see a thin, fast-moving cloud of dust mingling with the fog of the morning, shooting up and out of the shaft like water from a spigot. Tom spat. "It goddamned blew."

"Was it a boiler?"

"No."

"Then what?"

Tom spat again. "I told you. The mine. The whole damn thing."

"God is sleeping," Reese murmured. People were already moving slowly toward the mine; later would come the rescue crews, the reporters from all over, the Red Cross to feed everyone, and the tables set up by the local restaurants to supply fresh coffee to anyone who wanted it.

"I'll be damned," Tom said softly.

Christmas passed; the ducks were safe and the apples remained in the cellar. There were no official services at the Churches—most of the clergymen were down at the mine. So was nearly everyone else, there to help, to gawk, to see if they'd become a widow, or an orphan, or one of the lucky few to see their men emerge. Five men came out early on, but they had just been preparing to go down to work, and weren't actually inside when it blew. Still, the five were greeted with a cheer of such magnitude, it nearly eclipsed the earlier explosion, a rousing welcome followed by grasping hugs, grateful tears, and kisses that left clean marks on coal-dusted faces.

But most of the news was bad. It had all happened six hundred and twenty-five feet below ground—an explosion, born of the marriage of open flame and natural methane. It tore through the western shaft where fifty-four men had been working. The overcast had collapsed in the blast, cutting off ventilation to those miners who survived the initial cave-in. Volunteers from the nearby Pana Mine and the Red Cross did what they could, working to locate and bring up survivors, but as the days passed, found only rock and debris. On Monday, the rescuers finally broke through and found all fifty-four miners, dead.

Reese would remember everything about that Christmas with perfect clarity, but there were two things he thought of most. One happened that first night, Christmas Eve, as he and Tom tried to catch some sleep despite all the commotion surrounding the mine. The shack still smelled of the free ham dinner from the Red Cross. Reese lay on his bed with his coat draped over him, sweating under his knees, and Tom sat up in his yellowed long johns, drinking corn whiskey from a brown medicine bottle and grinning.

"Our worries are over, Reese," he said.

"Why?" Reese asked, drowsy.

"The Negris are dead," Tom said. He raised the medicine bottle to his lips. "Not a bad Christmas present."

Outside, a truck backfired, and Reese heard someone laugh in the distance. He pulled his coat up under his chin, rolled over, and fell asleep listening to Tom drinking and singing to himself.

The other moment Reese would long recall happened the next day. He'd gone to Snyder's to see Glorrie, with the pretense of buying a cup of coffee, even though he could get it for nothing down at the mine. When he got there, he saw two figures behind the Drew—it was Tom, he realized, kissing a girl. His hands were flattened against the whitewashed wall, and she had one foot curled slightly around his calf. It was Glorrie, and Reese saw the smile on her lips when she looked up at Tom, saw that hungry look in her eyes he'd imagined so often in his dreams.

Reese turned away and chided himself for the hope he'd allowed himself to enjoy. It had been obvious for some time which one of them Glorrie preferred, but Reese had tried to ignore it. He went back down to the mine, where at least the coffee was free.

They met because her line was the shortest. She was volunteering at one of the coffee urns, and Reese was struck by her resemblance to Glorrie, even though everything about her seemed slighter. She was thinner, certainly, and her hair was lighter—where Glorrie's was rich chestnut, hers was the color of ginger—but it held the same curl. She had the same look in her eyes, too, the soft allure he could see in Glorrie's, even if this girl didn't look up nearly as often.

"Hi there," she said to Reese, handing him a cup. "I bet you don't remember me."

"Of course I do," Reese said, taking it and nodding thanks. "Clara Sanner, right? Glorrie's younger sister. We met a few years ago in school."

"That's right," she beamed. "How nice of you to remember."

"I never forget a Sanner girl."

"It's Glorrie who people never forget. She's the pretty one." Clara twirled her hair and lowered her eyes again, inviting him to deny it.

Reese obliged, trying desperately to mimic some of the charm he'd seen Tom produce so effortlessly. "I bet she says the same about you."

Reese looked into Clara's face, as he would for years to come. He found something there calling to him, though he was never truly certain what it was. He finally decided it was love.

# Chapter Four

MOWEAQUA HAS TWO SENTINELS guarding its northern-most flank, right where Highway 51 interrupts the town line. On the east is the school, where children spend kindergarten through twelfth grade learning about the world beyond the fields. It used to be Home of the Moweaqua Indians, and there used to be a big chief's head complete with war bonnet painted all in gold up on the water tower, which, like the grain elevator, you can pretty much see from anywhere in town. Like much of history, though, the Indians gave way to the Raiders. Just saying Raiders sounded wrong, felt wrong. And so did the new colors: red and black. They probably let the students pick the new colors after consolidation. Red and black. The angst is blinding.

To the west, however, is something that's not likely to change anytime soon: the slaughterhouse. They call it a packing plant, but I think you should call a killing floor a killing floor. Some guys from my high school class ended up working there, but I knew I could never do it. There's a pen just outside the plant where they keep the livestock, and the haunted look on the faces of those cows out there—it's like they know where they are. Like they're dead already.

Our house sat just to the other side of the school, across the road and on a short rise overlooking the ball fields. This, at least, hadn't changed. My tires mumbled and spit the driveway gravel, popping beneath me in a familiar welcome. I turned off the truck. The barn loomed on my left, a wide thing with two windows up near the crook of the roof that always reminded me of eyes, staring out at the house, watching everything. And the windmill was still there, but the wheel at the top had collapsed, fallen over onto its side. It hung there stubbornly, its flat tail sticking out at like the pan of a broken shovel.

There's a photograph of the day the windmill was erected. Used to sit on Glorrie's mantle at her old house. It's the only picture I ever recall seeing of me and my Uncle Tom together. I was just a couple of months old when it was taken, and he passed on not long after. Glorrie told me the story. Not that the story was all that exciting—it was just us having a picnic on the lawn—but I liked the fact that we're all there, except Glorrie, who was behind the camera. Dad's smiling broadly, holding me tightly up on one shoulder, Mom's sitting on a blanket on the ground next to him and looking directly at the camera, and Tom's in the background, working beside a very young Earl. Glorrie told me I'd sat in her lap by the watering trough and watched these men work, witnessed them building something larger than themselves. When I was young, the windmill might as well have been a skyscraper. Now, its struts looked thin as reeds. Like the wind had used it up.

I saw Mom by her garden, unfolding a blue and green ribbed lawn chair. She was burning paper in the rusted fire barrel near the windmill. I couldn't see anything in the rowed patch beside her, which was odd. Usually, by this time of year she'd have a thick vine of squash showing, or maybe pumpkin for Thanksgiving pies. When I was growing up, Mom was always planting or picking something in her garden—flowers, vegetables, sometimes both. It had always looked perfect, all green leaf on black soil, perpetually sprouting. But there was nothing in the garden, now. Just some spaded black dirt.

She hadn't heard me pull into the driveway. I walked towards her, just about to say something in greeting, to put my hand on her shoulder, wake her from her gardening reverie, shake a few years off of her. She'd turn around, her face brightening, hug me, welcome me home. That was what was supposed to happen. Then we could commence fighting. It was inevitable.

Instead, as I got closer, she turned. "About time you got home," she said. She knitted her brow, and stood up straight. Mom was a small woman, always had been. I remembered seeing old photos of her, and thinking she was a very pretty girl back then, with a coy smile and sandy hair that folded over itself in waves. But the mom who I had grown up knowing had hardened like summer mud, especially after Dad died. Her face had hollowed, and her smile was weary, often forced. She cut her hair short, and the color drained from it until it was as white as a deer tail. She began to stoop, and eventually, her back took on a permanent bend. It was always hard for me to reconcile the people I would see in old photographs and the people I came to know as an adult. They seemed like different people entirely. I suppose they were.

Mom was wearing her housecoat, a long robe she had taken to wearing like a winter coat for yardwork. It was a flower print trimmed in yellow, its hem dragging in the dirt. She had the same eyes that had always looked right through me, blue things that could rip the truth out of the devil's mouth, as my father used to say. "I could use some help, if you've got the time," she said.

"Sure, Mom." I didn't know what else to say. *In your more lucid moments, you old loon, you ask for me,* I thought, but I couldn't really be angry. I was too busy being surprised at how good it felt to be home, to smell Mom's Chanel No.5, good to hear the wind whistling through the barn. There was a rustle of dying leaves in the apple groves to the south, and the sound of the sliding doors on the garage tapping lightly against the frame. I felt seventeen again, late from football practice. I cleared my throat and smiled, trying to elicit the same in response. "I just wanted you to know I'm here."

Mom nodded, impatient. "I can see that, James," she said, as though I were being an idiot. She turned and began to walk toward the cellar.

I was still looking for signs of Mom being "untethered," but so far, Mom was responding to me in the same way she had for years: distant, impatient, vaguely rude. Not only that, but I was grasping at anything that might have disproved Doc's shot-from-the-hip diagnosis. *My mother isn't nuts,* I'd tell Doc on the way out of town, *she's just mean. And she's always been a little out of her head.*

"So long as you're here, why don't you help me carry these chairs up?" Mom called from the cellar door. "I need three more. Four, I guess, now that you're home."

"Okay, Mom. Okay." I followed.

As we walked down the cement steps that descended into the blackness of the cellar, its musty odor surrounded me like a familiar fog. It tasted old here, always had, like brackish pondwater. Mom stepped over to the north wall where the shelves of jars sat, all with fruits and vegetables packed and waiting for the table. These had always been full of things you could barely recognize in the shadow of the cellar, things with soft, rounded shapes and indiscernible color. I used to play down here, and this wall had sometimes been that of a comic-book villain, bent on creating an army to conquer the world—the peaches were ears, the carrots fingerbones, the cabbage, brains. Stacked beneath the shelves was the lawn furniture: three chairs and a chaise lounge with an old copy of *Reader's Digest* stuck between the folded seat and back. The rest of the room was full of Glorrie's things, piled up and covered in thick plastic. The bare bulb hanging from a cord in the center of the room seemed to move slightly, even without a breeze, and the switch was on the wall by the stairs, and not a pull-chain. But still the bulb had always swayed a little, always rocked, throwing planes of light over the shrouded shapes of Glorrie's things, a jigsaw of shine and shadow, of peaks and valleys the likes of which Illinois flatlanders can only dream.

Most of the furniture was Glorrie's. I peeked under the tarps to see what was there, smiling at the memory of Glorrie and Tom's old house on Cherry, the one Tom had built for Glorrie just after he came back from the war on the very site of their old house, which had been little more than a shack. This was all that was left after the auction Glorrie'd had for the stuff she didn't care about, and had moved a few of her favorite pieces into the house when she moved in with Mom. What didn't fit but couldn't be parted with ended up here.

Glorrie had collected some nice things since Tom died. She always said Tom spent his money on living, not living well, but she made up for it after he was gone. There was the cherrywood bedroom set: a dresser, a chest of drawers, and a four-poster bed frame with an ornate, carved headboard that had been dismantled and set flat against the cool surface of the western wall. The silver filigree standing mirror covered in a black drape because it was bad luck to see yourself in a mirror by accident. Against the south wall there were boxes stacked up one on top of the other, some marked china, some clothes, with hats perched on top like crows on a line.

"They're over here," Mom said, "under the jam shelf." She still called it a jam shelf even though she'd had to stop storing jam there since my cousin Bryan and I got into a couple jars of strawberry when they were stored too low. Since then, Mom kept her candied apples on that low shelf, always my least favorite part of holiday meals. She'd tried to get me to try it again one Thanksgiving back when I was in high school, and I remember telling her we could get fresh fruit year-round now, we didn't have to keep preserving stuff like it was the Stone Age. My comment sunk like a rock in a well. Mom left the table, and Earl, Glorrie, and I ate in silence. Mom came down from her room only to do the dishes.

As Mom bent over slowly to pick up a chair, the dirty hem of her housecoat raised up to her ankle. She was barefoot, and her toes looked red and a little swollen.

"Jesus, Mom, where are your shoes?"

She stood up straight, and seemed to think about this for a moment, staring down at the chairs on the floor and wearing a blank expression. "Shoes?" she finally said, not looking up.

"Yes, shoes. Why aren't you wearing shoes? Come to think of it, why are you outside at all in nothing but a housecoat? You'll catch your death." I was immediately sorry for my choice of words, but Mom took no notice. I felt like I was talking to one of my students, and one having a slow day at that.

"I have to get these up to the lawn, James. Near the garden. It has to be ready for when they all come." She had this wild look in her eyes, locked halfway between fear and determination. "You coming home late from school doesn't help matters any, either. I know you enjoy Amy's company, but you have responsibilities here, too. We can't all afford to go gallivanting. There's work to be done."

I felt the hair rise on the back of my neck. Rod Serling could have stepped out of the shadows and delivered a pithy intro and I wouldn't have been any more stunned. Even though Doc Pistorius had told me something was wrong, there it was, standing before me and delivering a lecture I hadn't heard since my biggest worry was what to do after the game on Friday—or, rather, what Amy was going to let me do. But this—the tables had turned, and I was the parent. I was the one who knew better. It scared the living shit out of me.

"I know, Mom," I heard myself say. "I know, and I'm sorry. I didn't realize the time."

I grabbed a couple of the chairs. I guessed she was setting them up for whatever visitors came by today, and there would probably be more than a few once word of Glorrie's death got around town. Even as we spoke, down there in the cellar, there were probably ten to fifteen hams being baked, all to ease our pain. People would be bringing them over anytime, but I didn't think they would want to sit outside. It wasn't bitterly cold, but cold enough. "Tell you what," I said, moving toward her, "you go inside and put on some socks and shoes, and I'll take these up to the garden for you."

"And set up," she said. "They need to be set up, right around the garden."

"Fine. I'll set them up. You go."

She looked at the chairs, unsure as to whether she could trust me.

"Go, Mom. I mean it."

"I don't know where you think you get the right to tell me what to do, young man," she muttered, but she put the chair down and started for the stairs anyway. She walked slowly, shuffling her feet. I could hear them softly scrape against the chilled cement of the floor, then up the stairs, and farther up into the light. She muttered the whole way.

I took a deep breath and ran my fingers through my hair. I was into it now. I didn't know what I was going to do, but I was there, ready to do something. I found myself hoping Earl would come around soon, so at least there'd be someone I could talk to about it, which struck me as funny. I hadn't hoped to see Earl for a long time. Finally, I loaded the three lawn chairs over my left arm, and shut the cellar doors behind me. Mom was still standing out by the garden, looking down into the dirt. "Did you get some shoes, Mom?"

"Isn't it beautiful?"

"What?"

"The garden."

I looked down. "It's dirt, Mom."

She smiled, still looking at whatever garden she imagined. "Your father used to talk about the stalks like they were legs. Strong like legs, he'd say, but then, his one leg wasn't very strong. Still, I like to think of them that way. Strong like legs."

I looked again, this time closer, thinking I had missed a bud of something, whatever she had planted, poking through the soil, even though I knew it was too late in the year. There was nothing that I could see. I looked back up at Mom. "Please go inside and get dressed. Please."

She looked at me. "First the chairs, James."

"Okay, okay," I said, and began setting them out in a shallow arc, facing the garden. "No one's going to want to sit out here, though. It's cold. It's November. Who sits outside in lawn chairs in November?" I was talking to myself, which was just as well, since Mom was paying me no mind. "Who's coming by, anyway? Do you know?"

Mom looked at me as though I were the one untethered. "What's the matter with you?"

"Me?" I said. I watched her sit in the first chair she had brought out, stare down at the dirt again. "What the hell," I said, and took the chair next to her. I rubbed at my eyes. I was already tired. "It's good to see you, Mom," I said.

"Well, you too, dear."

"Been a while."

"Has it?"

"Yeah."

She smiled weakly, and patted my hand, but I could see in her eyes she didn't really know what I was talking about.

"So what are we going to do, Mom? I mean, what are we supposed to do now?" It was a serious question. I hadn't been around many funerals in my lifetime—there was Uncle Tom's, of course, but I was way too young to remember it. And then there was Dad's, but I certainly wasn't involved in its planning. I was barely conscious. Everything from that period seems to be in black and white, as though it were something I watched on television, and nothing I lived through. So I had no clue as to what you did when someone died. Did you call someone? Did you just drive down to the mortuary? Did you have to hire a minister, like you do at weddings? Maybe Earl would let me know, whenever he showed up. He always enjoyed telling me what to do. Or I could call Doc Pistorius, or Donnie. Donnie would know. And if he didn't, Meg would.

"Do about what, James?" Mom deadpanned, scratching her jaw and looking off into the distance.

"About Glorrie."

"For Pete's sake, just relax," Mom said, her face brightening as if all had become clear. "She'll be back any minute now. We just ran out of breakfast food, is all."

She didn't remember Glorrie was dead. Which meant she didn't remember the call from Doc Pistorius, or asking him for me. I wondered why, then, she was going to the trouble of putting chairs out for company. If there's no death, there are no hams, and no one to bring them. But with her apparent state of mind, I realized there really wasn't an answer for why anymore.

"Okay, Mom," I said. "But why don't we go wait inside for a while, all right? You can get dressed, and we can talk."

"We can talk?" she looked surprised. "That sounds nice. We don't really talk anymore, you know."

She let me lead her inside, my palm on the small of her back.

We went in through the back door and into the kitchen. No one used the front door save salesmen and trick-or-treaters. The kitchen looked the same, still colored like it was 1974, all yellow linoleum and orange countertop on chestnut-brown cabinetry. There was still the line of tall glass canisters holding spaghetti, flour, sugar, coffee, and tea, sentried against the wall and arranged in descending order of height. The same ceramic green frog, his gaping mouth stuffed full of rusty S.O.S. pads, still peered down over the lip of the sink. The only thing missing was the Folgers can of bacon drippings, which used to sit to the right of the faucet, nearest the range. Glorrie had called it "nauseating and unhealthy in every way" five or six Thanksgivings before, so Mom had threw it away and promised to use margarine to grease the pans.

"Go upstairs and get something on your feet, Mom. Jeez, it's almost as cold in here as it is outside." Weather had hit early. No snow yet, but it was threatening. I wondered if the ground was frozen yet. From what I hear, it's hard to bury a person when the ground works against you.

"It is chilly, isn't it?"

"Yeah, it is." I said. "What do you have the thermostat set on?"

"I don't know," she said. She was standing there in the middle of the kitchen, her hands crossed over her chest and absently scratching at her shoulders. She looked smaller than normal, standing the way she was.

"Where are your shoes?" I finally said. "Let me get them for you."

She looked around the room slowly. "I don't know," she said again, softly.

"I'll find them," I said. "You sit. And I'm turning the heat up."

"No," she said quickly, "Glorrie said not to touch the thermostat anymore. Don't touch it, Glorrie gets so upset."

"What do you mean, Glorrie said not to touch the thermostat?"

"She said not to. It's expensive, and it could start a fire."

"You just had a fire going in the barrel outside," I protested.

"Shhh," she smiled, putting her finger to her lips. "Don't tell Glorrie."

"I don't think that's going to be a problem," I muttered, and then, "I'm going to have to turn the heat up, Mom. It's just too goddamned cold in here."

Her head snapped up and her eyes locked on mine. "Don't you curse at me, James," she said, "I won't have it." It was a strange trans-formation. One minute, she was quiet as one of my freshmen on the first day of school. The next, she's my mother again, and I'm the school kid. She sat down at the window seat behind the kitchen table and looked outside. I took a deep breath. Through the kitchen window, I could see the garden, my truck, the windmill frame, and the barn beyond. I considered for a moment how easy it would be to be driving right now, how comfortable it would be behind the wheel instead of doing this, instead of dealing with my weirded-out mother and my aunt's funeral and getting shoes and being in this house again after so many years. So easy. Not now, I promised my-self, but soon. "I'll get you your slippers," I said, "and a blanket."

Mom curled up a little into herself, her knees to her chest, still looking out the window. Her breath streaked visibly on the cold glass pane.

I headed upstairs. The rest of the house was as predictable as the kitchen. I could have closed my eyes and gone from room to room to room and never hit a stick of furniture. From the kitchen, there was a soft arc around the end of the hardwood dining room table; from there, into the living room, a sharp left behind the brown velveteen recliner, and up the stairs. I've run the patterns at least a few thousand times. And there were patterns to run with Mom, too—ruts, really. It was the only way Mom and I knew how to be together—saying and doing things we hated, but saying and doing them all the same. The curse of history, I guess. There are things that stay with you, moments that you wish you could clip out of time, save in an album to thumb through whenever you want. And then there are those things that are left you, sometimes cultivated in and by you, things you wish you could bury like the dead in a cold November. It all hangs there like a stubborn ghost, the good and the bad alike. It all remains.

Up in the hallway, I turned the thermostat on. It was set at seventy-two, but the switch was off. The furnace grumbled to life.

"James!" Mom called from downstairs. "Did you just turn the heat on?"

"No, Mom," I lied.

"Well, it just came on."

I paused. "No it didn't."

"All right then," she said.

I was both amused and deeply troubled to be able to get away with something like that. I tried to focus on warming Mom up a little. The afghan was in the linen closet at the end of the hall, and her slippers were in the bathroom, sitting next to the tub. I scooped them up, slung the afghan over my shoulder, and headed back downstairs again. I could hear the opening and closing of doors, and I hurried down. "Here, Mom," I said, putting the afghan around her shoulders, "here's a blanket for you." She walked over to the coat closet and opened the door, peered inside, closed it again. "What are you looking for?"

She didn't answer, and went to the front door. She opened it, looked around, and closed it as well.

"Mom? Mom, what are you doing?"

She headed back into the kitchen again, still not making a sound, and I followed, watched her open the door to the basement stairs. I stepped in front of her and grabbed her by the shoulders. "Mom, answer me. What the hell are you doing?"

She looked up at me. She looked very frightened. "Glorrie isn't back yet. She isn't back yet."

"Mom," I said, suddenly sounding as tired as I felt.

"She was supposed to be home this morning. She told me she'd come back and make breakfast, and here it is almost noon."

"Yeah, Mom. Sit down, please." She sat back at her place on the window seat, and I took the chair across from her, leaned heavily on the table. "Do you remember Doc Pistorius calling this morning?"

"No. Did he?"

"Yeah, Mom, he did. Do you remember what he told you?" I didn't want to say it if I didn't have to. I didn't have to be the one to tell her sister was dead. The most important person in her life, gone.

"I don't think he called."

"He did, Mom. About eight, I'd say. Remember?"

"No."

"And then you asked him to call me."

"Call you?"

"Yes."

She raised one eyebrow. "Why on earth would I do that?"

I smiled, but Mom had looked away. She was sort of watching the floor, her eyes darting about rapidly. I shook my head. "I don't know. It surprised me too. But here I am. I came."

"Why would the doctor call? What did he say? Was it about Glorrie?"

"Yes, Mom."

"Is she sick?"

I took a deep breath, let it out decisively. "There was an accident, remember? At Fathauer's?"

"At Fathauer's."

"Glorrie was shopping for breakfast, remember?"

She looked up at me, then, and put her left hand to her forehead. "Yes," she said. "She went for apple butter. And pretzels, so we could make candy later. Pretzels dipped in chocolate. And we could play rummy this afternoon. I can still play rummy. Glorrie just marvels at the fact I can still play cards. Isn't that funny?"

I nodded. "Yeah, Mom."

"I have the chocolate, but not the pretzels. I keep the chocolate

59

in the freezer just in case there's something to be made."

"I'll get you some pretzels later, Mom, okay?"

"Don't worry about it, Glorrie's getting them."

"No, Mom," I said. "She's not." I watched her smile fade. Something had clicked in her head. "Glorrie fell, Mom. Do you remember?"

"No."

"She did. Someone at Fathauer's hit her with a cart or something. And when she fell, she had a stroke."

"He hit her?" Her eyes were wide, and they instantly welled with tears. "He hit her again?"

I shook my head. "Not again, Mom, just the one time. But she had a stroke, and she died before they could get to her."

"Oh, my Lord," she said. "She was only buying apple butter." My mother's eyes were wet and wide, like a baby's, her hands rolling around each other just below her chin, hunched over slightly. She was breathing heavily. I thought she might cry, but she didn't. "He shouldn't have hit her," she repeated, put her hands out to grasp mine tightly. "Not for that, not for that. It's not right. Not for that."

I returned her grip, watched her lay her head down to the vinyl tablecover, and gently stroked her fine hair. It smelled of talc. "Don't go crazy on me, Mom," I whispered, half to myself. "Don't go crazy on me."

"I'll try," she whispered.

We sat like that for a while. I could feel the cold air on my back and warm air from the duct overhead on my face. After a while, my mother said, "What will we do, Reese?"

"I don't know," I answered, and it took me a few minutes to realize what she'd just called me. Who, at the moment, she thought I was. Who, when talking to Doc Pistorius, she had really been asking for.

By four that afternoon, Doc had come and gone already, told me everything that had happened with Glorrie. The story was already making the rounds around town. She had gone to Fathauer's and got to talking with Freda at the counter about Bingo, which Glorrie and Mom hadn't been to in a while. Glorrie asked about apple butter, an innocent enough addiction she'd picked up on her Civil War tour of the South. The apple butter had replaced marmalade, from her London trip, which in turn had replaced her affection for cactus jelly from the Grand Canyon. You could always tell where Glorrie had last visited by what she spread on her toast. She was there in aisle two, reaching up for a jar, when a kid from Decatur took the turn around the endcap too widely, and in trying to pass her, glanced off her right side. Glorrie was thrown off-balance, did a half-turn on one heel, and fell to the tiled floor. Everyone within earshot said they could hear the bone in her hip snap, like a bell cracking with its last ring. She died on the floor, Doc said, a stroke, brought on by the shock to her system. Doc and I agreed it would have been a tough blow to Glorrie, had she lived. Breaking a hip is considered the beginning of the end, at least in Moweaqua. People talk about it like a death sentence: *Did you hear who broke a hip? What a shame. Won't be long now.* Glorrie wouldn't have liked it. Maybe it was a mercy she went the way she did. I don't know. Or maybe it's just human nature to defend fate.

Doc Pistorius also examined Mom and confirmed his earlier diagnosis: she was, indeed, untethered. Possibly Alzheimer's, but Doc said naming it wasn't nearly as important as dealing with it. He said she was still pretty high-functioning, but that status would probably change, and not for the better. Glorrie had been taking remarkably good care of Mom, Doc told me as he was leaving, and that such a responsibility was tough for anyone of any age to take on. He wasn't talking about Glorrie so much as about me, and what I should take on. Or, rather, shouldn't take on. He wanted to see her again, maybe the middle of next week. *I won't be here next week,*

I thought, followed by the familiar voice I think of as Dad's. *Then who will?*

Mom was napping, which is something Doc said she'd do a lot. The day was nearly spent, but I didn't feel like I'd accomplished much. I'd reunited with my mother, who apparently wasn't aware I'd ever been gone; I'd set out some moldy lawn furniture no one who'd come over that day even considered using; I broke my mother's heart in telling her her sister was dead, and then found out it wasn't me who she wanted help from, but my father, who had been gone for almost twenty years. All in all, it had been one bitch of a day.

My stomach growled, and I realized I hadn't eaten anything since my Egg McMuffin on the way out of Bloomington-Normal that morning. Not that food was going to be a problem for this visit—finding enough fridge space, maybe. Death in Moweaqua means one thing: food, and lots of it. Dozens of women whom I didn't know but knew me had been dropping off hot and cold dishes like we were a soup kitchen on the holidays. So far, the count was six sliced hams, two plates of turkey, and a deli tray; three casseroles: turkey tetrazinni, beef noodle, and something that smelled like tuna; mashed and scalloped potatoes; green beans with bacon, peas and carrot medley, lima bean bake; two plates of deviled eggs, one with relish, one without; potato, macaroni, and lettuce salads; bags of chips; tins of cookies, a chocolate cake with a cherry on top, and pies, pies, pies. I felt full just looking at it all. I pulled off a slice of ham. It was still warm, and some of the juice slid down my hand to my wrist. It was tastier than I had expected, and I found myself on my fourth slice by the time I heard someone behind me.

I swear to God, at first I thought it was my father standing there. It's not that Earl looks at all like my father; Earl was tall, yes, but thick, with a round paunch. His buzz-cut hair had gone all salt-and-pepper, his basset eyes were low and sad, and the crooked bridge of his nose had become more pronounced since I'd last seen him. It was the way he was standing more than anything, leaning on his right leg like my father did, his hands on either side of the door frame as though he were blocking it, John Deere cap in one hand, head cocked to one side. I felt ten again, thrilled and frightened and sad all in the space of a breath.

"Reese," Earl said.

"Hi, Earl."

"I wasn't sure if I'd see you."

"Well," I said, "I'm here."

"Yeah," he said, scratching the back of his head. He looked tired. I had surprised him, being here. Earl was used to taking care of my Mom and Glorrie by himself. He was the one Mom was supposed to call. He was, after all, the son who Mom wished she'd had.

Earl had said as much the last time I'd seen him, at Sweets a few years before. We fought like brothers because essentially we were—he'd already been taken in by my folks by the time I was born, after his mother Beatrice—Mom and Glorrie's younger sister—died. We got along well when I was young, but it all went south after Dad died. He went from scrimmaging with me in the backyard to lecturing me on barn safety, from wrestling with me in the living room to telling me to stop slouching and watch my language. Things never got better between us—he became the responsible adult, and I became more and more resentful of the place he'd taken, farming my father's land with my father's equipment. I was glad when he moved into a place of his own after that first season. He used to brag to me about how much money he made. From what Donnie had said, it sounded like Earl had saved some of it up.

"I hear Doc's been here," Earl said.

"Just left," I nodded. "He said Mom's not well. Said she needed to be watched so she wouldn't hurt herself."

"Nothing new."

"Really?" I said. I still didn't want to believe it.

"Yeah, really."

"For how long?"

Earl shrugged. "A while now. Glorrie was doing most of the work. And your mom has good days and bad."

I nodded again, picked up a napkin and wiped the ham juice off my fingers. I took a deep breath. I didn't want a fight, and figured I needed Earl's help in all this. So I decided to try the high road. "So how have you been, Earl?"

Earl just looked at me, shifted his weight so he was leaning fully on the doorframe, settling in for a talk short enough, I imagined, that he wouldn't have to take the time to sit down. "You need to call Howser's funeral home," he said, ignoring my question completely, picking at his ear. "Like I said, I had no idea if you were coming or not, so I went ahead with it. I'm just back from coffee with Gum." Gum Howser ran the mortuary, and was one of Earl's old fishing buddies. "We talked about it a little, already. I didn't want to waste any time." The words *waiting for you* were understood, and I didn't miss them, hanging in the air like that.

"So you thought you'd just make plans without me. Seems like you've been doing that a lot, lately." So much for the high road.

Earl sniffed. If he understood I was talking about buying the land, he didn't show it. I doubted he did. Earl was never one for subtlety. "Guess so, Reese. We've had to do a lot of things without you in the last few years."

I could feel myself bridling, could see the fight arcing out in front of us. This was what Earl and I did. But I pushed it down. The last thing I needed or wanted was Earl on my back. And it was the last thing Mom needed, too. Earl and I were too practiced at this, too ready to fall back into old arguments. So I tried the one thing I knew he wouldn't expect—a peace offering, albeit through gritted teeth. "Look, can I make you some coffee or something?"

He followed. "I told you, I just had some." Then, more quietly, "And don't play host for me in this house."

I turned back to face him. "What did you just say?" I straightened my back, felt the muscles in my forearms tense.

He sized me up. Earl had more than ten years on me, and was used to being able to push me around. He probably still could, though it would be a fair fight. I had maybe an inch on him in height, but he was heavier than I was. Stronger, too. I hadn't been in a fight since ninth grade, when I threw Jimmy Kaler up against the wall for snapping Amy's bra strap in the hallway. Jimmy was easily cowed. Earl wasn't.

"I said don't play host for me in this house." Earl's voice was louder, and small bits of spit flew from his mouth. "I'm in this house almost every day. I make coffee in this kitchen almost every day. I do the work that needs to be done around here. I mow the lawn. I paint the barn. I see that Glorrie and Clara are all right."

"Yeah, nice job, by the way. You took real good care of everyone. Glorrie's dead and Mom's nuts. Great fucking job."

His mouth hung open, his eyes narrowed. I'd wounded him, and he was surprised. "Go home. You don't belong here anymore."

"Belong here?" I snapped. "This isn't about belonging anywhere, you jackass. This is about me coming home to help *my* mother, and then getting the hell out. You're the one who doesn't belong here."

"You don't even know where the damn coffee is, hotshot."

I shook my head. A ludicrous challenge. And he was calling me hotshot again, the way he would when he teased me, back when I was a kid. "Third cabinet to the left of the sink, where it's always been. Nothing changes around here, Earl. I could be gone ten years and it would all be the same."

"Wrong, professor," Earl went to the third cabinet and opened it. There was almost nothing there anymore—no coffee, no spices, no tea bags, just a few packs of Sweet-n-Low and a stack of chipped dishes we used to take on picnics. He slammed the cabinet shut. "Neither Glorrie or your mom could reach up this high anymore, so I helped them move a lot of stuff around. So don't play host for me, Reese, and don't pretend to waltz back in here and start up like nothing's happened. You don't have the right."

I threw up my hands. "So you make me some coffee, Earl. You play the host. What the hell do I care?"

"That's the whole point," he said, muttering again. "You don't."

I let that one go. I leaned against the far counter, and watched Earl fill the coffeepot with water. Earl was actually going to make me coffee—a surprising move, I thought, given the circumstances. It calmed me momentarily—enough that I began to feel badly, again, for the way this had gone. "Earl," I said, modulating my voice, "we're getting off on the wrong foot here. Of course I care. It's just—"

"No you don't," he barked, pointing at me. His fingers were thick as bratwurst. I shushed him and then, in harsh but hushed tones, he went on. "No you don't. I've been telling your mother that you care for years now. Defending you, and against my better judgment, by the way. It was what she wanted to hear. She wanted to be convinced of that fact, and by God, I tried. But I could never quite do it, Reese, and you know why? Because you didn't show it. Not ever. You never cared, not like you should've."

I looked at him, then looked away, my arms crossed over my chest. I couldn't argue with that. I mean, I loved my mother, and I loved Glorrie. But I didn't see them. I didn't make the effort to look in on them. I didn't mow their lawn. I didn't paint the barn. I didn't move their kitchen stuff into lower cabinets. I chose not to. I said nothing, since there was nothing to say.

"Why are you even here, Reese?" Earl finally said, once the coffee was perking behind him. He shook his head, his anger apparently spent. "Why now? I honestly figured you wouldn't come. I really did. I thought I'd have to call you and tell you Glorrie had died, and you'd say you were sorry, and maybe you'd mean it. But you'd be too busy to come down, too busy to help with the arrangements, too busy to help with your Mom. But you're here. So you'll have to pardon me if I ask why."

I sighed. "Mom asked for me," I said. "Doc Pistorius called and told me Mom wanted me to come. So I did."

"She's been asking for you for years, Reese."

"I know," I said. "I never meant to hurt her. I just didn't have time. It wasn't her, it wasn't personal."

"She's your goddamned mother, Reese. Everything's personal."

He paused, looked at the floor for a while. "She asked for you specifically, huh?"

"Well, I thought she did."

Earl's eyes snapped up. "What do you mean?"

Part of me wanted to let him think she'd asked for me, and not for him. He was vulnerable here, I could see it in his eyes. But the less vindictive part of me—or maybe just that part tired of fighting—won out. I shrugged. "She was asking for Reese, so Doc Pistorius called me. Doc called me at work, and I came. But the truth is—"

Earl laughed in a short, grim breath. "The truth is, she was asking for your Dad. Am I right?" He shook his head, and his voice softened. "You drink your coffee." He straightened up, and tipped his cap back on his head. "I'll see you in the morning."

"All right."

He looked at me, took a long breath. "She has any problems, anything, you call me. We meet Gum at eleven."

"I'll be there."

"I'll pick you up, hotshot," he said, and he was out the door.

# Chapter Five

*1936*

THE PULL OF THE EARTH HAD BROUGHT IT DOWN, Reese thought—the pull of the earth and time. The western wall of the wood-peg barn had fallen in, perhaps a week before from the look of it. It was all busted board and splinter, the mottled color of white-wash, wood, and dirty, month-old snow. Reese gazed at the ice sparkling off a pile of old tack half-buried under plank, noticed how the roofline sagged in the middle, lacking the support to which it had become accustomed. The pull of the earth, he thought again, that's what rules things.

He turned from the barn, and put his suitcase down on the frosty mud of the driveway. All this was now his: house, stables, corn crib, orchard, acreage, barn. Except that one wall succumbing, nothing was different—and yet, everything had changed. His parents were dead. He was a landowner. He had become somebody, suddenly, by the passing of his father. It occurred to Reese he was now alone, but he felt no different than before.

Reese's parents had been quiet and hardy souls who lived off the land, and barely spoke a word to their son or each other unless there was need. His father Allen had been a stern man, never without a pipe in his mouth, from breakfast to bedtime, indoors and out. His mother Mabel had been a thin woman, and by the end of her days, her hands were bruised winter twigs. She had died in January, in her sleep, and Reese's father followed just six weeks later. The last thing Reese remembered the old man saying to him was he was tired of eating cold sandwiches.

Tom kidded Reese, the day of his father's funeral, called him "gentleman farmer," and knocked Reese's hat from his head. Reese was stunned, not so much because of the passing of his parents, but because someone had mentioned that Reese was now the last Moss in town. When someone talked about Mr. Moss, or the Moss place, it'd be him they'd be talking about. It was a hard thing for him to wrap his head around, being the last, being the only. He had always felt comfortable being unimportant. Now that he was someone, he wasn't sure he liked it.

Tom pointed out that Reese had been considerably better known in the community than his father since what happened back in '32. That's the way most people talked about the thrasher and the mine incidents both: "What happened in '32." It was shorthand. People figured if you lived through it, you'd understand; if you didn't, you had no business knowing what it meant anyway. But those things were history—dead like his parents, like the life he was now leaving behind.

Reese had built a life for himself, of a sort, over the past four years. His knee had mended well enough for him to get around, and though he'd never win any races, he was able to work well enough on the farm. He learned to budget his money and his time—to save a little during the growing season to get him through the winter. He'd lived with Tom until Tom and Glorrie had gotten married—they had gone to a show in Decatur one early summer night, and come back husband and wife. Tom knew a Justice of the Peace from some local bar, and he'd hitched them up for the price of a beer and a handshake. When they came home that night, Reese slept out on the porch, trying not to hear them.

So Reese rented a room above Nalbach's Harness Shop. Reese agreed to help out in the store, sweep up the place, keep it in good repair, and watch the property after dark, since Gus Nalbach had noticed some leather missing from his stock. Reese considered it a bargain. All he wanted was a place to hang his shirts and lay his head, and that's all he got. But he was finally on his own, leaning on no one.

Tom had quit farming completely after the fall of 1932. The country was still in the throes of the Depression, but things were getting better in spits and spurts—at least in Decatur, where companies were hiring again. Tom had landed a job up at A.E. Staley's, where they processed soybean. It was hard work, but paid all right. Reese met him for lunch there once or twice, and marveled at how big it was. He looked around and tried to follow all the pipes and lines running every which way, crisscrossing themselves and then leading away. He wondered if there were any one man who knew where they all went, if there was anyone who understood how the whole place worked. Tom said it wasn't possible.

He and Glorrie chose to live in Moweaqua because Glorrie didn't want to leave Clara behind, all alone. Tom didn't put up much of a fight—he liked Moweaqua, liked the way he said he was regarded there. He had respect, he told Reese, and didn't want to go anywhere where he'd have to impress people all over again. Besides, his house on Cherry Street was just becoming a home—Tom and Reese had knocked out a wall and put in a separate bedroom with a fireplace, and Tom was planning on putting in plumbing sometime, when he could afford it—or, at least, that's what everyone assumed he meant by "being rich enough to shit in the house." Glorrie sewed some curtains with red flowers on them, and there was always a fresh towel on the icebox door. Tom almost never wore the same shirt for days in a row anymore. He wore a smile more often too, though he was loathe to admit it, and about thirty extra pounds around his middle. They didn't have a car, so Tom caught a truck into work every morning with four other men from town. Tom tried to get Reese to join him, said he could get him an interview at Staley's, too, but Reese said he was fine where he was.

But with his parents gone, Reese had a new place to call home. A few days after the funeral, he gathered up his suitcase of belongings, made sure his room upstairs was clean, shook hands with Gus, and walked to his new home—or rather, his old home. He didn't know which to call it, but by the time he walked up the dirt driveway, he'd decided it made no difference. Things just happened, and it was the job of most men to follow the land, the weather, life's responsibilities, and those who seemed born to lead. To work quietly, and pray to do it well. That's all there was to it.

Reese picked up his suitcase, and headed to the back door of the house. When he tried the latch, he found someone had locked it, and Reese had no key. His parents had never locked their doors. He had to settle for going through a window like a thief in the night. This was how Reese came home.

Reese got married a couple of months later because he didn't know how to cook. He'd come to understand his father's last words all too well, having had little but cold liverwurst sandwiches since moving back home. Reese had no idea what half the gadgets in the kitchen were used for, and only a vague idea of how to operate the stove. He had seen his mother light it a thousand times, watched as she made pies, cakes, meats, and corn. But he'd paid no attention to any of it. Not to what was done in the kitchen, nor in the barn, nor in the rest of the house and surrounding outbuildings. It would take him years before he felt like he wasn't missing something important, something he was supposed to know but hadn't figured out yet.

But he didn't have to learn the ins and outs of the kitchen. That knowledge was for women, and for men to marry into, as Tom said whenever he brought over a hot plate of food Glorrie sent over. Glorrie kept mentioning Clara was a great cook, and that she had all the time in the world. It wasn't subtle, but it worked—Reese wasn't hard to convince. He asked Clara for her help, and she came over nearly every evening to help him, often leaving late after they'd talked for hours. He'd walk her home, and she'd smile, let him hold her hand. One Sunday, Tom and Glorrie came over for supper, and Glorrie asked when the two of them were to be married, seeing as how they were already everything but. Clara blushed, and Reese shared a look with her that was something of a promise, which only made Clara's cheeks flush deeper. Tom told Glorrie to mind her business, and that was the end of it. But it was that week when Reese struggled down to one knee while Clara was fixing chicken dumplings, and asked her to be his wife. "I have a place to call mine," he told her, though he still felt it was a lie. "I'd like to share it with you," which wasn't a lie at all. It made her cry and smile at the same time, and tears or not, Reese considered Clara's smile a thing to behold. As bright as Glorrie's—not as wild, but perhaps more kind. Clara accepted, getting down on the floor with him and kissing his face over and over again. They were married two weeks later at the Methodist Church on Hanover Street, and had a reception at the house afterward.

By seven-thirty, it was dark, and most everyone had gone home except Tom and Glorrie, her having volunteered to help Clara clean up, move her clothes in, and prepare for the wedding night. Tom and Reese had been relegated to the back porch to smoke and relax while the women got things ready. "Men only get in the way of good work," Glorrie said, and Reese wondered whether or not she meant that to be limited to cleaning the house. But out the door they went. Clara grinned and waved to Reese from the window, and Reese smiled back and went to meet Tom.

"You ready?" Tom asked, sitting on the cellar doors. Both Tom and the doors groaned, and he took a swig from his cup of warm beer. "For the wedding night, I mean?"

"I suppose so." Reese was drinking beer, too. He had been nursing it all night. He leaned back against the side of the house and breathed in the night air. It was cold, but the house had been too warm, with the fireplace and the people and the party. It was good to take in fresh air again. It felt clean. "I mean, it's not like we haven't..." He left the lie where it was. He and Clara had kissed some, and he had slipped a hand under her shirt once, touching nothing except her smooth stomach, and, barely, the soft undercurve of her small breast. "Anyway, I suppose so."

Tom laughed. "You'd better get a much happier face on before you walk into that bedroom tonight, or else this marriage might be over before it's begun."

Reese smiled. "I know," he said. "I do love her," he added, for no apparent reason.

"You'd better. Glorrie gets mad at you, you know who she's going to send to kick some sense into your head, right?" Tom laughed. "Not that I'd do it, mind you."

Reese didn't answer. He was looking up at the night sky, seeing all the stars, and trying to make pictures out of them, like the constellations he remembered reading something about once, many years before. "You know, they say there's a bear somewhere up there," he said, his mouth hanging open slightly as he tilted his head back.

"What?" Tom looked up.

"A bear. A big one and a little one, I think. And a scorpion someplace, and a guy with a club fighting it."

"What are you talking about?"

"Gods in the heavens," Reese said.

"Jesus Christ in a cup, don't let Clara hear you say that," Tom said, "or Glorrie neither. We'll both be at church three times a week and twice Sundays."

"They only thought there were gods, or something," Reese said. "Long time ago, in Greece, I think. They were up there, watching everything, just moving across the sky with the moon. They didn't move or do anything, just watched. The only one I know for sure is the club guy's belt—those three stars right there, in a line."

"That's a belt?"

"Yeah."

"No buckle."

"Maybe the middle one's the buckle," Reese said. "And I think the Big Dipper might be the bear, but I'm not sure. And then there's the North Star."

"That one I know. Brightest one up there."

"No, that's a different one, in the big dipper there. See it?"

Tom laughed, a short surprised bark. "Yeah, I see it." It occurred to Reese Tom wasn't used to being corrected.

Reese sighed. "You ever wish things were different? Wish for something you know won't ever happen?"

Tom snorted. "Hell of a thing to say on your wedding night, Reese."

"Not Clara," Reese waved him off. "I mean, like these stars. It

73

would be nice to know them all, know what's up there by name. My father knew them, some of them anyway. He had this thing where he'd say *gotcha* whenever he saw a cloud pass over the moon or the sun. But I never got to ask him why, just like I never got to ask about the stars. I know I'll never know now. I know I'll die looking up there, just like I am now, wondering about it."

Tom squinted at Reese, and took a long pull off his cigarette. "Jesus, you're boring." He shook his head, and leaned back against the cellar doors. "Boy, I don't know where you get this stuff. I really don't. And on your goddamned wedding night, no less. You should be thinking about that little girl in there, and all the things you get to do now."

Reese shrugged. "I guess. I mean, I am. But I still think about this sort of stuff now and then."

"I've been telling you, you need to get yourself a radio for the house," Tom said. Reese had never had the money for a radio, but enjoyed listening at the pool hall. Tom had finally broken down and bought one on credit at a store in Decatur, and Clara had been spending time at Glorrie's house, listening to what Tom called "goddamned love stories" during the afternoons when she could. "It's a wonder. You won't have time to think anymore."

Reese laughed. "A dream come true."

"I'm serious. You can listen to the WLS National Barn Dance right there in your living room. Hell of a thing, you know?" Tom finished off his drink, and tossed the mug into the soft grass so he wouldn't have to get up. "Speaking of barns, when are you going to fix that damn thing? You're going to need it pretty quick here, ain't you?"

"I guess," Reese said, tearing his gaze from the sky and looking at the pile of wood and shingle. "I'm just glad all the livestock was out of there when the wall went. We lost a few chickens that shouldn't have been out in the first place, is all. The horses were in the stable, and Dad had the cow slaughtered in October last year. He said he was sick of milking, and what with the grocers carrying fresh milk these days, he could afford to stop feeding her and have her feed him for a while. The meat was tough, but it was good. We still got some of it stored over at the packing plant."

"You going to get another one?"

"Another cow? I don't think so," Reese shook his head. "My father was right about that. But I'll need to store the machinery in there, once I figure out what's working and what's not. Some of it was damaged when that wall came down, but most of it is fine, from what I can tell."

"If you need any help, Reese, you just let me know."

Reese raised his cup to Tom, and swallowed the last of his tepid beer. "I will." Reese looked back up to the sky, watched Tom go into the house to refill his mug. Through the kitchen window, Reese saw Tom grab Glorrie from behind, kissing her neck like a wild animal. She laughed, tickled, and made a show of trying to get away, but she couldn't. Clara stood to one side, smiling, but walked away, deeper into the house.

The light outside dimmed as a cloud took the moon. "Gotcha," Reese whispered.

A few weeks later, Reese decided it was time to repair the barn. So he enlisted Tom's aid, and they put out the call for help, promising hot coffee and roast beef with potatoes for supper to anyone who'd come and lend a pair of hands to raise the western wall and put in a few nails where the wooden pegs were rotting away. Reese wanted the barn to be not just fixed, but improved, made more solid. He wanted to stop the leaks in the roof. He wanted to shore up the dirt floor where cold sheeted in and bothered his knee. He wanted to paint it red instead of the whitewash his father had used for so many years. Reese wanted the barn to belong to him.

They did it over the course of a rainy Saturday—Tom was there, and Woes showed up too, along with other men from town: Mike Hudson, Hal Bilyeu, Don Saddoris, and a few others who came and went over the day. Woes and Tom shook hands for the first time in years, having successfully avoided each other for a long time, up to and including Reese and Clara's wedding. Or, rather, it had been Woes doing the avoiding. Tom didn't seem to care one way or the other, and greeted Woes with a clap on the shoulder.

"How are you, old man? Holding up?" Tom said.

"Who's the old man here, Tom?" Woes countered with a smile. "Last time I checked, you had Reese and I here beat by a few years."

"Aw, I got you beat in so many ways, I can't keep track." Tom laughed.

"Thanks for coming, Woes" Reese added. "Really."

"Glad to help, Reese."

The men started, fueled by the energy of the morning and coffee and hot biscuits. They first built up a short wall of sugar brick on the west side, to protect the wood from rotting in winter, and then finished the new wall for the old barn with wood planks, complete with small, shuttered box-windows for ventilation. They patched the roof with tar, built a new ladder up to the loft, and used up an entire box of ten-penny nails stabilizing the rest of the joists, beams, and studs.

It was the first time Reese, Tom, and Woes had worked together since the day of the thrasher, and if it was uncomfortable for any of them early on, they fell into natural rhythms quickly enough that all discomfort was soon forgotten. Tom even sang a song Reese hadn't heard since that fall in 1932, a drinking song Tom had picked up somewhere and taught to Reese, Woes, Stupak, and even Jules. It was a bawdy thing about a can-can girl from France who would-would do her dance, and it was raunchy enough they stopped singing when Clara and Glorrie came out with fresh coffee. More than once, Reese looked over at Tom and Woes, marveling at how well they were getting on, as though Tom weren't the reason Woes had a broken smile. By day's end, Reese had a barn again, leaving just the painting to be done. The men ate until all the meat was off the bone and the potato bowl had been scraped clean, and then everyone but Tom and Woes left for home. The three men retired to the barn they'd just finished, to smoke and finish off the coffee.

Reese and Tom sat on a short pile of leftover wood planking against the new wall. Woes leaned on a wooden sawhorse facing them, warming his hands around a coffee cup, and sniffing at the steam rising up out of it.

"I'd better be getting back home pretty quick myself," Woes said.

"Where you living now, Woes?" Tom asked.

"Sullivan. Taking care of the parks over there, and working the grounds for a couple of the schools and such. It's not bad work."

"Sounds pretty good," Reese offered.

"Not like you, though, boy," Tom said, taking a flask out of his pocket and emptying some whiskey into his coffee. He offered the flask to Woes, who declined with a wave. He knew better than to offer it to Reese anymore. "You really struck it rich, with this farm and all."

"Yeah," Woes said. "You think you might want to hire us come fall?"

They laughed, but took it no farther. "Well, I don't know about striking it rich," Reese said, scratching his neck, "but I suppose it will be nice not having to worry so much anymore."

"Worries," Tom grunted. "You just got hitched. Your worries just got started, boy." Tom's eyes glanced at the back door.

Reese smiled. "You think so?"

"Hell, Reese," Tom said, "I know so. You married yet, Woes?"

"Nope."

"Well, don't. It's nothing but someone else telling you what to do. And the thing is, you're expected to do it. No arguing, no nothing. Just do it." Tom pointed at Reese. "You listen to me," he said. "Put your foot down early. Make her understand who's in charge on this farm, and who does what she's told. Cause it's tough as hell to get that across after ways have set."

"What ways?" Woes asked.

"You don't have the freedom that a man should," Tom said. "You're beholden to everything, especially to her. Now that me and Glorrie have an understanding, finally, things are getting better. But I had a rough time for a while. Couldn't do much of anything."

"Like what?" Reese asked. Tom was getting the swagger that had always bothered Reese. It bothered him doubly Tom was getting it while talking about Glorrie.

"Like staying late in Decatur to have beers," Tom said. "Hell, if my ride doesn't want to come home of a night, it ain't my fault. And besides, so long as I bring home the money, she don't have nothing to say about it."

"I guess," Reese said, but he didn't. Reese didn't want anything from Clara, really, except good care, someone to come home to and smile at, someone who'd hold him close and try to convince him for one more day he was doing fine. He didn't want to go out drinking. He wanted someone who knew how to work the stove, who didn't say anything when he passed gas. Someone who made him feel less alone.

Woes paid no attention to Tom. He looked around the barn and nodded. "We did some pretty good work today, Reese. I think she'll hold up a while longer."

Reese smiled, relieved to change the subject. "I think so too."

"How old is it, anyway?" Woes was examining one support beam as though he knew what he was looking at.

Reese thought for a moment, glancing around the hulking structure. He was still getting used to the fact the barn was his now, still getting used to owning things more substantial than his clothes and a pipe. "I don't rightly know," Reese said. "I know my grandfather built it, but I can't say when. It's the second barn to sit here, though. The first blew down in a twister—I think in aught-seven."

"Aught-seven, huh?"

"Around there," Reese nodded.

"Well, this one better stay up for a while," Tom said, "seeing as how much work we put into it today. Once we're done with the painting, that's it. Family or not, I'm not working on this damn barn again for a good while." Tom laughed, and took a drink of his coffee.

"It'll last, Tom," Reese said. "Don't worry." It still surprised Reese he and Tom were related now, if only by marriage. It made him feel guilty, though he'd never tell Tom. Besides, Reese thought, it was blood that bonded them together before, and blood that binds them now. Little difference.

"You're going to have to lock this place up good when you and Clara have kids, you know," Woes said. "Couple of kids from Sullivan just got killed last week playing in their daddy's barn. Seems they got hold of some poison somewhere, and before you know it, *pfft*. Gone."

"I heard something about that," Tom said. "That was in Sullivan?"

"Just outside," Woes said.

"You having kids, Reese?" Tom asked.

"I guess so," Reese said without thinking, though he and Clara had only discussed it in the most casual of manners. "Yeah."

Tom took another sip of coffee and looked over at the house where Clara and Glorrie were working. "Us too. 'Course, we're waiting a while."

"How come?" Woes asked.

Tom shrugged. "Lots of reasons. One more mouth to feed, you know? And right now, that's something I don't need. Besides," Tom winked, "me and Glorrie need all the practice we can get."

Reese gave a half-smile. "Well," he said, "I imagine Clara and I will have one sometime soon. Maybe more than one."

Tom clapped Reese on the back. "That's right, you lucky farming bastard. All the fun you want, and the result is free help out in your fields."

"I suppose," Reese said. He looked across the yard's brown grass to the kitchen window. Clara was standing there, lit up like a girl in the movies. Her blue apron was already dusted in flour, her brown hair was up in a bun and fastened with a pencil, and her hands rolled dough. Reese tried to see her eyes from where he sat, but couldn't. Clara was looking down at her hands, and was obviously engaged in conversation with Glorrie at the same time. Reese wished he could see her eyes, then—he needed to, at that moment, for whatever reason. Clara's eyes were piercing and blue, and soothed Reese in a way he found pleasing. It was he remembered best from the first time they'd talked at the Red Cross coffee urns, those eyes that had made him feel like he was worth something. She believed in him. She had from the beginning. Reese didn't know why, but he didn't want to question it.

Reese's knee ached from the cold, and he wanted to go inside and sit in his favorite chair, the one in the living room by the picture window. He wanted to light his pipe—he was now calling it his pipe, though it was his father's Dunhill—and drink in the blue cherry-smoke that reminded him of his childhood, while at the same time convinced him he belonged in this house, on this land. From his chair, smoking his pipe, he would watch the fields—even now, with nothing growing there, he would watch the snow falling in rows, or see the wind blow brittle leaves over the soil, and listen carefully for its whistle. Sometimes, he swore he could hear it, just barely; other times, he was sure it was his imagination, calling up some ghost from memory and replaying it like a flatland echo.

Since they'd been married, Clara had taken to standing behind him as he sat in the chair, sometimes leaning over him so closely he could smell her neck and hear her breaths in soft, irregular rhythm. She'd rub his shoulders, lay her cheek on the top of his head. It was then he felt her love most openly, then when he allowed himself to believe all this was his, that he deserved it all.

Tom rose suddenly, nearly tripping himself in his haste. "I want some more coffee," he said. "You guys want any while I'm in?"

"Not me," Reese said, "but you can take my cup."

"Mine too," Woes said.

"What am I, a waitress?" Tom grimaced a little, but took the cups. "Back in a minute," he said.

Reese looked over at Woes. "Don't let us keep you if you really need to go," he said. "Not that I'm turning you out or anything. But Clara and Glorrie will be in there baking for tomorrow's supper for at least another hour."

"I have a few minutes," Woes said, and then, after a pause, shook his head and laughed. "Tom hasn't changed much."

"No, I don't guess he has." Reese wasn't sure how Woes meant his remark, but it was true enough.

"He good to Glorrie?"

"I suppose."

"I remember how much you liked her a few years back. But I guess you married the next best thing." Woes' smile faded. "I didn't mean that the way it sounded."

"It's okay," Reese said, forcing a smile.

But Woes wouldn't let it go. "No really—Clara's no second best. Pretty girl, that one."

"It's okay," Reese repeated.

"I just always wanted to see you and Glorrie get together," Woes said. "Maybe it was just me wanting to see Tom not getting what he wanted for a change. But I thought she was right for you. I saw the way she looked at you sometimes, even when Tom was in the room, right there. I thought there was a chance. But Tom's a powerful force to reckon with, I guess, and he takes what he wants. Always has."

Reese smiled, this time genuinely. He'd never known Glorrie had made eyes at him, hadn't known she was really interested. He'd hoped, even dreamed, but never had any hard evidence of it. If he had...he thought, and then stopped. He realized that even then, he didn't know what he'd have done. Woes was right. Tom got what Tom wanted, especially back then.

"It's been good seeing you, Reese," Woes said, offering his hand. "Really."

"You're going to go while Tom's inside?" Reese said, clumsily rising to his feet and shaking Woes' hand.

Woes winked. "I'd better, while I still have my teeth."

Reese laughed. "Well, thanks for coming out. And for your help."

"Glad to do it. You take care, Reese."

"We should do this again sometime. Maybe have a picnic."

"That sounds real fine," Woes said.

"We will, then," Reese said, though he knew it was just an easy, social fib that eased the parting of friends become strangers.

"See you around," Woes said with a half wave.

Tom came back out just as Reese heard Woes starting up his truck. Reese and Tom talked a while longer, about marriage, children, their wives. It was all they'd ever talk about, anymore, Reese realized, all they'd ever have the chance to discuss. He looked absently up into the lit kitchen, where the two sisters talked and gestured and laughed. He loved Clara, and he had loved Glorrie. But that was long ago, Reese thought, repeating it over and over.

Somewhere in the fields, a mouse became the night's first meal for a hungry owl, and a breeze stirred some soil that had been packed down since the deep freeze. Reese shivered in the cold mouth of the barn, looking over at the figures in the window. He couldn't tell who was who anymore. It would be years before he'd come to understand what he'd only started to realize that night. People say things left unfinished are the hardest to get over. But what's often worse is what's left unbegun.

# Chapter Six

BY THE TIME I ROLLED OUT OF BED AT EIGHT-THIRTY, Mom had already been up for hours. Comes with the job description of being a farm wife. If your husband has to be in the fields by sunup, then you have to be up a couple hours before to perk the coffee, fry the eggs and sausage and potatoes, and then clean it all up and start on the next meal. So Mom had coffee on, eggs made. She'd moved all the other food out into the mudroom, which wasn't insulated, so it worked as well as a fridge this time of year. I didn't know if I was supposed to let her use the stove, but the coffee smelled good, and the house wasn't on fire.

"Morning, Mom," I said, grabbing a cup from the cabinet. I was still wearing the same clothes from the day before, though I was "going commando," as my students like to say, since I couldn't bring myself to wear the same underwear two days running. I wished I'd packed a bit better, but I hadn't been prepared for any of this.

"Good morning, James," Mom said. "Do you need me to make you a lunch?"

"I don't think so," I said. She'd done fine so far, but I didn't want her cooking anything else. I could just see Earl's smug look if I let Mom burn herself. "Maybe we could go out for lunch."

Her face brightened. "Really?" she beamed, and then put her hands to her hair to check it. "I must look a fright. Will you clean up here while I go get ready?"

"Sure," I said. "And we have to see Gum today, too, remember. Earl's going to be by in a bit."

"What are we seeing Gum Howser for?" Mom asked, wrinkling her nose. "I swear, that man smells of peat." I laughed, and she smiled and poked me gently in the shoulder. As she headed upstairs, she said, "And don't you go telling people I said so, either."

I wondered if I should remind her of Glorrie's death, but I dismissed it. I didn't have the energy to go through all that again.

Besides, I was enjoying our moment—it was the first really good time we'd had together since I got back. So I let it lay, as still and as quiet as Glorrie herself.

What would Mom say when she saw Glorrie in her casket? Could she deny her sister's death while looking it square in the face, while smelling the peat and the flowers and the formaldehyde all around her? My father's voice whispered, *How many times can you remind a person of something she refuses to know?*

Look for the silver lining. Whatever's happening to Mom, maybe it works in our favor, lets us erase the past few years and start again. It's like a psychological plenary indulgence, all my sins wiped clean just by coming home and walking through that door one more time. And maybe it's all right. Maybe it's an okay trade. Would Mom give up her future in order to recreate her past? Would anyone? Would I?

I sat at the kitchen table, drank my coffee, and listened to the whalesong of the old plumbing upstairs. I ate my eggs serenaded by those familiar sounds, and soon found myself wandering into my father's den. It was wood-paneled, with an oversized couch and a recliner dominating the room, both pointed at a Zenith TV I remember Dad buying. It had been a big deal, but was almost an antique now. There was a bookshelf in one corner, with a small filing cabinet next to it, and a desk next to that, with a manual typewriter. I wondered if the papers scattered around the desk dated back a couple of decades, too, but they didn't. Glorrie had been using the desk—I recognized the handwriting. I couldn't make much sense of them—they looked like they were written in shorthand. And then there was the neat stack of paper just to the right of the typewriter with a top page that simply read: *Memoirs.* Every page beneath it was blank.

Too much to ask for, I supposed, that Glorrie had time to sit here and write out her life's story, but I would have given my truck to read it. Glorrie would have been just the woman to do it, too, to chronicle the things she'd seen, places she'd been, all the things she'd done since her husband had died and left her with a decent amount of pension and insurance money she'd been savvy enough to invest well. She'd traveled a lot, but when she was home, I assumed she'd led the same quiet life Dad had. I missed her more at that moment than in all the time since I'd heard of her passing, looking at the stack of blank bond, at the typewriter that had been too poorly used.

I looked on the bookshelf—not much in the way of books, only some pictures in frames, an old program for the Moweaqua Centennial Celebration back in the 50s, other gewgaws from the various events that make up the history of a town and a family. Dad's hats were still here, too, on pegs by the shelf. Dad was big on hats, always wore one so long as there wasn't music playing. That was his rule. He took his hat off if occasion demanded it—and he claimed he could always tell an occasion by the music—dirges at a funeral, soft piano at a nice restaurant, choir at church, the national anthem at a ball game. When he did doff his cap, I would laugh at his permanent "hat hair," a ridge of graying hair on the back of his head. He knew I laughed, and I remember him smiling back at me as though it were something special we shared. He had his good brown fedora, hit fishing hat pinned with flies, the straw-hat Glorrie brought him from Florida with the bright flowers on the brim that he'd never worn but kept nonetheless. And then there were his caps. A few were true baseball caps: a vintage Cubs hat he never let me wear—belonged to an old friend, he once said—and a newer Cardinals one he'd bought at an exhibition game in Decatur. He didn't wear either of them, but kept them both as a physical reminder of the eternal quandry the baseball fan of Central Illinois found himself in. Cubs or Cardinals? Chicago or St. Louis? North or South? It was split pretty much evenly—and was the cause for many a feud at the coffee shop downtown. But one thing was agreed upon: no one around here, and I mean no one, rooted for the White Sox.

But my father's most important caps weren't related to baseball at all. Instead, they were giveaways by local companies looking to institute brand-loyalty or as free advertising. Bright-orange Caterpillar caps from the plant in Decatur, Staley's slate-grey numbers, red and white from International, green from John Deere and Van Horn Seeds. These were the ones he wore.

Dad walked with a limp, a continual give in his right hip. It embarrassed me when I was a kid, because I could never claim my father could beat up anyone else's. He seemed damaged, worn out, older than he was. We'd be out walking beans or detassling corn and I'd watch him move, watch him with pity. It always seemed to me he was about to topple over with every step, to crumple like an old dollar bill stuffed in a wet pocket, but he never did. Not once, so far as I saw. That is, until he fell that one last time.

I was only a kid when he died, but I remember the day as though it were the beginning of my life. The memories I have before it seem from another time, happening to someone else, fuzzy snapshot visions in sepia, made possible, I am certain, by pictures in my mother's albums. The memory is the first that has the full palette, Dorothy leaving the monochromatic farm and stepping into technicolor Oz. With Dad's death, everything became real.

It was an October Saturday in 1969. I had just finished watching cartoons, and was sitting at the kitchen table playing with the tiny green plastic army men Dad had ordered for me from the back of a *Superman* comic. I was waging war on the pitted oak surface, making huge explosions with spit and breath and imagination, moving my men into position, each one moving in exactly the right formation, in practiced patterns, to gain the most ground for the US forces, to move the lines forward and stamp out the Nazi hordes. While my men were performing complex military strategy, Mom and Glorrie were making supper and idle conversation.

Dad and Earl were starting to bring in the corn and I was killing time, waiting for them to finish picking a field with the tractors so I could grab a basket and go gather the leftovers by hand. Back then, the machinery wasn't as precise as it is today. Today's pickers don't miss an ear, not like they used to. But then, I could make all the money I needed to buy Christmas presents and still have enough left over for a month's worth of gumballs or a few comic books, or even a model of a Ford T-Bird with real rubber wheels and doors that opened and closed. I gathered the leftover corn, and sold it at the grain elevator, with my father's help. "Real little farmer there," the men would say as they weighed my grain, and would then hand me a stack of coins and a couple of bills—more than $10 on a good day. My father said he liked my initiative.

And so my war games were half-hearted. Usually, I played with ferocity, mimicking the battles I heard from Vets who hung out down at City Service, or stories Glorrie would tell about her war-hero husband of WWII. But that day, my mind wasn't even on the small-scale escalation happening there on the kitchen table. It was on the corn, and the prospects it brought.

I suppose that's exactly what my father wanted. He thought of me as the one to whom the farm would someday go, the one who would want the land, all the responsibility it held, all the rewards it promised. He told me it would all come down to me, but the idea that he should actually teach me everything seemed to strike him only occasionally. He taught me seemingly random things about farming from time to time, but mostly talked about how this was all mine, all mine. We'd walk beans together, pulling up the weeds by hand, a torturous job, but necessary, and one I'd helped with as soon as I was old enough to walk down rows without disappearing into them. He taught me their names, made me recite them like prayers in church. *What do I have here, son?* Jimson. *And here?* Milkweed. *This?* Cocklebur. *That?* Piemocker. *Good man, son. Have to know your weeds to tend your crops, know what's bad to grow what's good.*

About a week before he died, he took me for a ride in his tractor. He let me steer as we went down the swaying row of corn, me sitting on his lap up in the cab, the window open behind us, the familiar rumble of the huge machine under my control for the first time in my life. My father promised someday I'd get to operate the pedals, help him bring in the harvest. He and I would farm the land together. I told him I was ready right then. He said he had a lot more to tell me, and that I had a lot more to learn.

But my father didn't have a lot more of anything, as it turned out. He was gone by the next week of a heart attack. Earl was the one who broke the news, stepping through the door gingerly, almost as though he meant to sneak past us without anyone noticing him. For a moment he just stood there, and let the screen door swing slowly behind him. He took off his hat and held it in front of him, looking as though he were about to offer it to one of us—me, Mom, Glorrie, anyone. But he didn't. He was only in his early twenties, and my father was as much his hero as mine. I don't think he wanted to say it, like speaking it might make it more true. He just looked down at his boots, caked with black dirt, and breathed hard.

Glorrie went up to him, put her hands on his shoulders, ducked to look into his eyes. "What is it, Earl?"

"Reese." He looked up at each of us, one by one. This is the moment I recall with uncanny clarity. My mother was standing in front of the counter, holding a wooden spoon covered in corn batter. She was not yet a widow. My aunt stood rigidly before her nephew, who slumped lightly against her as though he were about to collapse himself, and the screen door reached its open limit behind him and stopped with a soft thump. The clock on the stove read 11:23. I held a mine-sweeper army man in one hand, and the prone-rifleman figure was on the hill created by the sugar-bowl, about to sniper him. The television in the next room was on, and I could hear people cheering at the University of Illinois-Michigan game. Somewhere outside, my father was supposed to be picking corn, and readying the fields for me. The cold air from outside smelled empty.

"Call Doc Pistorius," Earl said. Mom muffled a short cry with her hands over her mouth. I didn't make a sound.

This is where my memory starts to blur. Glorrie was on the phone; Earl talked to my mother for a while, and she was trying like hell to push her way past him, to go outside, but Earl wouldn't let her. He told me to watch her, to see that she was all right, and then he went outside. Mom broke down, hugged me for a long time, and I listened to her sob quietly, while at the same time I thought about the game on the TV in the next room, about the corn outside waiting in the fields, about selling it at the elevator and if all this was going to make that impossible. I don't know how long we sat there together, but I know we rose only when Doc Pistorius walked through the back door with a solemn look, put his hand on my shoulder, and took my mother into the dining room to talk.

I didn't know what else to do, so I went back to playing with my army men. They managed to take their ground, but suffered heavy casualties, and couldn't hold it. They quickly discovered they were pinned down on all sides. There was nowhere to run to escape the battle, so they kept fighting. They hoped for a miracle to save them, held strong for as long as they could, but in the end, it was a massacre.

Earl was late. Mom was resting upstairs, and I was in the kitchen trying to lose myself in a pan of soapy water, washing some dishes, focusing on the task. I washed a lot of dishes after Carrie and I split up. It helped to be accomplishing something, cleaning up what was a mess, putting things back in order, if only with the help of hot water, pearly soap, and sleeves rolled up to the elbow. But there weren't enough dishes from the breakfast Mom had prepared, and I found myself done all too quickly. I turned the water off, took the towel from the refrigerator door handle, and dried my hands as I leaned back against the sink.

It was almost eleven. I was supposed to be teaching sophomores about American Government right now, or do as well as a person can with sophomores. Tenth grade is the vast wasteland of high school. Freshmen are cowed, juniors are motivated, seniors are weary. Sophomores just are. But still, I wanted to be there again, felt like I was playing hooky being here at my mother's kitchen sink.

My eyes were heavy and I notice the wind had picked up a little outside. Leaves were blowing around, tumbling by and swirling up in invisible eddies of rushing air. I watched them dance, just watched them while I dried my hands over and over again on a damp dishcloth festooned with garlic cloves and green onions. The heat blew against my back, and the cold that stole through the window caressed my chest and face. It was very comfortable there, and I felt very tired.

I wondered if the weather would warm up for Glorrie's services. I recalled the story of my Uncle Tom's funeral—one of Glorrie's favorites, oddly enough. *Mud Run Cemetery*, she would say, *by God it earned its name that day.* Mud Run sat down south of Moweaqua, a good hour's drive down through farmland and tree groves, across a few bridges. It was the part of the state Mom and Glorrie's branch of the Sanner family hailed from, and most of their relations were planted in that soil already. It sounded like a strange place, the way Glorrie described it. Not only was the place fairly old, but it was also the lot where they had built a one-room schoolhouse at the turn of the century, complete with built-in desks. Mom and Glorrie's mother Rebecca had gone to school there for a time, before she married. It seemed out of place, wrong somehow, a school in a cemetery. But this was back when families would pack Sunday supper in baskets and eat it graveside so their dead family could be part of the reunion.

Tom had died this time of the year. November, 1957. Mom stayed home with me due to the weather that had started up during the visitation the night before: rain in hard-falling sheets, ditches overflowing onto the roads. By the next morning, the hillside leading up to the cemetery was nothing but mud. They slogged up through it, though, all of the mourners, and there were quite a few of them, according to Glorrie. Galoshes were of little use—the mud oozed through the eyelets or came up over the flaps and sank into them anyway; Sunday shoes were buried in wet soil. Tom had the wettest twenty-one gun salute in military history, a send-off for a hero of World War II provided by a lodge from Decatur that did that sort of thing for all veterans. They folded the flag draped across his casket and gave it to Glorrie. And that, as Aunt Glorrie used to say, was that.

I heard the door close from the mudroom, and assumed it was Earl. "About time you got here," I said.

But it wasn't Earl. "Nice to see you too."

I recognized the voice immediately. "Amy?" I said, spinning in my chair. Amy Lakin had been my girlfriend for most of high school, and for a while afterwards. We'd known each other most of our lives, from school and church, but only started dating in our freshman year. She made the first move, approaching me at the first high school dance, and simply saying *come dance with me.* I was hers from then on, until I went away for college years later, and over time left her behind with everything else.

And here she was again, just as pretty as she ever was, holding a plate of oatmeal-butterscotch cookies. Her hair wasn't as curly as it used to be—it was bobbed, now, one soft curve at the bottom, reaching up to her neck, her soft jawline, her little turned-up nose, and those cheeks that still held the slightest hint of fading freckles. She wore jeans and a black turtleneck, and looked for all the world like she'd stepped right out of a very good dream. She grinned when she saw me. "Mind if I come in?" she said.

I smiled back at her, so happy that I felt stupid. "So long as you bring the cookies in with you," I said, trying desperately to be suave while my chest felt like a kettle drum. "What are you doing here?"

She shrugged, sat at the table with me. "Heard you were in town, thought I'd come by, see if I could help. I heard about Glorrie, and your Mom."

"What about Mom?" I asked, my voice taking on an edge I didn't intend. It was a strong reaction, and a surprising one, even to me.

"Whoa, it's all right," Amy said. "You should know the way things go around here by now. Doc Pistorius' nurse tells someone, they tell two friends, and so on, and so on...." She punched me playfully in the arm. "Come on, don't be that way. Have a cookie." She pushed the plate of cookies toward me, and I took one. "People are just worried about her. I'm worried about her. And you, too."

"Me?" I said, my mouth full of cookie. "Why me?"

"Because you just lost your aunt," Amy said, "and sort of your Mom too."

Damn. I hadn't really thought of it like that yet. "Mom's upstairs asleep," I said, trying to laugh it off. "She's not going anywhere soon."

"You know what I mean, Reese. I had an uncle who had Alzheimer's. At the end, he was convinced he was living in Siberia, with the Russian soldiers he knew from the war. He'd never even been to the U.S.S.R., but he described it amazingly well. Talked about towns I thought he'd made up for sure until I got curious enough to look them up on a map, and there they were. Hell, he even spoke a little Russian towards the end, and I have no idea how he accomplished that."

"Really?"

"Yeah."

"Is he gone now? Your uncle?"

Amy nodded. "But I didn't come here to make you feel worse, Reese. I really came just to say hi."

"Just seeing you again helps."

"Yeah, right," she said, looking at me sideways.

"I'm serious. It's really good to see you."

"Sure. That's why you rushed home to dance with me again at the reunion." She winked at me.

Amy had helped organize a get-together for Moweaqua High just a year before. The invitation had arrived at exactly the right time and exactly the wrong time, just a week after Carrie and I had separated. I sat in our apartment, which had suddenly become *my* apartment, and stared at the invitation for hours, specifically at what Amy had scrawled at the bottom of mine in her familiar, looping hand: *Come dance with me.*

I didn't. Wanted to, but it was too soon, too soon for anything.

I wasn't divorced yet, didn't want to think I would be, didn't need an old love from an old life getting in the way. Still, I didn't refuse the invitation either. I didn't RSVP at all. I stalled until the night of the reunion, still thinking there might be a chance I'd decide *what the hell*, I'd go. I thought about dancing with Amy again, about how she used to clasp her hands around the back of my neck and stroke it with her thumbs. I thought about nothing else until I looked up from my TV the night of the reunion, and realized it was already nine-thirty. Too late.

I held up my hands in mock surrender. "Fair enough. You're right. My fault. I meant to go. I just...you know...with my divorce and all..."

"It's okay," Amy said. "You don't owe me an explanation."

I wanted to dance with her, then, just take her in my arms and dance, if badly, across the kitchen floor. But my feet stayed planted. "Well, I am sorry," I said. "I'm an idiot."

"That we can agree on," she beamed. All of a sudden the world seemed brighter.

We talked for a while. I told her about teaching, she told me about her work selling real estate up in Decatur. We dredged up some old times, too. She recalled the time I threw apples at the girls at a school picnic in third grade, how she and I used to steal out to the barn after football games and make out, and a few things in-between. What we didn't talk about was how I left, how bad that was, how much of an ass I was in the way I did it, just taking off one day and not talking to her, not returning phone calls, not caring, really, when they finally stopped. We talked about the good stuff, the stuff I needed to hear, the stuff she was kind enough to limit herself to. She kept saying she had to go, but then we'd get on another subject, carried away, and then she'd say it again. She was looking at her watch for the fifth time when we both heard the shower come on upstairs.

"Can she still do that by herself?" Amy asked. "Take a shower, I mean?"

I shrugged. "I guess so," I said. "She did yesterday, anyway. It never occurred to me she couldn't."

"She's still really high-functioning, then," Amy said.

"That's what Doc said, too. Of course, this is her third shower this morning, because she keeps forgetting she's already taken two."

"Oh, that's very funny," she said in the condescending manner you don't mind from good friends and old flames.

"I wish I were kidding," I said. "But yeah, she's okay. She still cooks like a champ."

"You're letting a woman with Alzheimer's cook for you?" Amy deadpanned.

"Hey, I was watching her closely," I said, lying a little. "Besides, she was making hamburgers last night, and I haven't had Mom's burgers in years."

"Even funnier!" she said, and shook her head, smiling again. "Seriously, you shouldn't be letting her cook. You have enough food here to last at least a week, maybe more. Honestly, it will probably spoil before you can get through it all. So no more cooking, at least for a while. Okay?"

"Okay."

"Okay." Amy smiled at me, patted my hand, and started to get up.

"You really have to go?" I said.

"Yeah," she said, slinging her purse over her shoulder. "I have a noon appointment with a couple who are looking for a house with a deck and a hot tub. I think I found a place that might work, but I keep wanting to tell them this isn't California, and it's not 1975, you know? Besides, find the house you want, and you can build that sort of thing, right?" She put on her sunglasses, and shook her head. "Anyway, I just came to check on you."

"So how am I doing?"

"Barely hanging on."

"Damn, I thought I was hiding it better."

"Let me know when the funeral is," Amy said. "And if you need anything," she scrawled her number on the notepad by the phone, "call me. I mean it."

"I will."

She smiled. "Good seeing you." She blew me a kiss, and left out the back door. I sat there for a moment, listened to her walk on the gravel, get into her car, the engine start. I listened to the motor all the way down the drive until she pulled out onto the blacktop and was gone. I drank in what was left of her presence, trying to evoke her again, remembering what it was like to get a kiss from those lips up close, not from across the room. I finally got up and ripped the page from the notepad, folded it neatly and put it in my wallet.

A moment later, Mom came downstairs again, wearing one of her church outfits, a light blue dress with a pillbox hat and matching purse. "You look really nice," I said.

"Thank you, James. Who was that I heard down here with you just a little bit ago?"

"Amy came by. She left these cookies," I held out the plate for her, but Mom waved it away.

"How nice of her. I always liked her."

"Me too. She sends her best."

"Good," Mom smoothed her pleats. "Are you ready to go have lunch?"

"After we go to Gum's, sure."

Mom looked stricken, and took a deep breath. "I was hoping I'd remembered wrong again this morning," she said quietly, and went over to sit at the window.

"What do you mean?"

"I thought I remembered something about seeing Gum Howser. I was hoping I was making things up in my head again."

"Do you do that a lot, Mom?" I said softly. I was using as soothing a voice as I could muster. "Make things up in your head, I mean?"

"Sometimes," she said, staring out the window. "Sometimes I think I'm somewhere else. In the past, I suppose, if that makes a difference. It all makes perfect sense to me, when I'm there, when I'm inside it." She looked back at me, her eyes wide and wet with tears. "It's Glorrie, right? We're going to see Gum about Glorrie, isn't that right?"

"Yes, Mom."

"She's died?"

"Yeah."

She started crying then, and brought a tissue up to her nose, one she'd kept stashed in her fist. She nodded, and wept in long, sobbing breaths. I put my hand on her shoulder, still wary of her fragility, not wanting to do anything that would snap her out of this moment of lucidity. She reached up with one hand and placed it on mine, squeezed it, and then just held it there on her shoulder for a while.

We stayed like that until she stopped crying so hard. "I need you to tell me what happened to Glorrie, James," she said. "I need you to tell me how she died, because I just don't remember, and I want to remember. I really do."

A wave of sorrow ran through my chest like a cold wind through an open window. I told her, as softly and as quickly as I could, about the circumstances surrounding the accident and the ensuing stroke. I told her the usual things—she went quickly, she didn't suffer, wondering in passing whether or not such trite assurances were ever actually true, not just something you tell to a grieving survivor. She nodded at this, let a few more tears roll down her cheeks, and then leaned against me gingerly.

I stroked her back with the tips of my fingers, the way I remembered she used to scratch mine in church when I was a very small child, resting quietly beside her on the wooden pew. "Earl's going to be here soon, Mom, and then we'll go make the arrangements for the visitation and the funeral."

"All right," she said. "I'm so sorry." Mom leaned on me more heavily. "I'm so sorry, James. I don't know what's happening to me."

"I know," I said. "It's okay, Mom. It's okay."

"No, it's not," she said. "It's not okay." She pulled up from me and wiped the tears from her pale blue eyes. They were as sharp as I remembered them from my childhood, and I knew then my mother was back. It wouldn't last, I knew. But for that one moment, Mom was my Mom again, all there, body and soul, and it made me happy.

"Mom, really, it's fine."

"You don't understand," she said, looking out the window again. "I'm losing my mind, James, the way I watched your great-grandmother Alice lose hers and Uncle Mont lose his. Alice did nothing but sing children's rhymes toward the end of her days. And Mont took to wearing nothing but a smile to greet the milkman and the ice wagon. I don't want to go that way, James, but I don't know how to stop it. I don't think I can. Sometimes it's not bad, and I just forget things a little. Sometimes it's a bit worse and it's like I'm watching someone else go through my life, and it's ever so familiar. I keep thinking I know that woman. What silly things she's doing. How funny. And then, sooner or later, I come out of it and realize the silly woman I've been watching has been me." She turned to pick up her coffee. "You know," she said, "I stopped drinking coffee ten years ago. Suddenly, I'm drinking it again, like I did when I was a young girl, without a care for what it does to my stomach." She took a few sips of her coffee and smiled at me. It was sad, but genuine. "I'm so glad you're here, James. I really am. Thank you."

I smiled at this undeserved welcome, late as it might have been, and put my hand on top of hers. I decided, so long as she was lucid, to push the envelope a little. "Mom, do you see yourself, you know, like you were saying, when you're calling Earl and me by Dad's name?"

Mom's smile vanished. "Do I do that?"

"Sometimes."

She looked out the window at her frost-covered garden of spaded earth, at the barn, at my truck, and at the empty fields beyond. "No," she finally whispered, trying not to cry again. "I must do that those times when I black out."

"You black out?"

"That's what I call it. Times I don't remember at all. Most of yesterday, but yesterday was a bad day."

"Yes, it was."

"It's like swimming. Like when I'd go swimming at night in the pond out by the creek when I was a girl. The water was so deep and dark it looked black, but it was fresh and clear. You could dive in from the oak standing beside it. And if you got to the very bottom, and opened your eyes, all you saw was blackness, like nothing existed for you, and yet you were seeing it. That's the way I feel sometimes, like I'm diving in and out of that old pond, going down to the bottom and coming up again. And when I come up, there's this splash and suddenly, the world comes alive again. I start to hear the world again like a person is meant to. That happened to me this morning."

"This morning?"

"When I came downstairs and found Glorrie's dinner in the microwave."

"You remember that?"

"Not really, but I knew it was Glorrie's when I found it. And I knew, all of a sudden, why she hadn't eaten it."

"Just like that?"

Mom nodded. "I cried most of the morning before you got up. I don't really recall you getting here yesterday. I'm so sorry. It must have been bad for you, seeing me that way."

I shook my head. "No," I said. "Don't be sorry. I'm just glad to be here." I felt a rush of emotion in my chest when I said that, maybe because I was happy to talk to my mother at her most together, or maybe because I realized not only was she slipping, but she knew she was slipping. It had to be the most frightening thing a person could go through. Or maybe it was that when I said I was glad to be home again, I was telling the truth.

"Earl's here," she said quietly, and sipped her coffee.

"What?" I asked, still lost in thought for a moment.

"Earl's here," she repeated. "Just pulled up. I had better put on a fresh pot of coffee for him."

"Don't bother, Mom," I said. "Soon as I'm showered, we have to get going. There won't be enough time."

"Nonsense," she said. "Gum will understand. That's his job. Besides, I know how long you take in the shower."

Mom was back, no mistake. This was the woman I remembered, the one fully in control of her domain, and brooked no argument. I had a sudden memory of the way she used to pace a fleeing chicken in the yard, and in one fluid motion scoop it up and snap its neck with a flick of her wrist. Then she'd amble back to the porch letting the chicken beat its wings for the last few pointless times. When the chicken was done, she'd sit on the porch, pluck it and dress it, all the while watching my father off in the fields, or later, watch me. And that's what she was doing now—watching. She was sitting up in her chair, back straight, peering over her cup, looking about her house and the grounds outside with a gaze practiced over fifty years.

I was home, and for the moment, so was she.

Gum Howser was a big man, not in stature, but in girth, in presence. He had a way of enveloping you, especially when you were on his turf. He greeted us at the door, wearing a brown suit made from some nappy fabric—or maybe that was just its age showing. He wore a pair of black suspenders to hold up his pants, and a bolo tie with a clasp of turquoise he said his son had sent him from Arizona. Gum was the second Howser to run the Howser Funeral Home of Moweaqua, and earned his nickname by busting out his four front teeth when he tripped and face-planted a headstone. His father had just laughed, and said he was a natural for the family business.

I noticed it was almost noon when Gum was hugging Mom hello. His manner was practiced gentility—not false, really, but not deep in its emotion. A man in his business works more for the family left behind than the deceased, even though it's the estate that's probably paying the bills. And Gum knew on which side his bread was apple-buttered. He knitted his brow after the short embrace, told Mom how sorry he was. He turned and solemnly shook Earl's hand, uttering his name once as he gestured him in. And then it was my turn.

"Reese," he said earnestly, taking my hand in a solid grip and chucking me on the shoulder. "It's good to see you back in town. Been a long time, hasn't it? Just sorry it had to be this way."

"So am I," I said. "Sorry we're a little late."

Gum frowned, bowed his head slightly, and waved his hands in front of him as though the apology were preposterous. "No, no, no," he said, "don't you think about that at all. We're here to fit to your schedule. At times like these, things get hectic."

"Thanks," I said.

The inside of the funeral home seemed to be one big room. It had walls—partitions, really—covered in purple fabric and could slide around on tracks fitted into the ceiling. From the look of the track pattern, Gum could either have one big room, or two, three, up to four smaller ones. One section was empty except for a gilded bier on rollers and a rack of night-blue folding chairs. The section just ahead of it had a series of metal stands, probably for flowers, and a wooden podium with a microphone. And then there were the sections to which Gum led us—fully furnished, with living room-furniture done in gold and maroon. I sat on the couch with Mom, and Earl and Gum pulled up chairs. Gum laid some papers down on the coffee table.

"Have a seat there, folks, get comfortable, and we'll get started in just a minute. Can I get anyone some coffee first?" Gum asked.

Mom declined, as did I, but Earl said he wouldn't mind some if Gum was having a cup too. Gum must have wanted one, because he nodded and walked back through one of the doors lining the back wall.

"Well," I said, "this is a nice place."

Mom looked at me. "It's a funeral home, James. They try to make them comfortable, but they can't."

I looked around. It was all so dark, so artificial. "I don't know how long it's been since I was here."

"Your father's funeral," Mom said simply.

I felt the hair on the back of my neck come to sudden attention. "Yeah," I said. "I guess that was here, wasn't it? I don't remember it very well."

"You were a kid," Earl said.

"And he was your father," Mom said. "And on top of all that, this is not a place that makes you want to recall it."

Mom was still surprisingly alert. Back at the house, while Mom had been upstairs getting herself some more tissues, Earl warned me it wouldn't last. She tended to slip in and out of these phases. She could be calling me Reese and expecting Glorrie to come home with the groceries again by lunchtime. I told him I understood, but I didn't want to believe it.

Gum came back with two cups. He sat down in his chair and handed one to Earl and the other to me. "Just in case you might want it later," he said as I took the styrofoam cup from him. I took a sip to be polite. "There's creamer and sugar cubes back in the kitchen," Gum offered, and rose halfway from his seat.

"You have a kitchen in a funeral home?" I asked, aghast.

"Reese," Earl started.

Gum laughed. "I know, folks are always surprised by that. But we have to have a place to make the coffee, now don't we?"

"I'm sorry. I don't need anything, Gum, but thanks. I didn't mean anything by it."

"Don't be sorry," Gum chided gently. "You have much bigger things on your minds."

We all chatted a while, inconsequential things, for the most part: what I was doing now, the weather, my divorce, how sorry everyone was to hear the marriage hadn't worked out. Mom didn't say much, but she seemed present, so I didn't worry. With a muffled clap of his hands, Gum suggested we get down to the matter at hand. "Did you bring the things we'd discussed, Earl? A Sunday dress, perhaps some incidentals?"

"Incidentals?"

"You know, a string of pearls, her wedding ring, a favorite hand-bag." Gum gestured with each example: at his neck for the pearls, his finger for the ring, even mimed holding a purse. "Items that meant something to her, that you'd perhaps like her to have."

*How about a jar of apple butter?* I felt like saying, but I suppressed it. "I don't know, I didn't hear anything about this." I looked over at Earl, who was pointedly not looking my way.

"Her navy dress with the matching jacket is out in the cab of my truck, Gum. I didn't know what else she might need, and didn't want to bother Clara about it just yet. But I guess you need to know now, huh?"

"Not just now," Gum said, "but soon. It doesn't have to be serious, either, or dressy, or anything like it, mind you. We buried Jim Hanneman just last month—you remember, Earl—and his family chose to have him interred with his favorite fishing pole. Had to curve that pole up and around his head like a halo to get it in there, but we managed. But you folks need to decide this for yourselves. Maybe you want to leave something with her, or maybe you want to keep it as a memento, to pass along someday. It all depends on what you want."

"That's the thing," I said. "Aside from the dress, which I suppose Earl has taken it upon himself to choose, I don't think we know exactly what we want."

"Someone had to," Earl said.

"Yes, well, that's true," Gum said, "but it's important everyone be involved with these decisions, so there are no hard feelings or misunderstandings that could linger."

"You have no idea," I said under my breath.

"I'm sorry?" Gum said, but kindly.

"Nothing," I said. "What sort of options are we looking at?"

"Well, we have a number of packages I'm sure Glorrie would have liked. Now here," Gum said, opening a brochure, "is what we call the Frontier model. It's a favorite here in town with those who can afford it. The casket itself is polished pine with gold leaf trim and a small gathering of wheat here stitched into the satin lining near the head. Its quite attractive. It would be a lovely choice for Glorrie."

"Wouldn't it be in her face?" I asked. Gum and Earl stared at me like I was simple. "The wheat, I mean? Once you closed the lid, wouldn't it be right in her face?" I envisioned the wheat drooping into her face and tickling her. She was dead, of course, and not likely to mind, but still, the idea bothered me, and made my nose itch.

"Well, it wouldn't be right in her face," Gum smiled somewhat patronizingly, "but it would be in the general area of the head, of course, yes."

"What does it matter, Reese?" Earl said.

"Well, that's another good point," I said.

Gum paused, and looked over at Earl, who shrugged. Then Gum looked back at me, smiled his funeral-man smile, and said "I'm sorry, Reese, but I'm not following you. What is?"

"That this sort of thing doesn't matter," I said, and took another sip of my coffee. It was strong and hot. "I mean, Glorrie was never much for frilly stuff when she was alive. I doubt she'd want us spending this sort of money on her now that she's gone."

"Jesus." Earl's voice was tired.

"Reese, you have to understand," Gum began, "a lot of the things in caskets today have to do with the people picking them out, not necessarily the people in them. The design, the details, all the bells and whistles—they're for the people at the visitation and at the funeral, so they see their loved one in the best possible light before they close the casket and—if you'll pardon me, Clara—not see them in this life again. This wheat isn't for Glorrie, though I do think she'd have thought it was pretty. It's for you, and Earl, and your family, and especially for Clara, here, so she can see her sister off in style."

The discussion went on like this for a while, me insisting that we not break the bank on a box that was just going to be covered with dirt anyway, and Earl saying that this was tradition and for the good of us, the family, and the community at large who would turn out for the services, and for Mom, who didn't say anything at all. It wasn't so much about the money—I don't know why I was arguing. Earl didn't seem to know either—he was more siding against me than siding with Gum. Finally, I became aware Mom hadn't said anything at all for some time, and I asked for her opinion. She just shrugged and looked down into her lap. It was not a good sign.

"Mom?" I asked, "are you okay?"

Mom nodded, and looked up and away from us, vaguely toward the windows at the front of the building. She stood up, suddenly, and walked toward them.

"Mom?" I said. "Where are you going?"

This time there was no answer at all. "She's just upset," Gum said. "People respond to stress in different ways."

"It's not that," I muttered.

We watched Mom walk over to the picture window at the front, lean against the glass, and look outside. I sighed.

"Great," Earl said. "Let's just get this stuff decided so you can get her home. This is too much for her."

"I think you're right," I said.

"That's a first," Earl said, and caught him wink at Gum.

"We do have some time if you want to let her calm down," Gum said. "But we really need to set up the details of the visitation today. We had her notice put in the Decatur paper this morning, and we're already getting calls from folks wondering when they can pay respects."

I made a mental note to buy the *Herald and Review*, just so I could see what they said in her obituary. It was curiosity more than anything else—I'd never seen the obit of someone I knew before. "I understand," I said. "Let me try to talk to her." As I walked away, I heard Earl starting to fill Gum in on what had happened the night before and this morning. Like Amy said, word was already out, though in hushed tones, like if you said it quietly enough, it wasn't gossip. When I got closer, I could see Mom crying. A hope kindled in my chest that maybe Gum had been right, that she was just upset. But it was soon put out, embers and all. "Mom, are you okay?"

She shook her head. "For a minute there, James, I thought I was arranging your father's funeral with Fred. I really did. Fred was sitting there, where Gum is now, and Earl was right there where he's sitting, only a lot younger. And then I saw you, and I didn't know who you were, and it threw me. I got dizzy for a minute, and the whole time I was trying to think just who you were—you looked so familiar—and part of me was saying that you were Reese, but the other part was saying that was impossible, that I was there to bury Reese, so he couldn't be sitting there, and it felt like my head was going to bust wide open, it really did."

"I'm sorry, Mom."

"No, it's me that's sorry, James. I'm so sorry I couldn't remember you."

"Stop apologizing," I laughed grimly. "Don't you worry about any of this, Mom. You just concentrate on yourself, okay?"

She nodded, and blew her nose quietly into a tissue.

"Do you want to go back and try to do this again?" I asked. "Or do you just want Earl and me to handle it, and then we'll go."

"I don't have anything to say," she said. "I can't remember what Glorrie told me she wanted. I can't even remember if she told me what she wanted. I just can't catch a thought. It's all I can do just to recognize you."

I patted her shoulder. "Just hold on," I said. "We'll get you out of here. Give Earl and me a few minutes to finish up with Gum, and then we'll go on back to the house and fix some lunch."

"I thought we were going out."

"Oh sure," I teased, "*that* you remember." She smiled a little. "You're right," I said. "We'll go to Wendell's, okay? You just make sure you're up to it."

She nodded, and I made my way back to Earl and Gum.

"How is she?" asked Earl.

"Not good," I said. "I think I need to get her out of here."

"She's going to have to be here for the visitation, at least, Reese. Maybe she should get used to the idea," Earl said.

"We'll cross that bridge then, okay?" I said. "Right now, she needs to go."

"All right, then," Gum said. "Do either of you know when you want to have the services? I assume you're going to want a visitation?"

"Why wouldn't we?" asked Earl.

Gum shrugged. "Some people don't have much in the way of family or friends still around who would come, or they were new to the area, what have you. It's just easier for some. But Glorrie still knew lots of people in town. She should have one—folks will expect it. But it's up to you."

"Okay, so she'll have one. When can we do it?" I asked.

"Tomorrow evening is open." Gum was checking his calendar. "Let's see...a Thursday. Quick, but certainly doable. And that would lead us nicely into a Friday funeral. We could start telling people the time when they called, and put the notice in tomorrow morning's paper."

I nodded. "Fine," I said.

"Say, four to seven? People could still come early if they wanted, or they could stop directly after work if need be."

"Three hours?" I asked. "Isn't that a long time?"

"There will be a lot of people, Reese," Earl said. Gum nodded in agreement.

"Fine," I said, "I just hope Mom can stand up there that long." Hell, I was hoping I could stand up there that long.

"I assume she'll be buried in Mud Run, next to her husband?" Gum asked.

I looked at Earl—he shrugged. "I guess so, yeah," I said.

"And what kind of casket have we decided on?"

I looked over at Mom. She was still against the window, crying softly. "I don't care," I said, waving my hand. "The wheat thing is fine. Okay with you, Earl?"

"It was fine by me a half hour ago," he said.

"Would Glorrie have liked it?" I asked.

"As well as anything else," he admitted.

"Okay." I said. "I'm taking Mom to lunch. Earl, can you handle the paperwork?" Earl nodded. I turned to Gum. "Is that okay?"

"Course, Reese," he said, standing and offering his hand. "We'll see you tomorrow night."

"Thanks," I said, and we shook on it. "Earl, we're going to Wendell's for lunch, if you want to meet us."

Earl looked surprised. "I don't know. If not, I'm sure I'll see you at the house later."

I nodded. "Okay, good. There are some things I want to talk to you about, anyhow." I hadn't gotten the chance to talk to Earl about the land, and I didn't want to do it in front of Mom. And the funeral and all the trappings seemed more important.

"Before you go," Earl said, "I wanted to ask you—do you know where Glorrie kept her shoes?"

"What is this, a riddle?" I asked.

"I'm serious. It's the damnedest thing," Earl said, half-talking to Gum now. "I can't find any shoes other than the beat-up ones she was wearing to Fathauer's the morning she died. That couldn't have been her only pair, could it?"

"You're asking me?" I said. "How would I know?"

"I don't know," Earl said. "I just thought I'd ask. Is it all right if she's buried in ratty looking brown shoes, Gum?"

"No one will see her shoes," Gum chuckled. "It's not going to be a problem."

"So we have a navy dress with a matching jacket, and you said brown shoes?" Gum was writing this down. "And anything else?"

"I picked up the purse she'd take to church with her," Earl said. He turned to me. "The beaded one she got in England years back, remember?"

"The one she'd keep her Smith Brother cough drops in?" I smiled at the memory.

"That, some tissues, and a few spare offering envelopes. They're all still in there. I thought I'd leave them."

"That's nice," I said. "I like that."

"Good," he said. "Are you walking, or should I?"

"We'll walk. Mom could probably use the fresh air."

I led Mom outside into the cool November day. We went to Wendell's for lunch, sat at the counter and both ordered a cheese toastie and some tomato soup. Earl didn't show, but that didn't surprise me. I told Mom about how I remembered going to Wendell's with her and Dad, eating pork tenderloin sandwiches and fries, drinking the soda that they'd never buy for the house, waving at folks passing outside the wall of windows, buying a pack of Lions Club mints on the way out. She laughed that I'd remember such a thing.

"You should eat, Mom." She'd barely touched her sandwich, and only taken a couple of token sips from her soup.

"I am," she said, lifting her spoon again. She was pretending to be annoyed, but she was smiling, at the same time. "Don't fuss."

I wanted to talk and keep on talking, to occupy her. I thought if I kept her mind working, maybe it wouldn't have the chance to slip. But I'd spent my memory of Wendell's and was grasping for straws. "I found Glorrie's memoirs in the den this morning," I said.

Mom's eyes snapped up at me, her spoon still at her lips. She lowered it slowly. "Really?" Her voice was small, barely above a whisper.

"Yeah," I said, cursing inwardly. What was I thinking, bringing up Glorrie? I wanted to take it back and let us return to the lunch we'd been enjoying. But there was no turning back. I pressed onward. "But that's as far as she got, I guess. Just the word "memoirs." Nothing else. It's funny, isn't it?"

Mom let out a small sound, maybe a moan, maybe just hmm. Her eyes glazed over. Whereas she'd been staring at me only a second before, now she was looking through me, seeing, perhaps, nothing but memory. I was losing her.

"Mom?"

Her eyes darted back to me. A sudden winter had fallen in her eyes. Her breathing seemed more deliberate, exaggerated.

"Mom, what's wrong?"

"This soup is thin," she said, and put down her spoon.

# Chapter Seven

## *1942*

REESE SHIVERED AS THE BARN DOORS SHRIEKED TO A CLOSE on frozen rollers. The March nights were still cold, so he turned on the light and the small space heater he'd bought at Farm and Fleet in Taylorville. He was once again grateful he'd had the sense to run electric out to the barn when he had, just a couple of years before. It cost a bit, but he could have light without risking fire, warmth without two coats and gloves, and a radio to keep him company. Clara grumbled about it all, especially the radio, saying he might as well move his bed out there, for all the time he'd be spending in the house with her. Reese laughed, and promised not to spend so much time in the barn, but he knew any time would always be too much for Clara. He'd also told her they'd get a horse sometime, but he'd grown used to parking the truck in what used to be the stable, liked the idea of not scraping the ice off his windshield every morning more than he liked the idea of keeping a horse. Or, he had to admit, a promise to his wife.

As he pulled out his chair to take a seat, Reese saw something out of the corner of his eye. It was down low, back where the hay bales stacked, and he peered into the darkness for a moment before deciding it was nothing more than his eyes playing tricks on him. The barn had long since stopped unsettling him, as it had when he first moved back to the farm. Even after it had been fixed up, it hadn't seemed fully his, as though the shadow of his father stood behind him, his voice resounding in every creak. Reese would work out there, but he'd have as much light as he could, damn the reckless danger of fire. And still he'd jump at every sound, stare fearfully at every vague movement in the dimly lit interior. But he'd grown used to the place—made it his. Perhaps the place itself had finally accepted him.

Reese had learned the sounds of the barn: the whistle of the wind through the cracks in the wall boards, the scattering of a mouse in straw, the shuffling of feathers from the old owl that roosted up in the crook of the loft. Reese came to love that owl, messy though she was, and despite her habit of scaring him half, bursting from her perch on high like an angry angel bearing the weight of God's judgment.

Reese couldn't see how the owl could have flown that low and then disappeared, though, and thought the shadow, peripheral as it had been, moved too slow and was too big to be a field mouse. So he turned his chair towards where he'd seen the shadows move, took his whetstone back to the sickle blade, and waited.

She emerged, striding into the half-light of the barn like a predator. A gaunt calico, a cat that looked as though it had seen war and barely lived to tell about it. She came within ten feet of Reese before noticing him, her ears suddenly erect, her stance defensive. The cat hissed at Reese in a way that made him grip the scythe in his hands more tightly, and think about where he'd do best to place a blow if need be.

Reese looked into the feral eyes of the calico and found himself angry at Clara. He'd told Clara not to feed the strays. They're not pets, not even barn cats. They're wild again, and dangerous. Maybe rabid. They were common on farms, but tended to move on if they didn't find someone stupid enough to feed them. Those were the very words he used—*someone stupid enough to feed them.* He wished, when he'd said them to Clara the day he'd caught her putting scraps out on the old maple stump near the corncrib, he could snatch them back and swallow them. But he couldn't. Clara refused to talk to him for nearly a week. That was a month ago. Things had gotten better since. Maybe this cat was just coming back to see if she'd feed her again? Reese patted his pocket, wishing he'd brought out his pipe.

The cat stood there, stock-still, eyeing Reese like her next meal. Reese knew there was something wrong. The cat was too aggressive for a stray, and she had a look to her eyes that made Reese's muscles tense. Then Reese noticed the cat was drooling a little, a thin line of spittle connecting cat to earth.

Reese reacted, standing suddenly with the sickle wielded before him like a sword, trying to scare the cat off, or maybe to provoke it into an attack, so he'd muster the courage in that instant to strike out and pin it to the ground with his father's tool. But neither of these things happened—the cat instead rushed towards Reese and then, at the last minute, diverted its path toward the barn doors, squeezing through the crack between door and frame and darting out into the yard. Reese peered out into the yard, and could just barely make out the calico diving under the stoop at the back door.

Reese spat, and felt his heart pounding. He wanted his pipe more than ever now, but if he were guessing right and that cat was rabid, he had to take care of it before it got to anyone. He wished he kept a gun out in the barn, like Tom was always after him to do, and tried to recall where he last saw his shotgun. He thought it was in his den, but he could have been cleaning it down in the cellar, too, where his workbench was. He cursed at himself, and spat again, trying to clean the sour taste from his mouth.

It was then when Reese heard rustling coming from the hay stacks, over where the cat had been hiding. For a moment he was afraid the calico had somehow circled around and come back in another way, even though he knew that was unlikely. He inched his way over to the bales, and peeked over the top of one of them. There, in the straw, was a knot of kittens still covered in blood and birthing fluid. There were five of them, two brown and white like their mother, two all white with brown paws, and one stark black against the other four. They were blind, crawling all over each other, mewing pitifully, spitting up white and red. They were tearing at each other and at their own skin, trying to get away from the pain of being born rabid. They were dying, and painfully, and even though Reese wasn't one for cats, he very nearly reached out to one, to stroke it and try to comfort it in some small, useless way. Not two feet from the kittens lay a small green saucer with a few table scraps still in it.

Anger swelled in him again like a rising sun, and he stormed out of the barn. "Clara!" Reese nearly screamed his wife's name as he walked towards the house, all fear now forgotten, but never taking his eyes off of the darkness under the stoop. "Clara!"

There was some rattling from inside the house, and then Clara appeared at the back door. "For pity's sake, Reese, what is it?" Her face was a confusion of concern and annoyance.

"Get my gun," Reese said.

"Your gun? Why..."

"Get it, and get it now," Reese said again, stopping about ten feet from the stoop. He figured ten feet was too far for the cat to leap, were it to attack, but it was close enough to where Clara could throw him the gun without leaving the relative safety of the porch. "I think it's in the den. And get some shoes on. We have something to take care of."

Clara frowned. She wasn't used to being talked to in this manner, and she very nearly said just that. But Reese's demeanor convinced her otherwise. "All right," she finally said, and went inside to find the shotgun and her shoes. She emerged not a minute later with both. "What's going on, Reese? What's the matter?"

"Throw me the gun, Clara," Reese said, "and then get back inside for a minute and put those shoes on. You come out when I tell you to."

"All right," Clara said again, tossing the gun to Reese. "What in heaven's name are you—"

"I said go inside."

Clara opened her mouth to protest, but didn't, and went.

Reese could see her peering out the window, but he needed to focus on what he was doing. He had to kill the cat, he knew. It was rabid, nothing he wanted to play around with. He checked the gun for ammunition, then bent to one knee to see if he could spot the cat. The darkness diminished as his eyes adjusted, and he could see two green slits staring back at him from beneath the porch. He brought his shotgun up, inched closer as he aimed right for those glowing eyes, and pulled the trigger. The recoil was worse than he'd expected, but he stayed up on his bad knee, grimacing with pain. The cat didn't make a sound, and for a moment, Reese was afraid he'd missed. Then the smoke cleared, and he saw the cat wasn't sitting up anymore. He watched it, to see if there was any movement, and then fired his other chamber just to be sure. This time, he got close enough to see the pool of blood. Satisfied it was dead, he put the gun on the porch and stood up, his knee screaming the whole time.

Clara opened the door. Her arms were crossed over her chest, and she looked frightened. "What was it, Reese?"

"Your cat," Reese said simply. "It was sick. Rabid. Probably dying anyway."

Clara put two fingers to her mouth. "Oh, no," she said softly.

"And it had a litter of kittens in the barn," Reese continued. "They're still in there. They're sick too. They won't live. They might last a few days of pure torture if I leave them be, but they'll never even open their eyes. We have to do something."

Clara stood there on the porch with one hand on her hip, and the other still covering her mouth. She was crying.

"And it's your fault," Reese said before turning on his heels and walking back out to the barn. He checked first to make sure the kittens were still there—they were—and then went to get his heavy canvas gloves. He pulled them on and grabbed his heavy rake as he went back out into the yard—Clara was still standing there on the porch, not having moved an inch—and he proceeded to pull out all the debris from under the porch—old leaves matted with fur and blood. There wasn't much left to the cat, now, which was exactly what Reese intended. He pulled the cat's remains out into the driveway, and then raked up more leaves to cover it. Then he turned to Clara. "Come on," he said.

In the mouth of the barn, Reese had Clara hold a burlap grain sack open. He scooped up the writhing ball of kittens with the straw beneath them and dumped them in with as smooth a gesture as he could manage. Clara looked into the sack after Reese put them in, and nearly vomited at the sight of them. They drowned them together, in the galvanized washtub out by the horse trough. Clara filled the tub while Reese held the bag, both of them falling into the practice of pretending they weren't dealing with something living. Reese plunged the sack under the water, holding it until the bag no longer pulsed. Reese told Clara to pick up one of the river rocks lining the drive and bring it to him, and when she did, he put the rock on top of the bag to hold it down under the water, just to be sure. They both stepped back, then, and Clara started crying again. Reese picked up the sack and tossed the rock back over to the edge of the driveway, and told Clara to go back inside, that he'd finish.

Reese threw the burlap sack on top of the pile of leaves in which the calico was buried, and then went and raked up clean ones from around the apple trees, covered the whole pile with those. Then he set the whole mess on fire, and watched it burn until the fire got down to the cats. That was when Reese stopped watching, and tossed a few pieces of firewood over the top of it all. He tried to avoid breathing the acrid smoke. He went back inside, suddenly very tired, and went to find his pipe.

"That cat ever scratch you?" Reese asked. His voice was flat, like someone asking a stranger for the time of day.

"No," Clara whispered. She was sitting at the table, shaking.

"You know if she did, we'd need to get you in to see the doctor right away. Right?"

She nodded.

"All right," Reese said. "The washtub needs to be scrubbed out tomorrow, with a wire brush. Use water from the stove, hot as you can get it. All right?"

Clara didn't say anything for a moment, and then took a deep breath. "Was it necessary that I had to watch, Reese?"

Reese looked at her over the rims of his glasses. "We've seen worse. You kill chickens all the time."

"This was different, and you know it."

"No, I don't."

"They were babies," Clara sniffed, and fat tears rolled down from her eyes.

Reese considered this. "They were dead already," he finally said. "And you're the one who fed them."

Clara looked at him as if she wanted to say something, but Reese cut her off before she could. "Don't," he said. "Don't."

Clara stood without a sound and walked upstairs. Reese left the house just as quietly, and went out to the barn to wait for the fire in the driveway to die.

Tom heard the story about the rabid cats a few days later, from Glorrie, who'd heard it from Clara, who still wasn't speaking to Reese. To Tom, though, it seemed like a cause for celebration, and he'd come over to the barn, found Reese, and congratulated him as though he'd just become a father.

"Damn right she had to clean up that mess," Tom said to Reese. He leaned against the barn wall. Reese was sitting. "Her mess, after all. Only right. Only right." Tom was a little drunk, but that was normal these days.

"I don't know about that," Reese said. "Clara seems pretty upset. I wish I hadn't done it now, but what's done is done."

"No," Tom said, shaking his head. "You did the right thing."

"I don't know," Reese said again.

"You apologize to her or anything?" Tom asked.

"No," Reese said. "But I probably should."

"Hell no you shouldn't," Tom said. "You knew what was best. You told her not to feed that damn cat, and look what happened. You were right, Reese, don't apologize to her. She's the one who should be apologizing to you, for God's sake."

"I just don't like the cold shoulder," Reese said. "It's been days now. She goes to bed before I do, gets up before I do, I hardly see her all day, and then I don't really see her at night."

"She still cooking for you?"

"Sure."

"Sounds perfect to me."

"You're funny."

"I'm serious. Wait it out. Remember, she needs you more than you need her. Now let's get out of this damn barn and head into town for some food. I'm buying."

Reese looked up at the high shelf where he'd set Clara's small dish, the one she'd fed the cat from, the one he'd kept from her like he was punishing a child. There it sat, the green Fiestaware saucer. He had no intention of ever giving it back to her, unless she asked. She probably thought it was lost—broken, perhaps, or burned beyond recognition in the fire that had consumed the cats. He could give it back to her, of course, but he knew he wouldn't. He knew that like he knew that he'd go to town with Tom, that he'd accept Tom's approval, that he'd feel a secret joy in it even at the same time it made him a little queasy. He knew all this, saw it laid out before him like someone else's winning poker hand.

Later that night Glorrie showed up at the back door, bleeding from the forehead and sporting a bad bruise on her cheek. It was raining outside, a cold rain that ate through to a body's core. Glorrie wore a scarf over her head, and held a red-stained towel to her brow. "I'm sorry," was all she said. Reese let her in the kitchen.

Reese wasn't shocked by it anymore. He didn't need to hear the story about this latest time, or the specifics, to know what had happened. Tom had beaten her again. The reason was always different, but reason was never the point, never good enough, certainly. What could be, Reese wondered, what could be good enough reason to take up against your own wife? He couldn't fathom it. Couldn't imagine doing it, anyone doing it, not even Tom.

But Tom had, many times. The first had been back in '37, in a fight over Tom's drinking. Glorrie had shown up in their kitchen in the early hours of the morning. It was a February, and there was ice everywhere. Reese had come downstairs to investigate the sound of a door closing and found Glorrie, limping and nursing her arm, which was bent at the elbow, her wrist cocked, her fingers curled helplessly. Reese helped her into a chair, and called for Clara, who came running. Glorrie tried to make some excuse about slipping on the ice, but when Clara asked how she managed to do that at two in the morning, Glorrie broke. It had been Tom, she said. Grabbed her by the shirt and swung her around, twisting her ankle. When she told him to keep his hands off her, he wrenched her arm throwing her across the room. Glorrie left the house as quickly as she could, even favoring her right leg the way she was, and drove to the farm. Neither injury had turned out to need special care, just rest. She stayed there for three days until Tom came to get her. Clara had told her not to go, and Reese had agreed she could stay as long as she wanted, but in the end, Glorrie went with Tom.

"You didn't try hard enough," Clara had later said to Reese. "You shouldn't have let her go back to Tom. You should have stepped in."

"She's his wife," Reese said.

"So what," Clara snapped. "He gets to hit her?"

"Course not," Reese said. "But it's not our place to decide for either of them what they should to do. They can work it out. Give them some time. Glorrie can always come back here, if she needs to."

"You mean if he beats her up again," Clara said.

Reese took a deep breath, said nothing.

"Useless to talk to you," Clara said.

That was five years back. They'd had several nights like it since, and many more when Glorrie hadn't left the house, when she'd just cleaned herself up as best she could and tried to forget. After a while, Reese offered to step in, to talk to Tom. But Glorrie had turned him down flat, said he'd just make things worse. Reese considered arguing this, but then he remembered Woes' teeth, remembered Jacobs, and let it go.

"What happened this time?" Reese asked, handing Glorrie a

fresh towel. He didn't call Clara down. They still weren't speaking, and he didn't know how Clara would act around Glorrie, even in these circumstances.

"He knocked me over the bed," Glorrie said, laughing at nothing and shaking her head. "Just pushed me right over it, and then I crowned myself on the bedwarmer. I knew I shouldn't have left that bedwarmer on the floor, I just knew it. But I didn't pick it up."

Reese checked her forehead as she switched towels. She was bleeding like a deer being dressed, a long gash over her left eye. "Damn," Reese said. "Keep some pressure on it. If it doesn't stop soon, we're going to have to call Doc Pistorius."

"I'll be fine," Glorrie said, easing back into the kitchen chair, her shoulders slumping. "I'm just tired."

"What do you need me to do, then?" Reese said.

"Talk to me," Glorrie smiled. "Just talk to me."

Reese sat down with her at the table. He still liked her smile, looked forward to it like a good meal. It brought something out in Reese that satisfied him, even if he tried to hide it from Clara. They sat quietly for a long while.

"You're not very good at talking, Reese," Glorrie grinned.

"I guess not," Reese said.

"I'm sorry to get you up in the middle of the night like this, I truly am. I don't mean to be a burden. If you want to go back to bed, I can just sit here for a while until Clara wakes up. I don't mind, really."

"No," Reese said. "I'm going to wait to check your head. You're bleeding pretty badly."

"I don't want to be a bother."

"You're no bother."

"I think I am," Glorrie smiled, "but you're kind to say so."

Reese sat in the quiet of the kitchen for a few moments, just listening to the silence. And then he said, "Tom shouldn't be doing this, you know. He shouldn't do you this way. You know, don't you?"

"Yes," she said. Her smile had faded, and she was close to crying again. "But I swear to you, I don't know what to do."

Reese scratched behind his ear. "Me either."

"Sometimes, Tom can be so sweet, you know? And I used to be able to talk him out of these fits he has, I really did. But that was a long time ago. Now, he just gets so angry, so fast. Some of it's the drinking. The rest of it, I don't know." Glorrie took the towel off her head to check, but the bleeding started again instantly. She put the towel back on the wound and pushed hard. She forced out a laugh. "I'm going to get some more magazines for this," she said.

"What?"

"Tom gives me magazines. After—after nights like this, he gives me magazines. He knows I love them, knows that with the paper drives and all they're hard to get anymore. But he knows some places in Decatur, buys them for me. I like reading about all these places I'll never go, all these things I'll never see."

"Like where?" Reese asked, leaning forward.

"Pikes Peak, for one," Glorrie said. "Highest place in America, I think. And then the Grand Canyon. New York City, maybe see a Broadway show. Hollywood, of course. I've seen pictures of the Florida Keys, and they look wonderful. And then there's all the places around the world, too. There's just so much to see, you know? And I'm here, and I love it here, I really do, but there are so many other places, so much else out there to see."

"That's why we have movies," Reese joked.

Glorrie rolled her eyes. "You men," she said. "That's just what Tom says. The Movietones are enough for me, he says. But you all miss the point."

"So what's the point?"

"Movies just show you what someone else saw. The magazines show you what you could see yourself."

"I don't see the difference," Reese said.

"That's because you're a man," Glorrie said. "But enough about me. Are you and Clara still fighting over the cat?"

Reese could feel his good mood slipping away. "I suppose we are."

"That was a dumb thing to do," Glorrie said.

"Her or me?"

"Both of you."

Reese laughed, looked away. "Maybe."

"You know what she's really mad about, don't you?"

"I thought it was the kittens."

"That's part of it. But do you even know why she was feeding the cat in the first place?"

"I guess I don't."

"She wants a child, Reese. A baby. She needs to feed something."

Reese felt gut-punched. It wasn't as though he and Clara hadn't tried, hadn't been trying, on and off, for a long time. He knew Clara wanted a baby, and he did too, and saw the practicality of it too, after a dozen years or so. Clara had told him once that having trouble conceiving ran in the Sanner family, but said she didn't care. Clara wanted to be a mother.

Of course, Reese thought with his luck, it would probably be a girl. Girls couldn't do much of anything to start with on the farm, and only got less helpful as time went on. They'd worry too much about their hair to pick up stray corn, too worried about their nails to walk beans. Reese had heard the stories from Hal and Cotton Bilyeu, two brothers who'd started a seed company in town, and whose wives had both given them girls their first time out of the chute. Of course, they'd kept trying, and eventually had boys—more than a dozen of them between the two—but it was the curse of the farmer, they said. The first to come out is always a girl.

It was an easy joke for men who married wives who could have kids, which, apparently, wasn't meant to be for Reese and Clara. It broke her up just to talk about it—she'd sit there on their bed and sob into his shoulder, and he'd feel as useless as a coat in summer. He'd look out the window to their land outside, and imagine children playing there, how that would make Clara smile, how satisfied she'd be then, how he might come in from the fields at night and smoke his pipe, sit in his chair by the window, and watch her playing games with the baby on the floor, hear their laughter rolling around him. How they'd both tuck this child in at night and go to bed themselves, happy to sleep in the knowledge that tomorrow would be the same as today, the process of watching a baby grow up and a wife grow happy. But it wasn't to be, and Reese didn't know how to change it, so he had suggested they put their faith in God, that if it was meant to be for them to have children, God would provide, and until then, it just wasn't time. All things in good measure, their minister had once said, and Reese reminded Clara of that, surprised and thankful he'd been able to recall it himself. All things in good measure, she repeated to him, and nodded. She seemed almost relieved to have put it in God's hands, as though she were tired of carrying it around in her own. She still cried, but she smiled at Reese in a way that made him understand it would be all right again. And it was, though Reese often considered that God really hadn't come through.

"God is sleeping." Reese smiled at his own joke.

"What does that mean?" Glorrie asked.

"Nothing," Reese said. "It means I need to check your forehead." He got up and knelt down next to Glorrie, lifting the towel off her forehead. Blood was still coming. "That's it," Reese said. "We need to call the doctor."

"It's the middle of the night, Reese."

"Yeah, well, that's why he has the big house on Hanover Street," Reese said, going to the phone to ring up the operator when he saw Clara standing in the gloom of the hallway beyond. "Clara?" Reese said. "How long have you been standing there?"

"Call the doctor," Clara said, moving into the kitchen, her expression betraying nothing. She knelt next to Glorrie. "How bad is it?"

"Not too," Glorrie said, but with the new attention, her voice was starting to shake again. "Not too."

"The bruise looks almost as bad as all the blood," Clara said, pulling a chair over to Glorrie and sitting. "How did smacking your head against a bedwarmer do all this?"

Glorrie didn't say anything.

"He hit you in the face, didn't he?" Clara pushed.

"I don't think he meant to," Glorrie said, starting to cry. "He's always been careful not to. Said I was too pretty for that." She laughed bitterly. "Or maybe 's changed now, I don't know. Maybe I'm just not pretty enough anymore."

"Don't say that," Clara scolded, but softly. "Don't say that."

Reese saw Clara looking at him, saw something in her eyes he'd not seen before. There was anger, yes, but he'd seen anger before. This time, there was something else. Determination, maybe? He wasn't sure.

"Call the doctor, Reese," Clara said. "Don't just stand there."

By the next morning, Doc Pistorius had put eight stitches in Glorrie's head, and left her to sleep in one of the upstairs bedrooms for a while. He pretended not to understand what was going on, but suggested that someone needed to help Glorrie stop having all these accidents.

Clara agreed. "We have to do something," she told Reese later that day. "You have to do something."

"What can I do?"

"Something," Clara said. "We can't just stand around while my sister gets beaten."

"Well, I don't know what. Tom doesn't listen to me. Tom doesn't listen to anyone."

"Tom does too listen to you. You think he doesn't, but he does. You might be one of the few men in the world who could get through to Tom, but you don't. You don't even try. You just sit at our kitchen table with her, talking."

"You tell me what else to do. You tell me."

"I shouldn't have to," Clara said, and went out to turn the dirt in her garden in preparation for the coming spring.

Two nights later, Glorrie steeled herself and went home to face Tom. Clara tried to get her to stay, at least for a while longer. But Glorrie refused, and said she had to go home, or things would be worse later. Reese offered to drive her because he thought it might make Clara happy, for him to do something.

"Park here," Glorrie said when they were still a block from the house. "I'll walk the rest of the way."

"It's still raining."

"I don't mind it." Glorrie was looking down the street, through the darkness. "I don't see any lights on."

"That good or bad?"

"Never know," Glorrie said. They were quiet in the cab of the truck for a few minutes. Reese thought she was summoning her courage to go inside. "I want to thank you," Glorrie finally said. "For helping me. I know it's a burden, and I want you to know I'm sorry."

"Please don't be," Reese said, and put his hand on hers. "You just be careful, all right?" He nearly said something about knowing what Tom was capable of, but stopped himself. Glorrie had enough fear without him defining it for her.

"I thank God I have you every day, Reese, you and Clara both. I don't know what I'd do without you."

"We're glad to help," Reese said, shifting in his seat. He didn't feel like he was helping. Much the opposite. "I'm just sorry you have to go through this. You don't deserve this, and Tom needs to stop."

"I know," she said quietly, squeezing Reese's hand tightly. "I just don't know what to do...don't know how to stop him. He's like a train, you know? Big and powerful, and dangerous at the wrong time. And usually, if you know the schedule, you can stay out of his way. But when you get caught on the tracks, there's nothing to save you. All you can do is run." Even though what she was saying gave Reese chills, she was still smiling.

For a moment, Reese saw in her the bouncy and beautiful girl who'd brought him coffee, who'd flirted with him sometimes, of whom he'd dreamed almost nightly. He saw her sitting there, hurting like a bird with a busted wing, unable to fly and probably just waiting for some cat to come along and kill it with a blow. Anger grew in him, and frustration. "I don't know what I can do," he finally said, "but I swear to you, Glorrie, I'll do anything I can to make sure you don't get hurt anymore. I swear it to you."

Glorrie's green eyes shone like a traffic light in the rain. She pulled Reese's hand up to her lips and held it there, for a moment. Reese was transfixed, and she whispered "Thank you" so quietly that it almost wasn't there. But it was, a slight sound that seemed to Reese like the sealing of a deal, as if he'd just promised her the world and she'd accepted. And in the moment, it made him deliriously happy. She kept his hand there, at her lips, and he felt her breath hot on him, felt the soft underside of her nose as it brushed the knuckle of his first finger, and then she kissed it lightly, smiled again sadly, and let it go.

She left the truck without another sound, and Reese watched her go as he listened to the beat of the windshield wipers and his own heart. He watched her go into her house, saw the lights come on, and waited to see if she was all right. He didn't know how he'd know for sure, but when she didn't come back out, he assumed all was okay. He looked at his hand, the one she'd held, gazed at it as though it was suddenly unfamiliar, and then, without thinking, put his knuckle up to his mouth and pressed it to his lips. He turned his truck back toward home, watching for Tom through his foggy windows and streaks of light.

By the end of the week, Reese had gone to talk to the sheriff. Jim Dawes was still the Shelby County Sheriff, even now as he was stretching toward his mid-fifties. Reese had gotten to know Dawes better over the years—they'd served on a parks committee together a few years before, and even though Dawes still looked askance at Reese every time he saw him, they'd gotten along well. Despite his age and his approaching retirement, the sheriff was as big a man as Tom, was still in better shape, and had a badge behind him. Reese knew Dawes was one of the few men who Tom had at one time been cowed by, and perhaps still was.

Dawes suggested they met at Wendell's, a new diner just opened on the north end of town. When Reese got there, it was mid-afternoon, and the place was deserted except for Dawes, who was already sitting at the counter sipping coffee and eating a slice of coconut cream pie.

"Reese," Dawes said. "Good to see you. You know Meg Parsons?" He gestured towards a waitress behind the counter.

Reese didn't know her well, but smiled and took off his hat. "Ma'am," he said. "Thanks for coming," Reese said to the sherrif, then ordered a coffee. "Would you mind if we took a booth over by the window?"

Dawes looked at Reese, and then at Meg, who smiled and shrugged. Dawes nodded, and they moved to the booth. "Why do I suddenly get the feeling this ain't going to stop with coffee and pie?"

"I'm sorry," Reese said, "but I needed to talk to you, and I didn't know how else to do this. I don't want it getting around, for a lot of reasons."

"Don't want what getting around?"

"I'm asking you to do something about Tom."

"Tom Horseman?"

"Tom Horseman. He's married to Glorrie, Clara's sister. One of the Sanner girls."

"I remember."

"Yeah, well," Reese sipped his coffee. "He sort of...well, he hits her."

Dawes put his cup down. "That's a shame."

"Yeah, it is. And I'm wondering what you might be able to do about it."

"Me?"

"You're the sheriff."

"That I am, Reese," Dawes said, folding his hands together on the table in front of him. "But this sounds like a family matter, not a legal one. And as much as I don't like a man raising a hand to his wife, there's not much the law allows me in situations between a married couple, especially on nothing but your say-so."

"It's happened more than once. A lot more than once. Doc Pistorius can vouch for what he's treated her for. And Clara and I have seen even more."

"I'm sorry to hear all this, I really am."

"But there's nothing you can do?"

"Not much," Dawes said, "but I'll keep an eye on Tom, and if I see something I can do, something I can get him on, I'll let you know. Fair enough?"

It wasn't enough, but Reese had no choice but to agree to it. He finished his coffee, paid the check, and went home empty-handed.

He didn't tell Clara about what he'd tried, about talking with Sheriff Dawes. He'd accomplished nothing, he reasoned, so why disappoint her again? But later in the week, as luck would have it, the sheriff called him, asked to meet him at Wendell's again.

Sheriff Dawes was sitting at a booth this time, again with his coffee and coconut cream pie. "Reese," he said.

"Afternoon," Reese said waving off a coffee. He took a seat on the cold, red vinyl of the bench seat. "You think of something since last we talked?"

"Better," he said. "I just got word that your friend Tom is in county lockup. Has been since last night.

"I hadn't heard."

"Seems like it's not an uncommon thing with Tom," Dawes said, "sleeping it off courtesy of the county. Only difference this time, Tom's gotten himself in a pack of trouble."

"What's he in for?"

"Drunk and disorderly, for starters. Destruction of property, both public and private. Assault on a police officer, if I want to charge him with it, not to mention resisting arrest. It's a long list."

"Wow," Reese said. "He must have had a lot in him."

"He and his buddies from Decatur, the lot of them. They tore up a bar just outside of Macon, roughed up some of the locals. We had a bear of a time bringing them all in. They're all looking at serious charges."

"I wish I could say I was surprised. So what are you going to do with him?"

"Now that, my friend, depends on you." Dawes took a bite of his pie.

"On me?"

Dawes nodded. "You know, in my family, they say if you eat a piece of pie like I'm doing here, from the crust to the tip, if you leave the tip as your last piece? You get to make a wish on it."

"They do, huh?"

"That's right," Dawes said, scooping up the last piece of his coconut pie with his fork. "You want to know what my wish is this time?"

"What?"

"I wish once and for all, you'd come clean with what happened on the thrasher back in '32." Dawes smiled and popped the tip of his pie into his mouth, chewing with a satisfied air.

Reese sat back in his seat. "Sheriff, I mean no disrespect, but explain to me how it would make a difference here? I mean, what do you need to—"

"You're asking me a favor. I'm asking you for one. That's all. Look, I'm not wanting to charge you with anything. I'm not wanting to charge Tom. Ancient history. But it's always nagged at me that the whole thing got smothered by what happened at the mine. It's always tugged at my heels a bit. I'm just looking to lay it to rest is all. And if I can do that, then maybe I can pull some strings with the Shelby County judge, and suggest to him that he give Tom this option: go to jail or go to war. Either way, he's out of your hair, and your wife's sister's, too, at least for a while. He'll no doubt choose to enlist, Reese. They all do. And for a lot of these guys? It's exactly what they need."

Reese looked at Dawes. There were always strings, he thought. Nothing is ever clean. But the deal was clear—in order to help Glorrie, he had to damn Tom. It was perfect, in a way, and yet, it was still betrayal, a crossing of the pact they'd made after the thrasher. Reese closed his eyes and called up the vision of Glorrie weeping into her hands, barely able to speak through her tears. He remembered her bloody forehead and her bruises, and mostly he recalled the feeling of her fear, the utter terror he felt coming off her as they talked and she recounted what Tom had done, about how she didn't know what she was going to do. He thought last about the promise he'd made to her on the spur of the moment in the cab of his truck as they parked down the street from her house on Cherry Street.

"So what do you say, Reese?" Dawes asked.

Reese took a deep breath. He didn't even know what he was going to say until he said it. "Tom threw him in."

Sheriff Dawes sniffed. "Yeah, that's what I thought." He reached down on the seat next to him, and pulled his hat on, readying himself to go.

"So what now?" Reese asked. "What happens now?"

"With Tom? I told you, the judge will give him a choice, and if Horseman's got any sense left in him, he'll sign up that day. If he doesn't, the judge can push a little, I've seen him do it. And before you get to worrying, Tom won't find out you were behind any of this, I promise you."

"Okay," Reese nodded, watching the Sheriff put down a dollar and some change for the bill. "Hey, Jim? What about the thrasher?"

"Just a wish on a pie-tip," Dawes smiled. "I told you I just wanted to know what happened for my own peace of mind, and I meant it. You didn't tell me anything I didn't already know anyway. Don't let it get you down. Besides, you did a good thing today. We'll get this handled. You don't worry."

"Yeah," Reese said.

"I'll let you know what happens," Dawes said, pulling on his jacket and trading a penny for a couple of mints off the counter as he left.

"Tom enlisted," Clara said, her voice feigning nonchalance. "I just got a call from Glorrie."

Reese looked up at his wife. She was in a long housecoat, with her jacket over it, leaning against the barn door's frame like it was an effort to stay on her feet. Her arms were folded across her chest, and her head was cocked to one side, but she had a smile on her face for the first time in what seemed like ages. No, Reese thought, as he looked at her, she was more than smiling. She was nearly beaming.

"He's a damn fool," Reese finally said as he went back to tinkering with the radio. It had stopped working a week back, and he missed the company. "But I guess we have to win this war."

"So you're telling me you know nothing about this?" Clara asked with an amused expression. "That you had nothing to do with him signing up?"

"Since when have I been able to tell Tom Horseman what he should and shouldn't do?" Reese asked. "Maybe he was struck with patriotism, Clara. Give the man some credit."

"Tom's an animal, and if he should be struck with anything, it ought to be a whip."

Reese looked up from his work. "Do you want me to say I'm glad he's going? Okay, I'm glad he's going. For Glorrie's sake."

"You should hear her, Reese. She's as excited as a girl on Christmas morning. More so. She's going on about how proud she is he's joining up, going to fight for the good of the world and all that, but she can barely restrain herself from thanking God he'll be gone for a while. And maybe for good."

Reese's head snapped up. "Don't—don't talk like that. He'll come back."

"It's war, Reese," Clara said simply. "Men die. Especially men like Tom. You don't think he'll go charging into whatever battle they put him in front of? And I'm not talking about heroism, either, I'm not talking about fighting bravely. I'm talking about not having the sense not to run right into a Nazi bullet. He'll get killed, all right—either that or he'll come home a hero, one of the two. And since Tom's not bulletproof, and since he's also fairly stupid, I'm betting on the former. So is Glorrie. You can hear it in her voice. She's already playing the part of the veteran's widow, and he hasn't even shipped out yet."

Reese sat back in his chair, reeling. "Please stop celebrating the man's death," he said. "He's going to war, not to the firing squad. Men come home from war every day. He'll come home, all right. He'll come home, but before he does, he'll realize what's important to him, realize the mistakes he's made. Tom will be a better man for this, Clara, he will. You'll see."

"Reese, I know you met with Sheriff Dawes. I know you two talked. You don't have to admit it to me, but I know you made this happen. You did something. You did it for me. And for Glorrie." Clara put her hands on Reese's shoulders, hugged him from behind the way she used to when they were first married. "And I love you for it. I really do. And Glorrie, well, she's giddy. I can't ask for more, Reese. It was the right thing, you have to believe it."

"I guess I do, at that," Reese said. "Have to believe it, I mean. I guess I do."

"Good."

"But he's not going to die."

"Whatever you say."

"And we shouldn't hope he does. Not even Glorrie, as much as it might be easier for her if he did. You don't send a man to war hoping he doesn't come back. It's wrong, it's just wrong."

"Okay."

"I mean it."

"I know you do," Clara said, and he could hear the smile in her voice. She kissed him lightly on the top of his head. "Thank you."

"Don't thank me," Reese said, annoyed. "Thank Jim Dawes."

"He never would have done a thing without you pushing, Reese, and you know it. He had no reason to. If not for you, Tom would be drunk right now, and drunk tomorrow, and Glorrie would be no better off. She knows it too."

"Glorrie knows?" Reese wasn't sure if that was a good thing.

"I haven't told her, but I expect she does. She knows you spoke with the Sheriff."

"Because you told her."

"We talked about it. It gave her hope, Reese, and hope is an important thing. Someone was finally doing something, which was a good sight better than us all just sitting around and cleaning her up every once in a while."

Reese sat back in his chair and sighed. "I didn't want to have to do it, Clara. I really didn't."

"I know you didn't, Reese, but Tom was the one who made it necessary. We all do things we don't want to do. Glorrie didn't want to be hit in the first place."

"I know," Reese said, "but that doesn't make it any easier."

"It never does." Clara was silent for a moment, and then she asked: "Do you think Tom has any idea you were the one who talked to Sheriff Dawes?"

"If he did," Reese said, "I might already be dead."

Reese sat there in his barn, gazing into nothing. Clara stood watching him. Moweaqua lay out there beyond the house, and on Cherry Street, a woman rejoiced quietly while her husband packed to go off to war. He never guessed who sent him.

# Chapter Eight

MOM WAS SEEING MY APARTMENT FOR THE FIRST TIME. We'd driven up to Normal first thing that morning because Earl had never come by to spell me the night before, and I didn't want to leave Mom alone. But the visitation would be that night, and I had to have some better clothes, fresh underwear, my toothbrush. I had been happy on the drive up, actually excited to show Mom my place. The moment we arrived, I realized my mistake.

"My, you can certainly tell a divorced man lives here, can't you?" These were Mom's first words upon seeing my apartment.

"I didn't really have time to clean up," I said, picking up some of the clothes that were laying around and hustling them into the bedroom.

"You know, I have a couple of end tables in storage, if it will help you keep some of this off the floor," she said.

"I'm fine on end tables, Mom, thanks."

"You have a lamp on the floor, James."

"It's a tall lamp."

"A tall table lamp, yes," she said, clucking her tongue.

"I haven't had time to decorate," I said.

"I can see that," she said. "Is it safe for me to sit?"

"Give me a break, okay? It's not that bad."

"No," she admitted, smiling. "You should see Earl's place, actually. At least you do your dishes. That's more than I can say for your cousin."

"That's something, right?" It was true. I might leave clothes laying around, and I might have a lamp on the floor, and I might not scrub the toilet as often as I probably should—and I was praying Mom wouldn't need to use the facilities and find out—but the kitchen sink was spotless. "You sit. I just need to throw some clothes into a gym bag, grab some stuff, and we'll get back on the road."

"All right" she said. "Can we stop at the Steak 'n' Shake on the way out of town? I wouldn't mind a hamburger for lunch."

"Sounds good to me," I said from the bedroom. I grabbed a handful of clean boxers and a few pairs of socks, and then went into my closet to pick out an outfit for the visitation and funeral. I didn't know what to wear, really, and didn't have a suit anymore, so I settled on dockers, oxford shirts, and a couple of sportcoats. I had it all together in a gym bag, a couple of jackets slung over my shoulder, when I heard the toilet flush.

"Pity's sake, James," she said when she emerged from the bathroom. "You're getting a toilet brush in your stocking this Christmas."

"I haven't gotten a stocking since I was eighteen years old."

"Well, you will this year. And it will be nothing but toilet brush and sanitizer."

"No orange in the toe?"

She smiled. "I'll get you orange-scented sanitizer, how about that, Mr. Smarty Pants?"

"Sounds fair to me. You ready to go? I think I am."

"I suppose so."

It was only when we were halfway back to Moweaqua, just on the outskirts of Decatur, when I realized I'd completely forgotten my toothbrush. About that same time, Mom started calling me Reese and planning Sunday dinner with Tom and Glorrie, and the weight of the morning fell down on me, and I sat there licking my teeth and listening to Mom call me the wrong name.

When we got back to the house, it was only just noon, but she had been tired out by the trip and her confused conversation. It was one of the kinder things about whatever was wrong with Mom—the worse she got, the more she slept. While she did, I decided to take a walk out in the old apple orchard out by the corn crib. I used to climb those trees as a kid, had fantastic apple-wars in the summer with some friends. We even had a flimsy fort built in the branches of one of the trees, and we'd pelt each other with rotting fruit for hours, falling down, getting up again, laughing the whole time. The day was crisp and solid, one of those days with a presence to it, one of those days you just know you'll remember later on. Maybe it was the fact that I was looking forward to the visitation in a way, anticipating getting this all done once and for all—or maybe it was just that I was wearing fresh underwear for the first time in a couple of days—but whatever the reason, I felt happy there, walking around the farm. There was nothing left to explore here, nothing to figure out, nothing to take you by surprise. I realized how much I missed that feeling as I walked out into the fields, now just rows of plowed dirt, and heard that voice. *This is all ours. As far as you can see, and farther. Dig as deep as you want. Jump as high as you can. Walk a mile or more, up to the creek. Ours. You can know this. There are no mysteries here.* I walked for a good hour or so, until I finally got to worrying about Mom, whether she'd awoken from her nap. I made my way back to the house, savoring every step.

When I came in the back door, Earl was sitting in the kitchen, sipping from a steaming cup, his coat slung over the back of his chair. "Don't you ever stop drinking coffee?" I asked, smiling.

"Nope," he said simply, not looking up from his newspaper.

"Mom up?"

"In the living room, watching the news, I think."

I took a seat at the table across from Earl. I wanted to ask him about the land, but didn't know how to broach the subject without starting an argument, something I was desperate to avoid this close to the visitation. I needed all the allies I could get, to help Mom get through it. I hadn't been to a visitation in years, and didn't recall the ones I had been to, so I wanted someone who was an old hand at it. Earl was it. "When did you get here?"

"About ten minutes ago. I saw you walking around out there. Taking in the sights, were you?" He put his paper down, and held his coffee cup in both hands.

"I guess so. You want a sandwich or something? We have ham."

"We have ham," Earl said, laughing. "Of course we have ham.

The whole town has ham. It should be on the damn town sign: Moweaqua: We Have Ham." He laughed, one of those tired, breathy things that escape you when you can't do much else. "Aren't you and your mom getting sick of ham yet? You've had it for three days now."

"The only ham I ever got in Normal was the shaved kind from the grocery, you know? The real stuff is sort of a treat."

"A treat. You have been gone too long."

"And Mom doesn't remember I'm her son half the time. I doubt she recalls what we had for lunch."

Earl laughed again. "I guess."

"One of the perks of losing your mind."

Earl smiled, and pointed at me in mock disapproval. "Hey, now, don't let her hear you saying that. She did okay yesterday, didn't she?"

I nodded. "For a while. But she couldn't hold onto it. It was too much for her. I'm starting to worry about the visitation and the funeral."

"Just starting, huh?" Earl scratched at the corner of one eye, trying to work the sleep from it. "What, you don't think she can handle it?"

"I don't know that she can—that's the problem. I don't think we can depend on anything from Mom right now. She's unpredictable at best."

"Sure, but what can we do? We can't very well keep her away from her own sister's services. People will ask where she is."

"I don't care if people ask."

"You should, damnit." Earl's voice got quieter, more intense, but I had no idea why. "So what would you tell them, Reese? That Clara's sick? They won't buy that. That she's mentally unable to come? That she's losing her senses? That's exactly what Glorrie wanted to avoid. She said so a hundred times."

"It's all over town, Earl," I said. "You yourself were filling Gum in on the details just yesterday. The word is out."

"And that's why people are going to want to see her there. They're going to want to know she's all right, even if she isn't. It's what Glorrie wanted, and I'll be damned if we're going to go against her wishes at her own funeral." Earl shook his head, and looked away from me. "This is just what I expected from you."

Now it was my turn to get angry. "What the hell does that mean? I've been here for three days dealing with this crap the best way I know how."

"Yeah, well I've been here for thirty years," Earl said, his voice getting a bit louder now as it grew more harsh. "And where have you been? I've been trying to help her the whole time, and most of the crap I was helping her deal with was your fault. I was picking up your pieces, hotshot, so don't you come in here and pretend to be all fine with the world, all Mr. Good-Son, come to take care of his mama. 'Cause I've been the one doing that for you. I've been the one doing that for years now."

"Yeah, well, it was me who she's been talking to, Earl. It was me who she asked for."

"It wasn't you," Earl said. "It was your father. You said so yourself. You being here now is nothing but a mistake, pure and simple, a mistake made by a confused woman at a time of a lot of grief. She didn't ask for you, Reese. You know she didn't. And I'm not going to have you waltz back into town like you suddenly belong here and do all the things Glorrie would've hated."

"What the hell's the difference, Earl? Why did Glorrie keep Mom's condition a secret? So she's losing it. So she can't remember what year it is, or mistakes people for dead family members, so what? Who cares?"

"I don't know," Earl said simply. "But Glorrie made it clear she didn't want anyone making a thing out of it. Said we couldn't be sure what she'd do or what she'd say, without meaning to. She said it was a matter of respect, and your Mom deserved not to be made the fool."

"She told you this."

"Yes."

"Before she died?"

"What sort of stupid question is that? I'm not the one talking to the dead, Reese, your Mom has a corner on that market. All I know is what Glorrie told me. All I know is the rules we've been playing by for a while now. And it's enough for me that it was what Glorrie wanted. She didn't want other people involved."

"I don't care about other people," I said.

"You said it, hotshot."

My fists clenched, and I was reminded of why Earl had traditionally not been on my Christmas card list. I turned and grabbed a cookie from a nearby plate on the counter, and chewed it as viciously as I could without biting my tongue. It was one of those moments where you know you're looking like an ass, but there's not much you can do about it. You've called the play, and there's nothing to do but run it.

"This is stupid," I finally said. "I don't want to fight with you about this. You're right, okay? I'm an asshole. I'm a complete asshole. But I still don't understand what that has to do with Mom staying home if she needs to."

"You don't know what she needs."

"Oh, like you do."

"Better than you."

I shook my head. "Can you stop riding me about old shit long enough to deal with Mom right now? Please?" He raised his hands in mock surrender, but he didn't look at me. "Are you paying attention to what's going on, Earl, or have you and Glorrie just been denying it for so long you don't see it anymore? It took her more than a day to hold onto the fact that Glorrie was dead. She wasn't even sure who we'd been planning to bury yesterday. She's not going to stand there and be cordial for three hours without someone figuring it out."

"She will."

"I don't think so."

"She will," Earl said. "I've seen her at church."

"What?"

"She and Glorrie went to church pretty much every Sunday, okay? I went with them once in a while—last time was just a few weeks ago. Your Mom wasn't much better than she is now, but she carried on conversations like everything was fine."

"She did?"

"She did," Earl said. He was calmer, but still on edge. "So she'll be fine. Just trust her, for God's sake. And let her tell her sister goodbye."

I clenched my teeth. My whole body felt tight. Earl was probably right. I hated it, but I recognized it was true. "I just want to do what's best for her."

Earl's glare faded slowly, and then he nodded. "Okay," he said. "Okay." He got up and walked into the living room to sit next to Mom on the couch. I'd forgotten she was there. I stood there in the kitchen for a while and thought about what he'd said. Nothing had been settled, not about Mom and not about Earl and me, either. The former, we would discuss; the latter we might never get around to.

But maybe we didn't have to. There was too much road behind us, too many potholes to hit ahead. Earl and I couldn't see eye to eye, even when we agreed on something. We were unpracticed. Or maybe just lazy, too used to denying the other the benefit of even the smallest doubt. It made me feel small. It had always been like this. I was tired of it.

I pulled on my jacket and told Earl I needed to run down to Fathauer's for a few things. He looked at me like he was trying to decide between anger and apology, then settled on just nodding again. I took it as a good sign.

It was chilly. The weather had cooled over the last few days, and even though it was early afternoon, I had to pull my jacket around me tightly as I walked to the truck, glad for the heater when it finally kicked in. I took the long way to the store, which meant that it took five minutes instead of two, but I was enjoying seeing town, the ways it had changed, the stuff that still remained. The main intersection was more or less the same. Ayars Bank was still on one corner, catty-cornered from Fathauer's, and on the other two corners were the American Legion Hall and the Oddfellows Lodge, up above some antique stores, a sewing shop, and Duez' Shoes, where I had gotten every pair of Buster Browns I owned as a kid. I was glad to see it all.

I pulled into the Fathauer's lot and stopped the truck. I knew I had to get back—the visitation would begin in a couple of hours. But it felt good being where I was, reminiscing about the past while surrounded by the comfortable trappings of the present: my truck, my travel coffee mug from White Hen Pantry nestled in the dash, Spiderman swinging from the rear-view mirror. It made me miss the place all over again, churned me up in a way I thought I'd outgrown.

I was a little nervous about going into Fathauer's—not so much because it was the place where my aunt died, but because I didn't really feel like talking to Freda. I didn't know her, and even though she was well-meaning, I didn't know what to say to her. Or, considering Earl, what I wasn't supposed to say. As it turned out, there was no need to worry. When I walked in the door, Freda was absent from the front counter. Some girl—probably a senior at the high school—stood there, filing her nails.

I walked down one of the narrow aisles, looking for the toothbrushes. I passed by the back of the store, and recognized the endcap near where I had been told Glorrie had been hit. I hurried past, not wanting to think about the accident. I wasn't a superstitious person, but I thought it was better not to tempt fate. I imagined Glorrie's ghost holding her apple butter, frowning. I found the tiny selection of toothbrushes: I could choose blue, yellow, or Scooby-Doo. I picked up Scooby-Doo—what the hell—and headed back up to checkout. On my way, I grabbed a bag of pretzels for Mom.

The girl at the front was still busy with her nails, and when she saw me approach, she smiled and put the emery board back into the little cylinder offering them for sale, four for a dollar. "Find what you needed?" she asked with a practiced smile.

"Sure," I said. She reminded me of my students, and I wondered why she wasn't in school at one-thirty. Didn't seem like my place to ask.

"This it, then?" the girl asked.

"I guess," I said, handing her a five. And then, as an afterthought: "Tell Freda that Reese said hello when you see her."

Her eyes perked up. "Reese? Reese Moss?"

I smiled, but I was scowling on the inside. "That's me."

She handed me my change, beaming. "My boyfriend is going to break your record this Saturday for Most Yards Rushing in a season," the girl said, counting back my change. "At least that's what he says."

I was surprised, genuinely. "I didn't know the record was still standing. Didn't they reset those records in the consolidation?"

"Oh yeah, but all the guys on the team think that's stupid. I mean, what's the point of having a record if all you have to do is show up all season? All the teams still have the old records written down, and still know them. They try to beat those, and if they don't, they don't count it." She shrugged. "It's a guy thing."

"What did they do with all the old trophies?" It had been tradition to keep awards in the cases in the hall, so as to inspire future generations of athletes.

"Sent them to whoever won them," she said. "Didn't you get yours?"

"No." I wondered if Mom had it at the house. That would have been my last known address as far as the high school was concerned. "Tell your boyfriend I wish him luck."

"His name's Kyle. Kyle Potts. Number 22. He says he'll have you beat by Friday's game. He's had a good season. The U of I scout is talking to him."

"Tell him to major in something useful, just in case his legs go on him."

"That what happened to you?"

I smiled. "No," I said. "I just got old."

She missed the sarcasm. "Well, it's good you finally came home for your mom and all. I've heard Freda talking about you. Your aunt used to come in here all the time. Really sad what happened to her. Sucks, really."

I had been around teenagers long enough to know "Sucks, really" was a fairly sincere and heartfelt sentiment, so I thanked her and grabbed my bag.

"Hey Earl," I said when I was back at the house. "Did Mom ever get an old trophy of mine? The one for Most Yards Rushing? It would have happened after the consolidation."

"Yeah," he said. Mom wasn't there, and I could hear the water running upstairs. "I thought Clara called you when they sent it over."

"No," I said.

"Probably upstairs in your old room, then," he said, turning his attention back to the television. "Look in the closet. I remember her rummaging around in there a while back."

My room was upstairs, last bedroom on the left, across the hall from Mom. She used to threaten to turn it into a sewing room once I was gone, but I knew even then that it had been an empty gesture. Even though I'd slept in that room for a couple of nights, I hadn't looked around much at all. Maybe I was too distracted, or maybe the room was just too familiar. I had missed the trophy—there it sat, propped against the wall on top of the dresser, along with a collection of other prizes from the past. It was the last thing I'd ever won, the last time I'd been honored. Most Yards Rushing. I felt a swell of pride in my chest, and a sense of relief the trophy wasn't lost.

Finding it spurred me to see what else I could find. When I'd moved, I'd just taken the stuff I'd thought I'd need in college, and left the rest. It looked like Mom had cleaned out some of the stuff she considered unimportant: stacks of magazines and comic books were gone, the few old toys I'd had left laying around had been pitched, even my old workboots.

I still had some shirts in the closet, old tees from high school, and stacks of old stuff, some of it mine, some of it Mom's. Under some of Mom's old family albums, I saw a yellowed Carson Pirie Scott shirtbox, the corners unglued and flapped up. I pulled it open and found a bunch of the old magazines I'd thought had been thrown away: a short stack of *Mad, Car & Driver,* that sort of thing. Towards the bottom, tucked inside an old copy of *National Lampoon* was something I thought I'd lost years ago. It was an old issue of *Captain America,* #116, 1969, where Cap switches bodies with his nemesis the Red Skull and has to convince his friends that he is, in fact, still Captain America. The comic was a great read, I remembered, from Stan Lee's script to Gene Colan's pencils to the *GRIT* ad on the back cover. It was the comic book Earl had bought to console me in the days following Dad's death.

I didn't remember saving this *Captain America,* or stashing it in this box with these old magazines for safekeeping, but it made sense. This was the issue that turned me on to Marvel Comics, my first. Until then, I'd been a Superman guy, and always had been. But this was a comic book that meant something, made important promises. Captain America didn't die in World War II—he was frozen in a block of ice, and came back from certain death to fight the good fight again. This was the lesson, and I believed. Nothing was forever, heroes never die, and there's always a happy ending. Always.

Visitations are strange things. You're already going through one of the toughest times in your life because you've lost someone for good, and everyone seems to understand that this is hard. They bring enough food so you won't have to worry about cooking. They give you time off work so you don't have to worry about money. All well and good. But then, the night before you're going to put that person in the ground and say goodbye forever, the time you're most emotionally unstable, they make you stand for hours in a receiving line, listen to the same things repeated over and over again. It's like a grief gauntlet.

*We're so sorry.*

*She was a good woman.*

*We'll miss her down at the church.*

*She did so much for people.*

*She's in God's hands now.*

*A better place.*

*If there's anything I can do...*

*Anything at all...*

*You just call me.*

*I mean it, now.*

*And it's so good to see you.*

*Sorry to hear about your divorce.*

People in Moweaqua mean it, too. They really do. It's not just talk—people look after each other. It's the up side to everybody knowing your business: there's always someone to lend a hand. And a ham.

Earl and Mom and I arrived a good hour before the service was scheduled to start, as Gum had suggested. Easier that way, I guess, to get all the worst of the crying out of the way before the other mourners come in. Gum and his son Ben met us at the door. We exchanged quiet, respectful hellos, and then they led us into the main room.

I didn't remember the last time I'd seen Glorrie. She was laid out in her casket, the one with the wheat sheaves above her head, with its mahogany finish and a cream-colored stuffed-satin lining. I had to admit it looked nice. Glorrie was just as I'd remembered her. She was a little more plump than the last time I'd seen her, though she'd never been a small woman, and she had finally let her hair go to its natural gray, rather than dying it her reddish chestnut. She wore the navy dress Earl had chosen for her, a strand of pearls she'd once said Uncle Tom had given her, and her beaded purse was clasped in her hands over her stomach. They'd made her up well—you could hardly make out the scar she had over her left eye—and she looked like she was sleeping, which is I guess what they shoot for. The only thing missing was her smile, which had been everpresent. Without the smile, she looked tired. Spent. Or maybe that's just what the dead look like.

Mom was on my arm, and when she saw Glorrie, she let out a little gasp and put her head against my chest. Earl, on her other side, put a hand on her shoulder in quiet comfort, and wore a grim expression himself. I think I may have seen a tear in his eye. I could feel tears running down my flushed face, too, which surprised me. I didn't know I had it in me. But the tears came, and when they did, it was strange. I didn't think just about Glorrie, but about Dad, too, and Mom. And, I had to admit, Carrie.

It occurred to me Carrie might show up. It was an outside chance, but word must have gotten around school by now that I had left, that someone had died, that I'd gone back home. Carrie would have heard, she would have looked into it. She'd met Glorrie, gotten along with her well. And with Mom.

Mom pulled away from me, walked gingerly over to the casket. Earl and I kept back so she could cry a little on her own, but I was ready to catch her if she collapsed, or did something—I didn't know what—that situation would require intervention. She leaned over her sister's body, and started talking to her, whispering. I couldn't make it out. I made out the word "forgive," but that was all. I guess it was something Mom needed to say, that she was okay with Glorrie leaving her the way she did. When she looked done, I went to her and put my arms around her. She smiled up at me, and I led her to the chairs where Earl was already sitting.

"Are you okay?" I asked. "Is there anything I can get you?"

She shook her head. "I just need to sit," she said. "I'll be needing to stand for a while tonight, so I better save my strength."

"That's a good idea," Earl said. And then to me he said, "I'll go get us all some water and some tissues." He went out into the front, and started talking to Gum.

"I just hope she's all right," Mom said, after we'd sat there for a while.

My heart sank. "What do you mean, Mom?" I dreaded the answer, afraid Mom was gone again, untethered, believing Glorrie was just sleeping, that she'd pop up at any moment and ask for her toast.

"I hope she's in heaven," Mom said, and then blew her nose softly.

"I'm sure she is." Seemed like an odd comment to make—weren't we supposed to assume heavenly admittance, not wonder if she passed muster? But so long as Mom still understood her sister was gone, it wasn't worst case scenario. Mom patted my hand, and rested her head against my shoulder. "Rest, Mom," I said. "People will start showing up soon, and we need to be ready."

And start showing up they did, ten minutes before Gum opened the doors. Even though I'd been warned, it still astounded me, the sheer number of folks who showed up—Glorrie knew a lot of people, but nearly everyone in town looked to be in that line, and then some. Folks from Bethany, Taylorville, Assumption, Findlay, Decatur, Pana—all over. As they filed in, we stood up and took our places in line. Earl pushed me to the first position, right in front of Mom—we'd talked about standing to either side of her before this all started, just in case something went wrong. That way, one of us would likely notice and do whatever we could to head off the problem before it began. I assumed Earl would take the head position, nearest the casket since he was the one who knew all these people—it was only when Earl, there in third at the end of the line, shook the first person's hand as the crowd filed in, calling each of them by name, looking straight at me as he said them that I realized that he was giving me a chance to identify them before I had to shake their hands.

Even with Earl there playing the greeter, I wasn't catching all the names. There were, blessedly, a few people early on who didn't know who I was, and didn't much care, apparently, since they shook my hand politely, some of them not even bothering to spare me a glance before looking over to Glorrie. These were mostly older people, I noticed. Some didn't even know Earl, or Mom. But most did, and most knew me, too.

The first gentleman I couldn't place was a short, white-haired old guy with eyes like a basset, who said he remembered me from the football field some fifteen years earlier. He also said he knew Glorrie from way back, and Uncle Tom and Dad, too. His name was Al Wozniak, and he went on for a bit about how he used to work the fields with Tom and Dad, back in the Depression. But I tuned him out, because I heard someone say something about Carrie off to my left and was trying to hear both voices at once. I said something about missing Glorrie already and wishing I knew more about her and my uncle and my father. Al's face brightened. He said he'd love to tell me more, to give him a call in Bethany sometime. I thanked him, told him that would be great, that I would try.

I tried to make conversation with everyone, but there were too many people with too many stories, each walking through this dimly-lit parlor like a silhouette. There were people who knew me as a child, from my football days, from my would-be farming days. I also got to meet some extended family I hadn't seen since the last big family reunion when I was eight—I know that's right because it took me and a second-cousin-once-removed ten long minutes to figure out exactly what the date of it was. I found out later from Earl the guy was a statistician for State Farm, and catalogued everything he could. Earl didn't seem to like him much, so I felt vindicated in not particularly liking him either.

And then, of course, there were the Moweaqua folks I knew and remembered well. Some of Earl's coffee shop friends, a group Glorrie had apparently come to be a part of, in the last years: Gale and Eloise Stewart who used to run the City Service and the Beauty Shop, respectively; Hal and Cotton Bilyeu, who once owned the Bilyeu Brothers Seed company out east of town by the water tower; Don and Rita Saddoris and a couple of their grandkids. And there were old friends of mine: the Barnes boys, Krista Pennie and Brian Williams from our youth group at the Methodist Church; a few others.

Buke Phillips and his Mom came by, Slater was with them, and not far behind them were Donnie and Meg Sweet. I thanked them for coming, told them I'd see them again before I left town, and it was one of the few promises I made that night I sincerely meant. It was all rolling along smoothly, and the time passed quickly. Mom seemed to be enjoying herself, and both Earl and I were relieved.

Amy came in about halfway through the procession. The emery-board girl I had talked with briefly at Fathauer's was right behind her. Amy looked beautiful, smiling and sharing some quiet joke with the emery-board girl. She caught my eye, and waved with a sad sort of grin. I waved back and pretended to become especially earnest in talking to the next person in the line.

It took a long time for Amy to get to the front of the line, but when she did, the scent of her was enough, just by itself. "Hi again," she said, giving me a hug. It felt so good to hold her, one hand on her delicate shoulder, the other in the small of her back, her face against mine, her breath on my ear. She was still thin and soft and strong in my arms. It was almost too much to take, and at the same time, not nearly enough. I gave her a squeeze and drew back slowly. She gave me a quick peck on the cheek. I felt it linger there, even after we had parted completely, tingling like that small part of my face had gone to sleep, like it had fainted dead away.

"Thank you for coming," I said. "For everything."

"You okay?" she asked, her hands still on my shoulders.

"Fine," I nodded.

Amy put her hands down, suddenly a little self-conscious. She gestured to the emery-board girl. "You remember my niece Crystal, right?"

"This is Crystal?" I asked, surprised. "God, I remember when you were born." I suddenly felt like every old guy I had shaken hands. Amy's older sister had had Crystal when we were high school freshmen, and we had lots of parties at her house when Amy was supposed to be babysitting.

Crystal smiled politely. "Yeah, we met this afternoon at the store."

"You didn't tell me," Amy said, frowning.

Crystal shrugged. "I forgot."

"Is your boyfriend still up for the game Saturday night?" I asked.

Crystal's smile widened. "Oh yeah," she said, "he's really stoked. I called and told him about you wishing him luck and all, and he really liked that. He told all the guys on the team. They thought it was very cool."

Amy cocked her head. "That's our Reese," she said, tweaking my cheek, "always cool."

"Thanks," I said.

"Hey, it's a home game, you know." Crystal said. "You should come out and see it if you can. If you come to the south gate, I can get you in free."

"I'll see if I can make it," I said. "I wouldn't mind seeing a Moweaqua ball game again."

"Central A&M," she corrected me.

"Right," I said.

"Why don't you go on ahead, Crystal? I think your Mom's supposed to be here any minute, and we were supposed to meet her out front." Amy nodded at her, and Crystal smiled back like it was some sort of conspiracy. Fifteen-year-olds aren't known for their subtlety.

"Okay," Crystal said, walking off without a glance at the casket. "Sorry about your aunt, by the way. See you at the game, I hope. I'll tell Kyle you're coming. He'll think that's awesome."

"Teenagers," Amy laughed.

"Yeah," I said.

Amy looked over at the casket. "I remember Glorrie," she said. "She was a very special woman. You always got the sense she knew what was up, you know? I remember sitting on the porch with you listening to her stories while we drank lemonade. She had some great ones, about her husband, about your Dad, about you. And she told them well, too."

"Yeah, she did. I'm just beginning to realize how much I'll miss her."

"It's always like that," she said. She looked down at her shoes, and then back up at me. She rocked slightly. I liked that she was nervous. It made me feel less alone. "Listen, when are you going back?"

"I don't know," I said. "Why?"

"I know I already said this, but I was just thinking if you needed any help or anything, or even wanted to just get out of the house for a while, you should give me a call. While you're back."

"I'd like that."

"Me too," she said. "What about the game tomorrow night? Were you serious about going?"

"Yeah," I said. "Might be fun. That is, if Earl can watch Mom for me. I suppose it would be uncool to wear the old school colors now, huh?"

"Red and black now, Reese," Amy laughed. "No one wears the old blue and gold anymore. Got to keep up with the times."

"You still go to the games?"

She shook her head, wrinkled her nose in a way I recognized down to my toes. "Not really. But I've been to a few in the last couple of years with my sister, ever since Crystal started cheerleading. It's fun once in a while."

"Sounds like it," I said. "I'll see if I can talk Earl into it."

"Call me if you can," she said. "I'll let you buy me some hot chocolate."

"Deal," I said. "I'll even get you some licorice."

Again, the wrinkled nose. "I'll pass."

I was surprised. "You used to eat that stuff all the time."

She shrugged. "Things change." She looked behind her. People had stopped waiting to come further down the line and bypassed us completely. "Oops," she said. "I'm holding up the line." She took my hand and gave it a quick squeeze. "You take care, okay?" she said, and then moved on.

My head was swimming, but I didn't have long to reflect on Amy.

Another couple I didn't recognize was already on me, talking about how good I looked, about how good it was I'd come home to be with Mom. A few of the people there asked about my wife, and I told them with as big a smile as I could muster that I was divorced, and courteously accepted their sentiments on that score, too. Toward the end of the night, I realized Carrie wasn't coming, and I surprised myself by feeling relieved.

By the last hour of the visitation, I was getting into the swing of it all, talking about old times and listening to the stories people had to tell about Glorrie, about Mom, about me, about my family. Mom knew nearly all of them, and Earl and I marveled about the way her mind just clicked into play, handily beating our feeble attempts at recognizing the people in Moweaqua who knew us. Earl had been right; Mom was holding up. It seemed as though nothing was wrong, that the last three days of mental roller-coastering were nothing more than a bad dream. Part of me knew they weren't, knew that Mom was just up for this, that she would come down.

It was a parade of ghosts all evening. They were faces of a different time, of a different life. Many were ciphers to me—recognizable, but only as people who lived in Moweaqua, as people who looked like they belonged here. These faces kept pulling me back in time, throwing me into a different reality. I would feel eight, then sixteen, then five, then twenty-two, then ten. I wondered if it was anything like what my mother went through daily. I represented something to them, too. A time past, a familiar face in their own haunted march down memory lane. It was good to see them, even the ones I didn't remember. Good in a way I had not expected, or even knew existed.

I mentioned this feeling to Doc Pistorius, who'd showed up with his wife right before the visitation was ending. He and I had gone out on the stoop to get some fresh air while his wife spoke with Mom a bit more. He looked unimpressed and amused at my small revelation, smiling at me over his pipe and taking a deep breath of the Moweaqua air.

"Of course you feel that way, Reese," he said slowly. He looked up into the cold night's stars. "Why do you think people come home again?"

# Chapter Nine

REESE SAT ON THE STEPS of what had been the Hotel Drew, scratched at the beard he'd been trying to grow out, watched the crowd around him. He wished Clara were with him, thought she should have been, to see everything going on. It seemed like the whole town was there. But Reese, alone as he was, didn't feel much a part of it. He was angry, sad, and frustrated, and furthermore, it seemed like he'd felt that way his entire life. He took out his pipe and lit it, wanting the smoke to burn up his mood or at the least provide him some company. The October sky was threatening, and Reese could smell rain. His knee hurt him, but Reese couldn't decide if it ached because of the coming storm or because of what he was waiting there to do. It was not a good day for celebration. Not a good day for much of anything.

Nonetheless, it was the first day of the Moweaqua Centennial. The town's first hundred years was going to be capped by a three-day party, an event the likes of which no one in town had ever heard. Highway 51 had been barricaded for the weekend, diverting traffic around town, and Main Street was closed down too. The square was already bustling with people, most of them edging closer to the bandstand where Mayor Howard was supposed to kick off the celebration at any moment.

Reese wasn't close to the grandstand and wasn't going to be able to see the mayor well, but he considered it appropriate that he survey this spectacle from the steps of what used to be the Hotel Drew. What had once been the finest hotel and restaurant in most of Shelby County was now just a locked-up storefront, and had been since right before the end of the war. Reese didn't even know who owned the building anymore. He didn't miss going there, necessarily—but he did miss it being there.

This was where he had said goodbye to Glorrie, after all. Or more precisely, where they said goodbye to each other. Reese sat back on the steps, and leaned on his elbows. The affair had begun this way: with Glorrie calling Reese to her, and with Reese being willingly led. And it had ended just as quickly: with Tom returning from war, and fear coming home with him.

Reese and Glorrie's affair had been a small thing, Reese thought. He was ashamed for having had it, but at the same time, he cherished every moment. They hadn't found themselves in bed often—that wasn't the point. It was more that they were playing out what might have been, the way young girls play house and make up stories about the way things could be. Glorrie would invite Reese to go to the Lyric Theatre downtown to see the new films—or rather, Glorrie would invite both Reese and Clara, fully aware that Clara didn't care for going to movies. She said it was too cold, that she didn't like the idea of sitting in someone else's chair. But Clara would insist that Reese go to keep Glorrie company, and so he would. And on those nights, Reese and Glorrie pretended to be a couple. They would have their date, though neither called it that, and laugh and talk and sometimes touch like they were kids, always careful not to cause any suspicions, not to raise any eyebrows. There was talk for a time, of course, but it stopped, having little tangible evidence to feed it.

Glorrie and Reese had kissed for the first time just a week after Tom left for Europe, one night when Reese had come over to patch up the holes in her walls, places where Tom had punched or thrown things right through the plaster. Glorrie made him supper—a roast duck, with potatoes and corn—and they ate together, talked about old times, about their school days, about the people they had known and the gossip they'd heard about them since. After dinner, they retired to the living room, where they listened to war reports on the radio, sitting on the couch together. They started at opposite ends of the couch—but when Glorrie got up to get coffee, she sat down right next to him. When she came back with cream for Reese's cup, she crossed her legs so her ankle brushed his knee. When he looked into her eyes, he kissed her, or he let her kiss him. He couldn't recall which.

They made love twenty-three times in the three years Tom was away. Reese kept track, as though the number itself was important. Sometimes, still, he'd think of her skin, her supple, giving skin, always warm and ready to slide against him in ways he'd dreamt of since he was in high school. He would think of the way her lips tasted faintly of cherries, the way her hair smelled of a thick row of sunflowers, the way her whole body encompassed his when they were in bed together. He would think about the way she would make him coffee or lemonade after they were done, as though he were coming in from the fields after a hard day's work, and how she'd sit on her knees behind him on the bed and rub his shoulders. He could feel her full breasts against his back, brushing his skin, relaxing him and exciting him all over again, and they would do it once more, slower this time, savoring every movement like it might be their last. He had never made love twice in one night to Clara, he realized, never in all the time they'd been together. He put the thought from his mind. He tried hard not to think about Clara and about Glorrie at the same time.

It had helped assuage his guilt that Glorrie felt badly about it, too. "Clara doesn't deserve this," Glorrie had said one afternoon, on a day when they had just come close to making love. Reese had stopped because Clara was weighing heavily on his mind. Her birthday had come and gone just the week before, and she was sick with worry because she wasn't yet a mother. She'd cried all morning, gotten hysterical a few times, blamed Reese for it all, saying it was all his fault, that there must be something wrong with him. Then, not ten minutes later, Clara had turned her rage inward. She shouted, "What's wrong with me? What's the matter with me?" over and over. Reese tried to soothe her; they sat in the kitchen and he stroked her hair as she cried. Then Glorrie called to see if he'd have the time to mow her lawn, and Clara told him to go, her voice suddenly flat as the fields. She went up to the bedroom and locked the door. So Reese had gone.

"She doesn't deserve this at all," Glorrie repeated.

"No she doesn't," Reese said. "But I don't know what to do."

Glorrie snorted, and let out a harsh laugh. "Get her pregnant, Reese," she said. "That's what she wants. What she's waiting for." Glorrie picked at a loose piece of thread on the bed quilt absent-mindedly. "But you know that."

"Yeah," Reese said, also staring out into space. "But it's not like we haven't tried."

Glorrie looked annoyed at this. "Well," she said, getting up suddenly, and smoothing her skirt. "Maybe you need to go see a doctor, Reese. Or maybe Clara does, I don't know. I just wish you'd both stop talking about it. Shit or get off the pot, like Tom says."

Reese knew that tone, and also knew what it meant when Glorrie started cussing and quoting Tom. It meant she was in no mood for anything, even for being reminded he cared for her. It was these times when Reese felt most alone—when he couldn't talk to Glorrie and couldn't talk to Clara and had no one else. He rose from the bed and wordlessly went out to mow Glorrie's lawn, leaving her standing in her bedroom, her arms crossed over her chest, staring disconsolate into the mirror.

But everything had ended abruptly with Tom's return from the service in the summer of 1945. It seemed the whole world was celebrating after V.E. Day, and the parties went on for weeks as troops came home in waves. Tom finally made it home again on a rainy Saturday at the end of May. He'd stayed a week or so in New York to celebrate with his buddies, and then caught the bus that would bring him back to his home, his friends, and his work. Back to Moweaqua, back to his wife, and perhaps back to habits of which no one had yet dared speak. That day back in 1945 had been all blues and grays and chilled winds; it had been late spring, but it felt like fall, like October. Like today.

Reese and Glorrie waited together for Tom to return. Even though the Hotel Drew had just shut down, its front awning kept the stoop dry enough for them to sit there out of the rain. Most of the windows up and down the street still had slogans such as Welcome Home Heroes painted in them, and flags hung from each streetlamp like apples on trees. One of the apartments above a storefront had a window open, and Harry James' Skylark, one of Clara's favorite songs, wafted down like fine mist. It was supposed to be a good day, Reese thought, when a man comes home from war—but it was dark, even though it was barely afternoon, and the steady drizzle washed the street in a glimmering haze. The clouds looked like they had edges, sharp against the flat sky behind them.

Clara was already at home starting dinner for the four of them— a ham spiked with clove, whipped potatoes, and cornbread, Tom's favorite meal. Reese and Glorrie hadn't taken the time to change their church clothes after dropping Clara off at the house. Glorrie wore her brown flower-print dress and the matinee of pearls Tom had sent from overseas, and Reese pulled at the sleeves on his gray wool suit Clara had recently bought for him in Decatur. Reese didn't like the suit at all—it itched, but he had to admit it kept him warm. Reese took off his hat, and held it in his hands, staring into it as though he might pull something from it to get him through the day. He felt Glorrie pat him on the shoulder, but when he looked over at her, she was looking up the road.

Reese knew he was about to lose her. He wanted desperately to kiss her, one last embrace he could remember for the rest of his days. He didn't recall when their last kiss had happened, exactly, but he knew it hadn't been enough of a kiss to carry him.

As bad as Reese felt, he was also worried for Glorrie. He wanted to believe things might be okay, that Sheriff Dawes had been right and that Tom had stopped drinking while he was away fighting, that he had spent the rage he always seemed to carry like a rucksack spilling over with bean. Reese had tried to convince himself of this for weeks, ever since the telegram came informing Glorrie of the Tom's imminent arrival.

"Thank you for coming," Glorrie finally said, after they'd listened to the rain for a while. Glorrie's knees were pressed together tight, her elbows resting on them, her tight fists supporting her cheeks that were the color of ruddy morning.

"My pleasure," Reese said, forcing a smile.

"I almost believe you," she said.

"Glorrie—" Reese began.

"I don't expect you to talk about this, Reese," she said in what was nearly a whisper, "and I'd think you were a fool for doing it if you did. But I've enjoyed your company while Tom's been gone. I'm going to miss you. I will. But I'm glad my husband is coming home. I've missed him, too. Despite everything."

"I expect you did." Reese said. He regretted it as soon as the words left his mouth. His was a response that invited discussion. A shrug would have been better, or a noncommittal grunt. That's what Tom would have done. Reese didn't want to go into this any more than they had to.

"Does that surprise you?" Glorrie asked quietly.

Reese sighed, looked at her a moment, and decided to try the shrug. But the gesture came too late to be of any effect. "I don't know, honestly. But I don't think anyone could find fault with you for missing your husband."

Glorrie looked out into the street. "Did you miss him?"

"'Course."

"You want to hear something odd?"

"Sure."

"I've missed Clara, too." Glorrie said, and she started to cry. She took a handkerchief out of her purse, and wiped away some of the tears.

Reese sighed. Even his wife's name felt heavy, especially now that Tom was coming home. "I have too," he said, and he meant it.

"You know, she's a good girl," Glorrie said. "She's lucky to have you."

"I don't know about that," Reese said. He wasn't feeling like he made anyone lucky—quite the opposite. "There's a lot we don't—"

he didn't finish. "I don't know. But she's a good woman. Yes she is."

"I envy her, Reese," Glorrie said. "I envy what you could have with her, if you tried. If she tried."

Reese smiled, and shifted his weight. "I don't know that trying is enough. I tried for a long time before you and I—before Tom went away."

Glorrie put her hand on Reese's thigh and squeezed. "Keep trying. Please," she said. "For her, for you. I want you to be happy. I've seen you happy now, Reese, and it looks good on you. You deserve to be happy, and so does my sister. Don't just live life, Reese. Don't go back to just living, and that being enough. Seduce it. Romance it." Glorrie smiled again, this time a motherly thing, like the sort of thing a child gets when they've done something misguided. "And do the same to Clara. It works wonders."

Reese blushed. He didn't know what to say. This wasn't the woman he'd been sleeping with, the woman he'd chosen over his own wife. This wasn't the woman he thought he might love, love like Clara, perhaps more. This Glorrie was the old Glorrie—the sadder, wiser woman who seemed to know her fate and mourn it at the same time. Not knowing what else to say or do, Reese asked the question he'd wanted to ask for years now. "Do you love him?"

Neither of them had ever said love, not while kissing, not while in bed. Never. It seemed like saying the word was the one step that would go too far, as though his promise to Clara was still unbroken, without those three words. I love you. And they'd never talked about love in terms of Clara or Tom, either.

"He's mine," Glorrie said, "so I guess I have to love him." She paused, and shook her head. "No, that's not fair. I do love him, in a way. I love him for what he could do, for what he could be, if he wanted. I love him for the promise I made to him years ago. But I can never say it without some sort of qualifier, you know? It's been a long time since I could. I love him despite everything. I love him anyway. I'm not sure a person should do that, really, to love someone anyway. Anyway should never come into it, I think. But it's all I have, all I've ever had."

"I'm sorry." Reese didn't know what else to say.

Glorrie laughed, and cupped Reese's cheek in her hand as though he were a child. "Oh, that's perfect," she said, "that's perfect, Reese. Of course you are. Tom gets drunk and beats me up and you're sorry, like you're trying to apologize for him, to make up for what he does. My God, I do envy Clara, Reese. And I hope you love her like I know you can."

Reese had nothing left to say. They sat on the steps of the Hotel Drew in the foggy rain, both waiting anxiously for Tom to return.

And so it had ended, and with the loss of his first love, Reese had been able to try and rebuild his relationship with his second. He tried to take Glorrie's words to heart, and be as good a husband to Clara as he had been a boyfriend. He wooed Clara all over again, starting by taking her to the movie house with a new coat and a folding chair, so she wouldn't have to sit in someone else's. Clara giggled at that, a sound he hadn't heard from her in years. He took her on drives in the country in his new truck, and parked the car near the creek, kissed her as though they were teenagers again, and she laughed and said she was too old for such a thing, even though she loved him thinking she wasn't. And he made love to her twice in one night, until she was too out of breath to giggle, laugh, or say a damn thing. He noticed she smiled more, and that filled him with the same sort of sudden and unexpected glee he'd gotten used to being with Glorrie. Reese let himself fall in love with his wife, all over again.

Of course, it hadn't been easy. Even with Reese's courting, it took months of asking for Clara's forgiveness for his inattention before she finally seemed to grant it. Reese knew he was apologizing for far more than that, and it occurred to him Clara might have a sense of it, as well. But Clara responded, and their marriage slowly improved. Reese had to remind himself that even if it did end up bringing him closer to his wife, he couldn't think of his relationship with Glorrie as a good thing—that way lay nothing good. Even then, in the middle of the revivication of his marriage and his love for Clara, Reese had a dream that Glorrie had come to him and asked him to run away with her, and he agreed. Sorry as he was to tell Clara goodbye, he went because Glorrie had asked. He put the dream out of his mind, just like he did with his memory of his affair with Glorrie. Or, at least, he tried.

But on days like this, here on the steps of the old Drew, he couldn't help but think about what had gone before. He wished again that Clara was sitting on the step below him so he could wrap his arms around her, put his cheek in her hair, and she'd hold onto his forearms and tuck them under her chin like a blanket on a cold night. But she was at the house with Glorrie. Again.

Reese scratched at his beard. He hated it, but growing it was what he was supposed to do. All of the men in Moweaqua had been encouraged to grow out their beards in honor of the Centennial, as had been the style in 1852, and the women were supposed to dress accordingly. And everyone in town seemed to embrace it—for a while. Men greeted each other with "How's the beard?" and a stroke of their chins. There were holdouts—Don Saddoris, for one, thought the whole thing silly and refused to participate. Reese admired his conviction, picked at the wispy hairs he'd managed to sprout in the past weeks, and wished he'd done the same.

Mayor Howard took the podium, welcomed everyone to the Centennial, and a cheer went up that shook the windows of the Oddfellows Lodge and Ayars State Bank. He said a few words, then announced the coming attractions: a free bean meal courtesy of local businesses; the next day, a bicycle parade, a doll show, and contests like pie-eating, sack races, a candy-kiss scramble, a marble shoot, and a greased pig grand finale. Saturday was the Big Parade, complete with a pageant at the new school site, and square dancing to follow, and televisions set up all night long so that everyone could watch.

Reese didn't cheer with the rest; his mind was elsewhere. It wasn't that he didn't care about the new school. It was being built a stone's throw from his driveway, right across the street, and he'd lent a hand building the bleachers for the pageant. He and Tom had worked together on them for three days, with a team of other local men: Don Saddoris, Gale Stewart, and Doc Pistorius, to name a few, and they'd done a good job. What they built was sturdy enough, the superintendent said, to keep after the Centennial had ended, to paint and then use for school events for a long time to come. The men were proud. They went out for pie once the last nail had been hammered, and they toasted with coffee to their expertise. Then Tom went out, got drunk, headed home, and threw Glorrie through the glass of their screen door when she asked him where he'd been and what he'd been drinking. Clara was with her back at the house, pulling slivers of glass from her hands, arms, face. They'd sent Reese into town so as to keep up appearances.

Watching the sisters together was what made Reese think Clara knew more about him and Glorrie than she let on. Though he thought she'd forgiven him, if she knew, Clara wasn't as quick to do so with Glorrie. Clara was quiet around her now; it was subtle, but there. They didn't laugh as they had. It was all business now—Glorrie would come over to be cleaned up, and Clara would oblige. They hardly spoke; Glorrie sat, nearly asleep, and Clara would daub at her sister's forehead with a wet cloth. Reese had been only too glad to be sent off. He didn't know how to fix whatever it was between Clara and Glorrie; it had been going on for years, and his strategy of waiting it out hadn't worked. To her credit, Clara still cared for her sister enough to help her, but that was all; the freeze, as it was, never fell to thaw.

So Reese attended the Centennial by himself, though no one seemed to care much. He saw a few friends there with their wives and families, and he waved as though nothing were wrong. They waved back, and that was about it. But they weren't whom the show was for. He was there to make sure Tom came.

Reese wasn't sure Tom had ever stopped drinking, or beating on Glorrie, as Glorrie had claimed he had when he came back from the war. Or maybe it was just hope kindled in a brief respite, a honeymoon of sorts that lasted too short a time. There was no doubt that Tom was drinking again, and that he'd gotten worse over the last couple of years. Doc Pistorius was starting to ask questions not just of Glorrie, but of Tom, which only made things worse. Glorrie stopped going to Doc for a while, and began walking up to the farm again to get cleaned up after what she came to call a "bad day." But Tom guessed where she was going, and always came to find her. Each time, Glorrie would hide herself in one of the upstairs bedrooms, and Reese and Clara would be able to convince Tom she wasn't there, that he'd best go home and sleep it off. And so he had. Glorrie was worried about what he'd do if he were to find her there, what he'd do to all of them. Hearing her worry for him made Reese feel like a child.

He hadn't seen Tom yet. Tom wasn't one for celebrations that didn't include liquor, and since this was still officially a dry town, there wasn't much draw for him. Reese figured he was home sleeping off the rage and the drunk, trying to get sober enough to get into the pool room that night. Tom could usually be found there on the nights when he didn't have to work the next day, and he'd gotten time off from the plant for the Centennial even though he knew damn well that he didn't intend on being a part of it until Saturday.

Saturday was the Big Parade, and Tom was one of the men picked to ride on the "Johnny Came Marching Home" World War II float and throw candy to the kids. Tom told Reese he liked being able to play the big-shot war hero again. "Sometimes I miss the war, Reese," Tom said, and took a drink from his boot flask. They were out in the barn, smoking after Sunday dinner. "Is that crazy? Guys dying all around me, and I miss it. That make me crazy?" He laughed.

*I think it does*, Reese had thought, but he didn't say it. That was all going to change today. Reese had had enough—enough of the way Tom treated Glorrie, enough of the way he treated everyone. There wasn't going to be anymore of this kowtowing, Reese thought, rubbing his knee. Tom was going to listen to him. He was going to get an earful. Things, Reese had decided, were going to change.

Over the next few hours, the crowd milled about, waiting for supper and taking in the free entertainment provided by the local lodges. The Shriners had their clowns, and the Oddfellows had set up a dunk tank—sink a man, get a prize. There was a magic show over in front of the Ayars' Bank, and Reese recognized Charlie Walters there under that top hat, doing card tricks with the same deck that all the lodge brothers played poker with every Wednesday night. Reese sat back and kept his pipe lit, waiting for Tom, wishing it could be any other way.

By four-thirty that afternoon, the clouds had broken up and the chance of rain that had looked a certainty earlier in the day had gone with them. The free bean meal was served, and people lined the streets holding paper cones filled with baked beans and ham, topped off with thick squares of honey cornbread. There were potato chips from Crane's up in Decatur, and Borden's had donated five-gallon buckets of ice cream for dessert to go along with what the Ladies' Society had baked.

Reese had no intention of going down to the tables—his stomach was in knots and the last thing he needed, he thought, was beans. Still, he liked honey cornbread quite a lot, and the beans wouldn't be too bad if he only ate a bit, and maybe some of that ice cream might actually soothe his stomach, once he thought about it, and then he wondered if Bernice Stombaugh had made any of those peanut-butter buckeyes he liked. He rose from the stairs and went down to get in line and wait. If nothing else, the food was something to take his mind off of Tom.

The beans were good, all thick and full of molasses, and the bread was just as fine as he'd imagined. Bernice hadn't made any of her buckeyes, but she'd brought some frosted brownies, so he balanced one atop his cone of beans, and made his way back to the steps. He ate, hoping that Tom would hurry up and get there already. What Reese had to say to Tom was a thing better said in a relatively public place. "Relatively" because it wasn't something Reese wanted anyone else to hear; public so that Tom couldn't lose his temper as easily or as completely. There was an upstairs at the pool hall. Reese thought it would be a good place to talk. A safe place, in every sense. Reese was counting on this.

The sky darkened, and the pool room started to do business. Reese steeled himself, rose, and went in. Frank Zimmer owned the place these days—Dave Craven had long since died, and it had changed owners three or four times since then, so many that when it came into new hands, no one bothered calling it so-and-so's pool room anymore. Frank greeted Reese with a quick nod and what passed for a smile—Frank wasn't much for conversation. He generally sat behind the counter and watched the TV he'd bought to attract new customers a year before. Folks in town had just started to buy television sets—Reese was thinking about splurging for one for Clara this Christmas if he could save enough—and the pool room TV did bring people in, especially when there was a ball game on. Folks joked that Frank bought the pool room just so he'd have a place to sit and watch television without his wife getting after him.

Reese was one of the first ones there that night—he didn't know whether it should be crowded or not, what with the Centennial, but he figured that there'd be at least a few men who wanted to get away from their families, or single guys looking for company. Reese went up to the big table, the one that was original to the building when it was built back in the 1800s. The table was broad and short, with dark green felt and leather-padded pockets, and it was heavy. Those players who tried to nudge it a little only ended up bruising their hips. Reese racked up and started playing, taking his time. He'd gone through three games and two Coca-Colas by the time Tom walked in the front door.

Tom looked bigger than he used to, but maybe that was Reese's trepidation talking. Tom was with a couple of guys who Reese had met before, guys Tom worked with up in Decatur. They were drinking bottled beers, and one of them carried a bucketfull behind him, making some small gesture to hide the fact that he had it. It was illegal to have beer in a public place, but it was clear from the nature of their entrance that they'd done it before, facing no resistance. Frank didn't give them a first look, let alone a second.

"Reese!" Tom exclaimed. "What the hell are you doing here?" He put a hand on Reese's shoulder. "Reese here saved us our table, guys. Someone give him a beer." He turned back to Reese. "Nice beard, by the way," he laughed. "You been growing that what, a day or so?"

"Two weeks, thanks," Reese smiled. "Yours came in well. You could scrub pots with that thing."

"Itches like crazy," Tom said, scratching at it. "I'll be glad to shave it off when this nonsense is over."

"Me too," Reese said.

"Well, won't be long now," Tom said, picking a cue from the wall. "Glad you're here, Reese. We could use a fourth."

"I'm not really here to play," Reese said, taking a deep breath. "I need to talk to you about something. It's important."

"C'mon. It'll be fun," Tom said. "You know these guys, right? Bob and Vic—they work the line up at Cat now, but they used to be at Staley's with me."

"I think I met them at that picnic a few years back," Reese said, nodding to them. The one Reese thought was Vic handed him a freshly opened beer. "But I really just need to talk to you, Tom. That's why I'm here."

"One game, what do you say?" Tom said. "Drink your beer, relax. We got time. I ain't going nowhere."

Tom started talking to Bob about some people that Reese didn't know, while racking up the next set. Reese set his beer down. "No," he said. "We need to talk right now."

Tom looked up at Reese, his face somewhere halfway between annoyed and surprised. He shrugged. "All right. Okay."

"No bottles on the tables," Frank said from the front.

Reese picked up his beer and put it down on a small table over by the row of chairs against one wall.

"So talk," Tom said.

"It's private. Upstairs?" Reese said, and then looked at Bob and Vic. "No offense meant." Vic waved it off, and Bob just nodded.

Tom sighed and scratched the underside of his chin. He leaned his cue against the table. "Okay, then. You lead."

Reese nodded, and the two started up the wooden staircase. Tom yelled down "You guys keep that beer cold and don't start without us."

The second floor was where Dave Craven used to have duck pin lanes, but that had died off quickly when the Moweaqua Bowl opened right up the street. Now, it was just a dark and dusty place used as a storeroom for all the stuff a place accumulates over years of operation. There was junk lying around everywhere—a broken pachinko game over against one wall; the old stools that used to sit in front of the soda fountain downstairs; the fountain itself one of the owners had installed to get a younger crowd in the place, and which the next owner had taken out to get them to leave. The only reason anyone came up here anymore was to use the toilets up at the top of the stairs.

Tom surveyed the room. "What a pile of crap," he said. "Can you believe someone actually decided to keep all this?" He shook his head, pulled out a cigarette, and lit it from a book of matches. "What's on your mind, Reese?"

Reese considered Tom's query—there were many answers to his question. Finally, though, he settled on one. "Glorrie," he said.

Tom stopped, and slowly turned his head to look Reese square in the eyes. He took a long drag on the cigarette as he flipped the match away into the darkness. "What about her?" His voice went suddenly cold.

"I don't know how to say this, so I'm just going to say it out flat. You need to stop hitting her, Tom. It's gone too far."

Tom cocked his head, and blew out smoke. "You think so, do you?" Reese nodded, but Tom kept going. "You think I need to stop hitting her. Well that's just great. Just great, Reese, really. Thank you very much, you stupid son of a bitch, for coming in and speaking your mind. Now get out." He took another puff on his cigarette, turned, and started pacing a little. He looked jumpy. "Get the hell out."

Reese paused. He hadn't expected this. He didn't know what he'd expected, really. A denial, maybe? He wasn't sure. Reese stood there in the darkness, not speaking, but not moving.

"I mean it," Tom said, his lit cigarette hanging from one corner of his mouth, the cherry at the end glowing like a railroad lantern. Tom hands were up, palms facing out as though he were surrendering. His fingers were tight and slightly curled, like claws, and he pointed to the door. "Get out of here before we're both sorry."

"Not this time, Tom," Reese said. "I can't. I promised Glorrie—"

Tom came around quickly, with an open hand swinging. Reese saw it coming and realized he couldn't get out of its way, even if his knee didn't make him slower than most men. Tom hit him squarely in the side of the head, driving his ear up against his skull and pushing Reese back onto a pile of folding chairs. The legs of the top chair bit into his back, but only for a moment; Tom picked him up by the front of his shirt and threw him again, this time toward the windows on the far wall. Reese flew across the room, and his face glanced off the padded seat of a stool. He fell amongst the chrome stool legs like a shot doe. "I told you to go," Tom said, his voice of a tenor Reese hadn't heard since Tom had knocked out three of Woes' teeth. It occurred to Reese this was the voice Glorrie had heard many times more. "I told you to get the hell out," he said, his voice rising in pitch, almost pleading. "I told you to go."

Reese checked his teeth with his tongue—none seemed loose. He put a hand to his downy jaw and felt blood, warm and wet, trickling down from his ear. He could taste it in his mouth, too:

salty liquid copper. The inside of his cheek felt ragged, furrowed like a plowed row of soil. It flashed over him that perhaps Tom had found out about him and Glorrie, but he quickly discounted the idea. If Tom knew anything about them, Reese wouldn't have had to find Tom. Tom would have found Reese.

Reese scooted backwards, rising up on his elbows, pushing his body back with his heels towards the wall. Tom was silhouetted in the light from downstairs, his face only dimly lit from the refracted light coming off the street below. Tom didn't seem to be coming towards him, or moving at all, except for his labored breathing, his shoulders heaving up and down.

"What the hell," Reese said. "What the hell, Tom?" His voice was soft and wounded and wet from blood. Reese felt like crying, but anger held it back.

Tom's breath still came heavy. "You hurt?" he said in a low voice.

"Yeah," Reese said, "yeah, I am."

Tom came forward, then, but not aggressively, and Reese sat stock-still and let him. "Jesus Christ, Reese, I didn't mean to. I swear to you I didn't."

"What do you mean you didn't mean to?"

"Your ear's bleeding," Tom said. "I think it's split at the top." He reached over to brush away some of the blood.

"Get your hands off me."

"Reese," Tom said, shaking his head, "I didn't mean to hurt you. I'm sorry. I just—I just—I didn't mean it." He tried a wry smile. "Hell, if I had wanted to hurt you, Reese, I would've taken you out at the knee first, right?"

"You think it's funny?" Reese said, glaring.

"Hey, what the hell are you doing up there?" Frank called from downstairs.

"Fighting," called back Tom, and then smiled down at Reese like it was a shared joke. "We'll be down in a minute, Frank. Go watch your TV."

Reese's ear started to throb, and his lip was ballooning. "What in God's name is wrong with you, Tom?" Reese asked.

Tom's smile disappeared, and he sighed and shrugged. It took a minute for him to say anything. "I don't know," Tom said, and it sounded like a real answer. "I don't know about anything any more, you know?"

"No," Reese said.

Tom sat down next to Reese and looked up at the lights from the window dancing on the ceiling. "When I was in the war, I knew what I was supposed to do. Every time I woke up, I knew my objective. My job was to go out there, risk getting my head blown off, and do my best to take out the bad guys. I've been home for six years now, Reese, and every morning when I get up, I don't know what my objective is."

"You go to work, you do your job," Reese said. "You protect your family."

"I know all that," Tom said, "but it's not enough. It doesn't feel right. You know what I mean?"

"No."

"I didn't have any questions back then. There were these people who I was supposed to kill before they could do the same to me, so I did it. I was supposed to. They gave me medals for it, told me I was a hero."

"It was war, Tom," Reese said, "I'm not saying you did something wrong. But saying you feel lost because you can't kill anything anymore is just crazy."

"That's not what I'm saying."

"What, then? And what the hell does it have to do with hitting your wife? Or me?"

Reese could feel Tom tense up next to him. Tom leaned forward, stretched to pick up the cigarette he'd dropped, and then re-lit it. "You want one?" he said, taking out the pack.

"No."

Tom sighed. "It don't happen that often, Reese. It really don't. Not that it's your business."

"She's Clara's sister, and I've known her longer than you have. Besides, I know how often it happens, Tom. I know how long it's been going on."

Tom looked at Reese long and hard. Reese was thankful they were sitting side by side, because Reese wasn't sure that given the opportunity Tom wouldn't have hit him again. Instead, Tom just stared at Reese, then turned away and pulled hard on his cigarette. "Still none of your business. You don't know me anymore. You don't know Glorrie either. You don't know the kind of shit she's capable of." Tom's dry-throated laugh came up with clouds of smoke. He pulled back his hair and pointed to a jagged scar over his left eye. "You know where this came from? Glorrie and a piece of firewood. I have another one on my shin where she stabbed me with a crochet hook, if you want to see it." He took one last drag on his cigarette and then scuffed it out on the floorboards between his feet. "I'm sorry I did you that way, Reese. Sometimes, I end up doing stuff I don't mean, but I never wanted you to be on the receiving end of it. I hope we can forget the whole thing. How about it?" Tom held out his hand.

Reese accepted it, not knowing what else to do, and the two shook hands. "There you go," Tom said, grinning. "You have Clara look at that ear." He hopped up to his feet, and grabbed Reese by the shoulder to help him up, too. "Unless you want to come down and play pool for a while?"

Reese shook his head. "No."

"Suit yourself," Tom said. "Am I going to see you Saturday?"

"Saturday?"

"The parade," Tom said. "I'm in it, remember? I thought the four of us could meet up once it's done, maybe have some supper together after whatever bullshit they have going on down at the new school."

"Sure," Reese said. "I guess."

Tom put his arm on Reese's shoulder and led him slowly to the stairs, where they stopped at the top. "You know they're gonna give us candy to throw off the float? Little wrapped pieces of butterscotch and taffy and gum. Don't that beat all? Throwing candy out to kids—it's a strange world, Reese, swear to God. When you and I were kids, we were lucky just to eat, and sometimes we had to steal to do it. There wasn't nobody throwing us sweets." Tom snorted. "Hell, sometimes my father depended on me to get him food, you know? Many was the day when I'd go picking out in the orchards, fill up my shirttail until old man Beemer would run me off his land. Then I'd go home and we'd eat those things until we were sick, my father and I. And he'd promise to get us some real food soon. And sometimes he would. And now, I'm sitting in a jeep, a hero throwing candy." He laughed.

"Yeah."

Tom stopped to light up another cigarette. "You sure you don't want to play a few games? We could still use a fourth, and that ear don't look too bad."

Reese shook his head, and watched as Tom disappeared down the stairs, heard him boom *All right, who wants to play some pool?* and clap his hands together, talking to Bob and Vic like he didn't have his best friend's blood on his knuckles. Reese put a hand up to his ear, and felt the grit of the drying wound. He turned and went into the men's restroom, but it was filthy. He used the sink in the women's, where there was at least a cake of soap. He washed himself up, and stared at himself in the mirror for a long while.

Reese moved through the crowd at the Centennial as though he were a stranger. He kept his head down and his hat on, to hide his ear. He walked through the throngs of people, his face burning him, and kept walking until the laughter and celebration was just a rumbling buzz behind him. When he got home, the first thing he did was shave.

Reese didn't tell anyone about that night, about what he'd attempted, or about the result. Glorrie had asked him to do it. Clara had chided him for avoiding it. But he told neither of them that he'd tried. Better to be thought of as unwilling than unable. Clara noticed his ear when he came out of the bathroom, slick-faced again.

He lied and told them someone in the crowd had thrown a Coke bottle and split his ear, and Glorrie and Clara cooed over him. Their nursing only made him feel worse for failing. That night was the first time in their thirty-year friendship when Reese had ever stood up to Tom. And it wouldn't be the last.

# Chapter Ten

EVERYTHING IS SHARPER the mornings of funerals. You realize that all those things you take for granted are things someone whom you cared about won't enjoy again. The way sun attacks your eyes when you first step outside. The crunch of late autumn leaves. The smell of morning frost on soil. The pop of gravel, a truck's door shutting. The taste of the coffee and fresh bread, the feeling of padded folding chairs, of cloth coats, of hands offered in apology, of comfort, of duty.

I was in front, right behind the hearse, down to Mud Run that morning. It was a strange day—the sky was clouded over, and a heavy mist had fallen on the surrounding countryside, wrapping around trees and crops and homes like hands grasping for something to hold onto, but finding no purchase. Mom and I were alone in the truck, and she wasn't any real company. She hadn't said a single word all morning—nothing at all. I couldn't tell if she was someplace far away, untethered, or just in mourning.

Earl had offered to ride with us after I told him about how Mom was doing, but I let him off the hook and told him to make his own way down there, that I might want to stick around for a while, have a look. I wasn't sure I was going to be all that much company either, and the trip south to the cemetery was long. Took a little over an hour to get down there, past old fields gone to seed, past dilapidated old homesteads, their roofs caved in, over old bridges and older trestles. Our part of Illinois seemed abandoned that day, as though it were a place that had once supported life, but now supported little more than the dead. And those coming to see them off.

The fog got thicker as we went south, and the procession got slower. But the slow and the quiet seemed to match the day, afforded me the opportunity to muse over Mom, Glorrie, Amy, everything. I thought about making this drive again with Amy, just to take it in more fully, to see it all with her next to me. I didn't know if she'd been down here before, and I found myself wanting to show her.

We finally pulled up along the chain-link fence along the lower edge of the cemetery. Someone had tried to plant a row of flowers along the front, but they'd withered in the autumn air, and no one had yet cleaned out the rows, now full of drooping yellow and faded pink. In the center of the fence was a wrought-iron arch, at the top of which was spelled out in thick, black capital letters: MUD RUN.

I got out of the truck and checked the hill. It didn't look muddy. Maybe a little damp, but nothing to wear boots for. The cemetery was just how I had pictured it, the headstone jutting crookedly from the ground like teeth, the grass green and wet and thick, the trees draping over the whole area old, wizened, and broad. Near the top of the hill, where the cemetery leveled out and then stopped at a grove of trees in the distance, I could see the tent set up over about twenty chairs and a yawning hole in front of an existing stone. My Uncle Tom was buried there. I didn't remember the man, except through Glorrie's stories, but it was nonetheless unsettling to see his grave. And one more thing was strange—the schoolhouse was missing. I had been looking forward to finally seeing the old place Glorrie had mentioned so many times in her stories, but from my quick scan of the area, I didn't see anything like it.

I shivered. The day was biting cold, and I pulled my overcoat tightly around me—or rather, my father's overcoat. I'd found it in the downstairs closet the night before, and thought it'd be warmer than my jacket. Nicer, too, made from a thick salt-and-pepper wool with a silk lining. I'd found a matching hat on the shelf above it, too. I was surprised when I tried them on and they fit me well, especially when Mom mentioned that Earl had worn it once in a while, but he'd gotten too big. She told me I should take it, that I should wear it. Said I looked dapper.

Earl, Gum, and Ben walked up to me, and Gum asked if we were ready to carry the casket up to graveside. I nodded. With a nod from Gum, Ben led Mom off by her arm, a hand lightly guiding her shoulder. He didn't say anything to her, and she didn't seem to notice someone else had taken my place.

Earl and I took the front of the casket. Gum and Gale Stewart had the middle, and Don Saddoris and Hal Bilyeu took up the rear. At first, it struck me as sad that Glorrie didn't have enough close relatives to fill out the pallbearers, but I knew how close her coffee shop group was, and that she'd have been thrilled to know it was they who wanted to carry her those last few yards. On Gum's word, the six of us pulled the casket off the rollers in the hearse and bore her through the gate and up the hill.

"Sure is cold today," Hal said behind me.

"Least it's not raining," Don said.

"Remember Tom's funeral?" Gale said.

"That was a day," Gum agreed.

Earl looked behind him to the four men and nodded. "That it was."

We hoisted it into the frame that had been scaffolded over the grave, and the casket clicked into the cold metal. We were offered the front row of seats, but I declined and went to stand next to where Mom was sitting. As I took my place beside her, she reached up and took my hand. Her skin felt fragile and cold, like the glass of a barn window in winter. People filed in and found their places around the grave. It was a sea of black, with spots of white handkerchiefs and gloves, and the breath clouding out from each attendee's face added to the mist in the air. Doc Pistorius and his wife were there, as were Donnie and Meg. I saw Freda, too, with a couple of the women from Bingo, and she was crying, a tissue held under her nose, both hands clasped like she was praying. A few other women were crying, too, but all the men stood there like stones. They were farmers, most of them, and even though the harvest was done, there was still plenty to do before winter set in. It was a good turnout, especially for Mud Run. Glorrie would have been pleased.

Reverend Simmons from the Methodist church stepped up and spoke for a short time—the usual stuff. Told a story about Glorrie volunteering at a women's shelter in Decatur, her faithful attendance at church. It didn't last long. Brian Traughber, from the church choir, sang the *Lord's Prayer* to finish things off. I had never heard it sung before—to me, it had been a string of words I memorized in Sunday School so I could earn a prayer button—but the way Brian performed it was haunting, and something close to beautiful. Gum took single white roses from the bouquets set out around the casket and handed them out to everyone, including me. I took it, gratefully, but I wondered what I was supposed to do with it. I shook Gum's hand, then the preacher's, then Don's and Hal's. I looked around for Earl, but he was already deep in conversation with a guy who I recognized but couldn't place.

Mom and I stared at the gravesite for a bit, and then Mom said, "I'm going down to the car." She abruptly turned and started walking.

"You want to stick around and see Tom's headstone with me?" It was covered with a tarp—keeps the dirt off, I guess, while they dig. I wanted to see it before I left. I didn't know if I'd ever be here again.

"No," she said. She didn't even turn around.

I watched her make her way down to the car. She walked slowly, choosing her steps down the steep ground, kept her eyes on her shoes. Her bent arms flew out from her sides here and there, as her heel bit too far into the soft earth, or she almost lost her balance. It was then when she looked like a girl, someone nearly as close to her birth as she was to her death.

I turned back to the gravesite. The casket was still above ground, and Gum was talking to a couple of men in overalls, the ones who were there to lower Glorrie into the ground and cover her up with a couple of yards of dirt. I pulled the tarp covering Tom's headstone down. It was a simple thing, weathered and beaten. Wasn't much to it—just his name, and the dates of his birth and his death. Glorrie's side had nothing but her name.

Earl cleared his throat as he approached. He wore a brown suit under his trenchcoat, and one of those hats with the fuzzy earflaps. He stopped next to me, and faced the same direction, shoulder to shoulder. "Well, it's over," he said.

"I guess so."

"I see you got your flower."

"Yeah, I guess I did. Are we supposed to do something with them?" I smiled, glad to have something to talk about.

Earl smiled back. "Press it in a Bible," he said. "That's what Glorrie and your Mom would do, anyhow. Me, I just wear it until it isn't a flower anymore." He opened his coat and pointed to his lapel where he had stuck his white rose in the buttonhole.

I nodded, stared up at the sky. It was slate gray. "I appreciate everything you've done."

Earl looked at me askance, trying to get a read, see if I was serious. He shrugged. "Haven't done much."

I shook my head, kept looking up. It was easier to do this in profile. "No, you've done a lot. More than I ever gave you credit for. More than I did."

"Don't worry about it."

"You didn't have to do it, any of it. I realize that."

Earl took a deep breath and turned toward me, but looked past at the grove of trees. "I never really had my own family, Reese. When I came to live with your folks, it was like I had started all over again. I always envied you for what you had. Your mom, your dad, the farm, the house. And I never could understand why you didn't appreciate any of it. Why you didn't care."

"I did," I said.

Earl shook his head. A blackbird passed overhead. "Maybe you did, I don't know. But I never saw it."

"I'm not sure I knew I appreciated it back then. But I did."

Earl laughed quietly. "You know what's funny? A week ago, I wouldn't have believed you."

We stood there a moment, Earl and I, now facing different directions—me, down the hill and into the cemetery, Earl, up slightly and to the trees beyond. A breeze picked up and I rubbed my hands together. "Wasn't there supposed to be a schoolhouse around here somewhere?" I asked.

Earl turned and paused, looking as though he'd been reminded that we were in conversation. "Yeah," he said, pointing over his shoulder with this thumb. "Down there, not too far from the fence to your left."

I looked, but nothing was there. "I don't see anything."

"It's there," he said, "what's left of it, anyhow."

"They tore it down?"

"Fell down. Too bad, too. There was a lot of history in that old place."

"Sounds like you knew it pretty well."

"Sure. I've been to this old place way too many times. I'm tired of coming, to be honest with you. I imagine this might be my last, though."

"Really? How come?"

Earl looked at me and half-grinned. "Everyone who's bought a plot here," he said, and spat as he paused, "is using it now."

"I guess that's true, huh?"

"Yeah," he said. "I might come around again someday, maybe on Memorial Day. But honestly, it was Glorrie who used to insist on it, so I doubt I'll actually get to it. I'd want to, I guess, and I'd feel sort of bad about missing it, but you know how it is."

"Glorrie used to drag you out here, did she?"

"Me and your mom. But we'd never get around to seeing Tom's marker up there on the hill. Not once that I can recall. Glorrie never even mentioned his name when we were here."

"Never?"

"Not to my recollection." Earl sniffed. "She told some good stories, but not all her memories of him were good ones."

"How do you mean?"

"Nothing worth talking about," he said. "They had their problems, like any couple. And Tom had his, like any man."

"Like what?"

"Nothing worth talking about," Earl said again. "Anyway, Glorrie and Clara were usually too busy remembering the good stuff, telling their stories, complaining about what a shame it was that my mom isn't here with everyone."

"She's not?"

He shook his head. "Buried down in Missouri."

"Ever been there?"

"Don't even know where it is. And now that Glorrie's dead, and your mom—well, I don't know that I could find it now if I wanted to." He took a deep breath. "Anyway, we never got around to old Tom. Not once."

"Maybe Mom will want one of us to bring her back next May?"

Earl looked at me, then. I couldn't tell if it was because I had mentioned that Mom would ask him or me, or that he didn't think she'd even be around by May, or what. Whatever it was, he shook it off. "Maybe, to see Glorrie. But I sort of doubt it. It was more Glorrie's thing. She might still want to go see your dad at the Oddfellows' Cemetery, but that'll probably be it."

"Yeah, I've been wondering about that. Why isn't Dad buried here?"

"Don't know," Earl admitted. "I remember Glorrie thought he should be, but your Mom wanted him in town. Maybe she just wanted him nearby. She bought a double for them."

I nodded. "Mom never liked going. It always felt like she was going for my sake, and when I was there, I never knew exactly what I was supposed to do."

Earl laughed. "Glorrie used to talk to them. I remember her and your folks bringing you out here like they were showing you off at a family reunion or something. Glorrie would take you to a stone, tell you to wave to grandma, stuff like that."

"So I have been here before. I don't remember it."

"You were a kid." Earl looked behind him, back to the grave.

"We should head back. These guys can't start burying her until we're out of sight."

"Okay," I said. "Before we do, though, can you at least show me where the old school was? I'm curious."

"What about Clara?"

I looked down to the truck. Mom was asleep in the passenger seat, her head leaning up against the foggy window. "She's okay for a bit," I said. "But we should probably hurry."

Earl nodded and walked haltingly down the hill, trying to maintain his footing as he let gravity pull each foot down hard in front of the other. "It should be right down this way."

We went down the hill slowly, and Earl took the time to show me where our relative's graves were as we passed them. We weren't taking the direct route to where the school had been, but I didn't mind it. It was interesting to hear all the stories. I never knew I had a great-uncle named Orlando, or that an old and distant cousin was a cattle rustler, and had been hanged for it.

"Over there is where your great Aunt Molly is buried," Earl said. "She was pretty old when she went—hundred and six. You were just a baby then. Aunt Molly had brothers fighting on both sides of the Civil War, lived through it all. And over there are your Mom's folks. They were good people. Grandpa Paul died of heart disease, I think. I don't recall what took Grandma Mattie." The litany of names continued, for a good fifteen minutes, short biographies and highlights of their lives. I was amazed not only by what Earl knew, but by what I didn't. What I had never bothered to find out.

"Over here is where the school used to be," Earl said, leading me over to a bunch of grasses on an overgrown mound. Now that I was closer, I could see remnants of an old wooden building, tangled in with the grasses. "Door was on this side," he said, pointing to the uphill-side of the mound, "and there were wooden stairs leading up to the floor. All this dirt was a sort of storage place, I think, sort of like a half-basement. Plus, they had to make the floor straight, since this was built on a slope."

"It was all wood?"

"Except the foundation. That's why it all fell in. I think they carried most of the wood away for scrap, or else people wanting a souvenir carried it off, piece by piece."

"That's too bad."

Earl shrugged. "No harm in it. It would just sit here and rot, anyway. There's this one woman from town who took a bunch of it and used the wood for frames around her paintings. Some were of this very schoolhouse before it fell. I saw a few up for sale at the Raspberry Tea Room in Elwin a year or so back."

"You go to the Raspberry Tea Room?"

"Glorrie liked to. Your mom, too," Earl said. "They have good pie."

"Well, the frame thing sounds like a good idea, actually," I said, "but I still don't like the idea of people carrying off things from sites like this. It keeps other people from seeing it, too."

"Not much to see, now," Earl said, kicking at some dirt. "But when it was still standing, it was like something out of a book. Made the hair on the back of your neck stand up just to look at it. Going up in was even better."

"You were still able to go in?"

"Yeah, a few times. The one I remember the best was when I was probably nine. Mom and I were out to visit, and we all came down: your mom and dad, Glorrie, Mom, me. You were still bug hunting—wouldn't be around for a year or so, yet."

"What did you come out here for?"

"Memorial Day, maybe? I don't remember, but I think it was spring. Your dad lifted me up into the school, over the boards of the steps. They were already rotting away, even back then. There was a weak spot in the floor, too, near the back, so I couldn't go too far, but we looked around a little. It was sort of spooky being in there, let me tell you. Your mom was standing at the door, right here," Earl stood where the steps had been, and gestured up above him, "telling me how Grandma Mattie had gone to school here when she was my age. How she used to walk a few miles to school, across a hollow where they'd cross by swinging on vines."

"I remember the story," I said. "Didn't Mattie have a younger brother who couldn't walk or something, and she had to carry him all the way on his back?"

"Yeah," Earl nodded. "Roy had polio, and couldn't move his legs much at all. So Mattie carried him. It's a good one, even if it wasn't true."

"You don't believe it?"

Earl looked at me. "About the vines? I used to. I guess it's possible. Strong women have always run in our family. But I'd imagine them swinging across this big old ravine, like Tarzan or something. What it probably was—and this was Glorrie's guess, mind you—that there was this little creek somewhere between here and their house, and they swung over it when they needed to." Earl shrugged. "But it's a better story the other way."

"Yeah," I said, looking around in the overgrown foundation. "So what did this old school look like on the inside?"

"Pretty small. There were holes in the roof, so it was dark in there, but not bad. There was this broken-slate board on the front wall, cracked all over the place. The teacher's desk and chair were long gone, of course, but the children's desks were built right in, and they were still there. They were two-seaters, and there were maybe ten of them altogether. I remember sitting at one, running my finger around the lip of the inkwell. It was stained with old, black ink. They all were. That was what got me, sitting in the seat, touching the ink. It was proof that some kid had sat there before me. Felt like it wasn't that long ago. I guess it wasn't really."

Earl and I walked around to the far side of the mound, and saw more wood and debris in a pile behind a partially-collapsed wall. Something small and white caught my eye laying amongst the pieces of wood and stone. I thought it was bone. But as I got closer, I saw it was an old porcelain doorknob, cracked neatly in two pieces.

"Hey, look at this," I said, reaching in and holding it up to Earl.

"Huh," he said, taking it from me. "This is the old knob from the front door."

"Was it still on the door when you were here?"

Earl nodded. "Door didn't latch anymore, of course, but the knob was still there." He handed it back to me. "Pretty good find, there, Reese. Keep it."

I considered it, wanted to, but my earlier words haunted me. I tried to justify taking it to myself—if I left it, I reasoned, someone else surely would. In the end, I couldn't do it. Seeing it was enough. Even if someone else takes it, I thought, it won't be me. "Nah," I said. "Let's let someone else find it, too."

"Suit yourself," Earl said. He was looking up the hill, his hand over his eyes. I looked up where he was looking. Gum was making his way down the hillside, and his son Ben and two men with shovels were still busy behind him. "I guess Gum's ready to head back. You and Clara really should have driven with us, Reese."

I waved him off. "It's okay," I said. "We'll be right behind you. You heading straight to the house?"

"I'll want to change first," he said. "But then I'll be over. We going to have supper?"

"Someone's got to eat that ham."

"True enough," he said. He started to walk back toward the path leading out of the cemetery and to the cars, and then he turned and said, "You know, Reese, you're looking more and more like your father all the time."

I smiled. "It's the coat." I watched Earl walk away, and waved to Gum. He returned the gesture, and then the two walked down to their car.

I looked down at the doorknob, and felt another pull to take it. I picked it up and turned it over in my hand. It was cold and smooth. I walked back across Mud Run to where Grandma Mattie and Grandpa Paul were buried, placed the old piece of cracked porcelain on the flat surface of Mattie's headstone. I put my white rose on Paul's, right next to her. I waved to the grandparents I never knew, and then turned to go home.

★ ★ ★

Earl and I made an agreement to talk about things that Sunday. Mom was eating with us, and we didn't want to talk about either the land or what we were going to do about her, in her condition, while she sitting with us at the table. So we ate, and we talked about old times, about Glorrie, but mostly about Earl and me and Dad. Like how Earl once paid me a quarter to kiss this girl he liked, Denise Webb, on the playground at school. Or how Dad pulled both of us behind his car one winter, on an old flipped-over car hood that was tied to his bumper, and how we flew twenty feet when Dad took a corner too fast. Or how Dad would say these things out of nowhere, like *God is sleeping*, or *Gotcha*, when a cloud would pass over in front of the moon. It was comfortable and fun, and Mom was still laughing when she went up to bed.

Earl got up and took some of the plates over to the sink. He came back for the rest of the dishes, and stopped, looking at me and smiling.

"What?" I said.

"You look like hell," he said, and turned to go back to the sink.

"Kind of you to say so," I said, groaning. "I need to get some sleep."

"Maybe." Earl turned on the water and put the stopper in the sink. "Or maybe you just need to get out of the house."

I shrugged. "I'm going out tomorrow night, anyhow, remember? You said you'd stay home and watch Mom while I went to the game."

"I remember, hotshot," he said. "But don't give me this 'I'm going to the game' crap. You're going to see Amy, and the whole town knows it."

"The whole town, huh?"

"And surrounding areas."

"Okay, well, fine, but I don't want to leave you here by yourself for two nights in a row. Why don't you go out?"

He turned and leaned back against the sink. "Nowhere to go.

I'm tired. In for the night. I'll just crash in front of the TV until you get home. I was thinking about sleeping in the den, actually, so we can talk in the morning."

"Sure," I said. Glorrie's bedroom was empty upstairs, of course, but I didn't blame Earl for not wanting to sleep there. Seemed too soon.

"Good," he nodded sharply. "Donnie asked me today when you were going to come by the bar, and I told him I'd get you down there soon. So if you feel like it, go. He said he owed you a beer."

I wondered if Donnie had told Earl about my initial reaction when he'd spilled the beans about Earl wanting to buy the land. It didn't matter—or at least it didn't seem to matter to Earl. "That he does," I said, getting up and grabbing the overcoat from the peg on the wall. "I guess maybe I will go."

"Say hi to the guys for me."

"Will do," I said. I wanted to thank him again, but he had already turned back to the sink.

It was colder, and the moon was bright and nearly full. I pulled my coat tightly around me, jogged out to my truck, and got in as fast as I could. My breath was white in the darkness of the cab as I fumbled for the keys. I sat there as the truck warmed up for a moment, and then pulled out of the driveway and headed north.

I walked into Sweet's not ten minutes later. There was a small crowd around the big-screen TV, watching the beginning of *Miami Vice*. Donnie and a few of the guys were at the bar—Buke, Slater, Larry, and someone I didn't recognize, about my size, maybe a little younger. Donnie waved me over to join them.

"How's it going, son?" Donnie asked. "Didn't expect to see you tonight."

"Didn't expect to be seen," I said. "Earl gave me a furlough. Can you get me a Natty Light?"

"If you want," Donnie said, reaching under the bar. That was the good thing about Donnie. He always knew when to ask questions and when not to. Had perfect timing, that man.

"Good enough."

I joined the guys at the bar, taking a seat next to Buke, who was on the end nearest the door. Next to him was Slater, followed by the guy I didn't know, and finally Larry Breeker. "Hey, Reese," Buke said. "Long time."

"Yeah," I said. "How's the slaughterhouse?" Last I knew, Buke and Slater both worked there—Slater as the day manager, Buke as meat-shaper.

"Packing plant," Slater corrected me with a smile.

"Still bloody," Buke said. "Hey, you know Duttings, here?" He pointed to the new guy with the neck of his Pabst.

"No," I held out my hand. "I'm Reese, Reese Moss."

Duttings took my hand and shook it firmly. "Harris Duttings," he said. "From Bethany."

"Originally?"

"Yeah."

"You play any ball in high school? What year'd you graduate?"

Duttings shook his head. "Didn't play, but I remember seeing you. You used to be pretty good."

"Yeah," Buke said, "And now he's gotten all soft in the middle. Living in the big city makes a man slow."

"Could still take you," I said, grabbing my beer from Donnie.

"Big talk, Natty Light," Buke said. "You want a Perrier chaser with that?"

"Please," I scoffed. "Bloomington-Normal is not the big city."

"Bigger'n here," Larry chimed in.

"Your wife's ass is bigger than here," Buke said. Larry began to protest, but let it go and laughed too.

It was good to get back in the rhythms of liquored conversations, of stale cigarette smoke, and of dim lighting with a beer chaser. Even Duttings got into the conversation here and there. It was unnerving, the way he interacted with these people I had known for so long. In a way, I resented him being there, despite the fact he seemed a fairly decent guy. Another guy I didn't know came in the bar—his name was Jackson, I think I heard someone say—and asked Duttings if he wanted to shoot some pool in the back room. Duttings excused himself, and the group was back to those I knew again. I was relieved, and when I got up to pump a quarter into the juke box—some old Johnny Cash—I came back and took his seat.

Donnie brought the conversation around to the funeral, saying it all seemed real nice and that Glorrie would have liked it. Everyone toasted to her, then, and said the things you're supposed to say. I was tired of hearing them.

"So how's your mom taking all this?" Donnie asked.

"Not great," I admitted.

"Must be hard," Slater said. "Your aunt was living with her out at your farm, wasn't she?"

"Yeah," I said. "Mom depended on her for a lot."

"Like what?" Larry asked.

I shrugged. "A lot," I said, not wanting to go into it all just then, not wanting to face it at all. "She has trouble getting around as easily as she used to," I said. "And Earl and I are worried about whether or not she can live by herself."

"That bad, huh?" Donnie asked.

"Maybe," I said. "I was thinking maybe she'd be okay. I mean, I don't want to put her in a nursing home if she doesn't need to go, you know?"

"Man, if I could put my mom in a home, I sure as hell would," Buke said.

"Liar," Slater said. "You're the biggest mama's boy in this bar." Buke looked at him with a raised eyebrow, and Slater flushed and held out his hands. "It was a joke," he said, "a joke."

"Nah, I'm kidding. It'll be tough to put Mom away when I have to. If I have to." Buke took a drink. "But I figure she'll completely lose her mind one of these days. And I can't take her. Hell, she won't even come in my house because she says it smells like dead cows."

"Doesn't it, though?" Larry asked.

"Yeah, Larry," Buke said with a patronizing scowl. "Of course it does. I work at a slaughterhouse."

"Packing plant," said Slater, more out of habit than anything.

"Right," Buke said without missing a beat. And then to me, with a grin, "I gotta tell you, though, the smell? My dogs love it."

I laughed. "Yeah, well, it's going to be tough for me, too," I said. "If we end up having to do it, I mean. But I can't take care of her either."

"What about Earl?" Donnie asked.

"He's got a living to make, life to lead. What can he do?"

Donnie shrugged. "If she can't take care of herself, Reese, I don't see what choice you have."

"Yeah," Slater said. "It's not like those places are prisons or anything, anyway. My grandma was at the one here in town until she died. I went to see her every Sunday."

"Of course you did," Buke said. "And I'm the mama's boy."

Slater ignored him. "It wasn't a bad place. The folks who run it are really nice. They're not like a few places I've heard of up in Decatur."

"That part's true, Reese," Donnie said. "I had an aunt up at one home in Decatur, and that place scared the shit out of me, let me tell you. The whole place smelled like piss, and there was this guy at the front door who would tug on your shirt sleeve as you left and beg you to write the governor and ask him to release him."

"Are you kidding?" Buke said.

"Nope," Donnie said. "Swear to God. This guy got to know me, see, and he'd follow me around, and tell me how his son had stuck him in there because he wanted his money, and if I helped him get out of there, he'd give me a thousand dollars."

"Just a thousand?" Larry said.

"Thousand bucks used to be serious money," Slater said.

"Still serious money to me. So what if the guy was on the up and up?" asked Buke.

Donnie paused and considered the question. "I'd feel really shitty, thanks. And I'm out a thousand bucks."

The night went on like this for a couple more hours. We played pool, watched the news, argued about politics. It was just like old times, and I was grateful for how easily I was able to slip right back in. I finally left around eleven—slapped a twenty down on the bar, said my see-you-laters, and headed back outside. I recognized nearly everything that was parked out there—Donnie's jeep, of course, Buke's motorcycle, Slater's red Civic, Larry's old silver Impala. My truck sat among them, looking for all the world like it belonged there, too.

I looked up at the sky. It was darker than it had been when I arrived—the moon had ducked behind a cloud and disappeared. *Gotcha*, I could hear my father say. *Gotcha.*

It had all been too easy. I'd been lazy, lulled into that state where you can make yourself believe whatever you need to get to the next thing, the next day, the rest of your life. Mom had been good, Earl was right, she'd been up for the challenge of burying her sister; she'd pushed through it just like I had. But now Glorrie was in the ground.

When I walked in the back door, I could hear the TV on in the living room. Earl was sprawled out on the couch asleep, a half-eaten bowl of popcorn on the floor beside him. I figured Mom had gone upstairs to bed. I took off my coat, slipped off my shoes, grabbed a couple of slices of ham from the fridge, and sat down in the recliner to watch the end of Carson. After about twenty minutes of dozing, I decided it was time to hit the sack.

I don't know what it was that made me check on Mom. I pushed her door open—carefully, since it whined when it opened too fast— and expected to see her lying there in her bed, sleeping soundly. She wasn't.

I checked the bathroom first, but it was dark and empty. Then back to her bedroom, this time announcing myself, and turning on the light when there was no answer. Nothing. Her bed had been slept in, but she wasn't there. I checked under her bed, where there were just a bunch of empty shoe boxes, her closet with a week's worth of dirty clothes, my room, Glorrie's bedroom, and back downstairs.

"Earl," I said, and then louder, when he didn't wake the first time. "Earl!"

He woke with a start, and smacked his lips. "Wha—" he started, and then, through slit-eyes, "What, what the hell's the matter?"

"Mom's gone," I said simply, ducking into the den to make sure she wasn't there.

"She's asleep."

"Not in her bed."

"She's not up there?"

"She's not up there."

"Damn."

"Has she ever disappeared like this before?"

"Not that I know of." Earl was standing, now, and walked over to where I stood in the kitchen. "Maybe she's fallen someplace and you just missed her."

"I've looked in every room," I said. "All over." My voice sounded more gruff than I intended, but I was angry at myself for letting my mind wander. For the moment, it was as if all my senses were operating at heightened levels, that I was noticing every minute detail. There was a small smear of red on the flowered clock in the kitchen—spaghetti sauce? The faucet was dripping in an odd cadence, the water dropping into a cup sitting in the sink in threes: *drip, drip, drip,* pause, *drip, drip, drip.* One corner of the fringed rug on the linoleum was folded over, dog-eared like someone left it and meant to hold his place until he came back to it.

"She's got to be outside." Earl said.

"Wouldn't you have heard the door?"

Earl shrugged. "I sleep pretty hard."

I wasn't wearing a coat, or even shoes, and Earl was worse off, sporting only a pair of boxers and a T-shirt. Neither of us seemed to notice. I ran over to the cellar door, but it was locked tight. Earl called from the garage that she wasn't there, and that the car was still there, too. We were both heading for the barn when we heard her. Mom was screaming bloody murder.

I bolted for the barn and pushed my way in. The huge front door was on rollers, but it was still heavy, and Mom had somehow pushed it far enough to allow her thin frame through.

The barn was only half-lit by the beams of dusty moonlight that filtered through the slat roof and side windows. Mom was kneeling on the dirt floor, holding her hands to her chest, rocking back and forth slowly, muttering something to herself and sobbing. She was bleeding from cuts on her arms, especially, but I could see red specks spreading on her pink nightgown. She was ghostly, her face pale and anguished, moaning, wavering there in the barn's dust. All around her were scattered pieces of bottle, as well as what they had once held. The shelves on the eastern wall were bare, no longer storing what they had for countless years: caked pucks of old paint, mason jars of rusted nails, long-dead seeds, and powders and liquids of all sorts, in an array of colors: blues, whites, reds, and browns. These were bottles I had been warned away from as a boy. And tonight, my mother had smashed them all, then collapsed in the debris.

Earl and I rushed in, taking care to avoid the glass. We dragged Mom up and away from the field of shards, the both of us lifting her over it all and sitting her gently in the chair by the desk in the corner. I switched on the desk lamp and knelt down next to her, tried to comfort her, but she was inconsolable. Most of her cuts looked minor, but what she'd been cut with, what could have gotten in those wounds, I didn't know.

Behind me, Earl flung the door open wide, headed outside, and came back with the hose running. He washed the powders and small pools of liquid that were left into the dirt of the ground, until what was left was a muddy pit of what looked to be brightly-colored gems, shining up in the moonlight from their half-buried bed in the earth.

I looked over at Earl and sighed. "Fuck."

Earl shook his head, and tossed the hose down on the ground.

"What in holy hell is she doing?" he muttered. He grabbed an old horse blanket from the cab of the tractor and tossed it to me. "Keep her warm."

I tossed it back. "You use it. She doesn't seem to be cold, but you look half froze." I wasn't kidding—Mom felt hot, like energy still roiled through her from the inside out. Earl couldn't even stand still, he was shivering so badly. I reached out and took Mom's shoulder to lead her back to the house where we could all at least be warm and clean up. But Mom wasn't done surprising me. She recoiled as though my touch burned her, threw her hands up as if to defend herself from an attack, and pushed me back hard enough to send me flat to the ground. I felt something dig into my head, just over my left ear. My hand went up to it, and I drew back blood. Looking down, I saw what looked to be a broken piece of an old green dish.

Mom started screaming again, only this time I was the object of her rage and not some wall of old bottles. What didn't I see in her eyes, in that moment? Rage, fear, sadness—they were all there. Her face was flushed, her look feral. I was afraid she might stroke out right there in the barn.

"Do you think you can get away with this, Reese?" Her voice dropped to a hateful whisper. "Stupid! Stupid! Do you really think no one will ask questions? This isn't 1932! This isn't the old days! This wasn't the way to solve anything, I don't care what she said, this wasn't the way!"

"What?" I asked, getting up on my knees and reaching for her again.

She pushed my hand away. "Don't touch me! If you think you can ever touch me again, you have another thing coming. Maybe she'll touch you. Do you even understand what you're doing? What she's doing? Do you understand anything? Do you honestly think you can do something so...so evil, and everything will be fine? That no one will know? Let me tell you something, everyone will know, and then we'll pay for it, all of us. You, my sister, me, everyone."

"Mom?" I said quietly. But she was somewhere else. Untethered.

"You think this will solve everything, that you can just go against God Himself and break His commandments and then be absolved?"

"Absolved of what?" Earl asked, and I looked at him, my eyes wide.

Mom ignored Earl completely. "God will punish us. He'll punish you, He'll punish her, He'll punish me just for knowing about it. Just for knowing and not doing anything. God isn't sleeping! God isn't sleeping! He's watching. I'm watching, you weak son of a bitch. I always have been." Her anger suddenly washed away like dirt in rain. She slumped over and began crying. It was at once the most terrifying and the most pitiful thing I had ever witnessed.

I shook my head, trying to make sense of it all. I was transfixed by my mother's fury, and bewildered by what she'd said. I was afraid I was seeing her slipping away for good, so I reached for her again, leaning in towards her, hoping to bring her back. "Mom, it's James," I said, lifting her chin to look at me, still ready to snatch my hand back if I needed to. When I was satisfied she saw me—really saw me—I pulled my hand back, folded my hands like I was praying, and said "We need to go in the house. Forget about all this for now. Forget about Dad, forget about Glorrie—"

Mom flicked her arm and backhanded me across the mouth. I fell back again and sat on my heels. Earl ran over—I don't know why, maybe to restrain Mom from beating the crap out of me—but I stopped him. I wanted Mom to have her say. It seemed like something she needed to get out, even if I didn't understand any of it.

"Don't you ever speak to me about my sister, Reese," Mom said. "Never, ever again."

"All right," I said. "All right."

She brought her knees up to her face, then, and began to cry again. After a few minutes, she stopped, but didn't move at all. Earl was still, and I just sat there in the cold of the barn, letting myself sink down to the ground, kneel before her. I felt my lip swelling, felt a drop of blood fall from my ear to the wet earth. My eyes never left my mother. She looked like a newborn kitten just opening her eyes: tired, innocent, lost, and an utter mystery.

"God may forgive her," she said to me, "but I never will."

# Chapter Eleven

## 1957

REESE HAD NEVER WANTED TOM DEAD. Not after Tom had thrown a man in a thrasher, not after he'd knocked the teeth clean out of Woes' mouth, not after what he'd done that night at the pool room. Not even after all Tom had done to Glorrie. Everything he continued to do, unchecked. Reese hadn't wanted the man dead. Never before.

"I'm tired, Reese," Glorrie said. "And I'm done with him."

Glorrie sat on the desk in the barn, and Reese was leaning back in his chair and smoking his pipe, his feet up next to her. She looked tired—her shoulders were slumped, and her eyes were heavy and dark. Tom had been on her again, Reese was sure. He'd seen her angry before, and he'd seen her despair. But he'd never seen this—Glorrie was calm, certain, and more than a little cold.

"I know you are, Glorrie," Reese said.

"You should be too," she said.

Reese was, but he had more to think about. It had been a time of new things, that November in 1957, and anything seemed possible. It had been a good year for farmers. Prices were up, and the crops had been the best anyone had seen in years. There had been just enough rain, just enough sun, and science seemed to be coming up with better pesticides and weed killers every year. Moweaqua was afloat in ready cash, and families all over town were spending—on garbage disposals, television sets, dishwashers. But Reese and Clara chose to save their money, at least for a while, since they had other things to buy: diapers, a crib, formula. Clara had finally had their baby.

She'd found out she was pregnant just at the start of planting, and by the end of harvest, she'd had a boy. Named him James after Clara's father, and gave him Reese as his middle name. "James Reese Moss," Clara had said as she presented him to Reese for the first time. "Just like his Daddy."

Reese smiled, looked down at this little person, so helpless, his eyes shut with sleep, his skin pink and new. Reese didn't know what to say then, and that hadn't changed much since they'd brought the baby home. It wasn't that Reese was unhappy, but fatherhood had taken him by surprise. He had pretty much decided that having children was something that wouldn't ever happen. Clara was forty, after all, long past the time when women usually had children, past the time when it was relatively safe. So when Clara told him she thought she was pregnant, he didn't believe her. And when Doc Pistorius confirmed it, Reese was half scared out of his mind—not that he was going to be a father, but that in trying to have a baby, his wife would be taken from him. Instead of becoming three, Reese thought he would become one. Alone. He started half-planning his life once his wife was gone, once the whole thing went horribly wrong and she died. They weren't dreams, but Reese was ashamed they weren't nightmares, either. He was even more ashamed that what scared him most was the thought of Clara dying in childbirth and leaving him with a healthy baby. He didn't know what he'd do, but he knew what he couldn't do: take care of a child by himself.

He couldn't care for Earl on his own, either. Earl had been Beatrice's boy, Glorrie and Clara's younger sister who'd married young and then moved to St. Louis with her husband. They'd had Earl, and then divorced a year later. Beatrice got remarried almost immediately to a man named Setts, who sold insurance. Reese had met Setts once—a gambler who never stopped talking. From what Clara and Glorrie said, that was Beatrice all over—nothing but bad choices, right up to the time when she decided to cross the street against the light and a Studebaker took the legs out from under her, cracking her skull against the pavement. They had all gone down to Missouri for the funeral and the reading of the will—Glorrie and Clara had been against going at all, seeing as how Beatrice was going to be buried in the cemetery down there and not up at Mud Run. But they went to see their sister one last time. A lawyer had talked to Tom and Reese both, apart from the women, to warn them about what was about to happen—that Beatrice had left custody of Earl to her two sisters.

"Shit," Tom spat, and walked off. He had been expecting money, and getting a child instead, as Tom put it later, was like inheriting a debt that grows every day. Glorrie wanted to take Earl because she couldn't have a baby, but Tom wouldn't hear of it. Reese considered Tom's refusal a blessing, because he would've worried for the boy. Glorrie sported tell-tale marks now and then, but said nothing about them anymore, and neither Reese nor Clara asked. Clara said she was glad not to see her sister as much, since it was hard to see her done the way she was by Tom, and harder still that Glorrie continued to put up with him. Reese didn't know if Clara were truly glad for Glorrie's absence, but he was. He'd done the best he could for her, but nothing had changed. Maybe, he thought, Glorrie felt the same.

Once Clara said that she and Reese would take Earl, Glorrie came around more often. Clara promised Glorrie they could raise Earl together, just like Beatrice had wanted. No one consulted Reese about any of it, but in the end, he didn't mind. He liked the boy all right, and Reese realized Earl had no other place to go.

Earl turned out to be a level-headed boy, contrary to his mother's reputation for bad choices. He did his chores, minded what he was told, kept his head down, seemed eager to learn. Reese tried to get the boy to go play, to leave him alone, but Earl wanted to work, and Reese finally gave in. Earl reveled in it, said he wanted to become a farmer too. Reese was happy for that because he thought he might finally have someone to pass all the land on to.

But all that was before Clara had given him a son of his own. Earl was still close to Reese's heart, but James was closer, even as an infant. Reese tried to hide this, from Earl, from Clara, from himself, but he was afraid he did a poor job of it. So Reese made an effort to do special things with Earl, like putting up the windmill. It was supposed to be special, anyhow, and it would have been. But Tom showed up, and he was a problem. Tom was always the problem.

"You owe it to Earl," Glorrie said, swinging her legs under the desk.

"I owe what to Earl?" Reese asked.

"You owe it to Earl to be fed up with Tom. And you owe it to me, and to the baby, and to Clara. To all of us."

"What does that mean? So what if I am fed up with Tom? What if I am? I sure as hell can't do anything about it." Reese gestured to his knee, but he knew it was a weak excuse. He'd tried and failed, and he still remembered walking down the stairs at the pool room, the snickering of Tom's friends, Tom telling them to *stifle it, fellas, or else.* That was the worst part. Tom being the one to defend him.

"What it means is that we do something about it. Something to stop what happened today from ever happening again." Glorrie looked him straight in the eye.

Reese hung his head. He wished he'd put up that damn windmill on his own, like he'd originally planned. If he had, he'd be inside watching his new television set with his feet up, smelling the chicken frying in the kitchen.

Reese had been wanting to replace the old windmill near the driveway for years, but hadn't been able to put the money together. But this year, even with the new baby and the TV, he'd been able to find enough ready cash, and he had promised Earl he could help assemble it. Earl loved his erector set, and to him, putting together a windmill from the ground up was the same thing in real size. But the plan soon escalated out of Reese's control. Clara planned a picnic so the baby could come out if it wasn't too cold, and so Reese could spend time with both the boys. And then Glorrie decided she and Tom would come help. Reese accepted all this cheerfully enough—he could use another set of hands, he reasoned, and besides, it sounded like it might be fun. A day out for the men of the family, the sort of thing you remember years down the line.

The work had gone fine, at first. It was cool but sunny, and the air was still enough that they worked without jackets all morning and through Sunday dinner. Glorrie and Clara came out with the food so they could eat while they worked, Glorrie carrying the basket, Clara cradling the baby in her arms. Dinner was ham sandwiches instead of the usual turkey—Clara always stopped making turkey about a month before Thanksgiving—and Glorrie had made her scalloped potatoes, though neither Reese nor Tom took any because they didn't want to mess with using a plate.

Reese leaned against the horse trough while he ate, savoring the meat, the air, and the day. Clara sat on a blanket, feeding James from a bottle, happy as Reese had ever seen her. Glorrie was next to her, dividing her attention between watching Reese Jr. and helping Earl fix a plate of food. At ten, Earl was already a strapping boy. He ate like a stray dog, his round face already buried in a sandwich piled too thick with ham and cheese slices. And then there was Tom, who stood up against the half-constructed windmill, looking back into the fields behind the barn.

Tom finished his sandwich and Glorrie handed him another before he could even ask. Reese noticed that he virtually ignored her, now, only addressing her when she annoyed him. And yet, Tom was as friendly to Reese as ever, like it was still 1932 and they still shared the old shotgun shack that used to sit on his Cherry Street lot. Tom slapped Reese on the shoulder, complimented himself on how straight the frame was so far. He told Reese a new joke he'd heard at work about the niggers up in Decatur, then took a drink from a hip flask he'd fished out of his jacket pocket. Reese could smell the whiskey on his breath from where he sat on the trough. He laughed politely, stretched and rubbed his aching hands, and said it was time for him to get back to work.

Glorrie pulled out her new camera. "I want to capture the moment with all these handsome men," she said. Clara looked suddenly uncomfortable, but demurred, smiling and nodding curtly, then looking away. Reese picked up his baby, held him on his shoulders, one hand behind his tiny back. Reese marveled at how fragile his son was, how full of promise. Tom grunted something about getting back to the job, and pulled Earl by one strap of his overalls to the windmill in the background, where they started to work. Glorrie took several pictures before Tom spoke up.

"Enough with the pictures," he snarled.

"I want to take enough so that at least one will come out," Glorrie said, snapping a couple more.

"Take the baby and get inside," Tom said.

Glorrie did as she was told, scooping up the baby from Reese, gathering the remnants of the picnic lunch with Clara. The sisters walked back to the house, not saying a word.

Tom's anger, as it turned out, wasn't directed at her after all—the problem that day was Earl. He was young, unused to managing Tom's anger, and ignorant of Tom's temper. He didn't know what to do, didn't know what not to do. Tom got more surly with each drink, and less patient with the boy, who was bored and passed the time playing with the tools Tom had spread out on the ground. Some were Reese's, some were Tom's, but Tom didn't like anyone playing with his tools, especially the leather-rolled tape measure he'd bought off a guy up in Decatur.

There were three times where Earl annoyed Tom that afternoon. The first was when Earl didn't get Tom the tool he'd asked for quickly enough. Tom launched into a string of curses that embarrassed Reese and made Earl giggle. Earl apologized, and Tom was mollified.

The second time, Earl had started to climb up the frame of the windmill. Tom pulled him down with a quick jerk on one of his legs, and Earl came tumbling down hard, sprawling out on the cold ground and looking up at his uncle with new fear. He wasn't hurt—Reese checked—but he was cowed. Reese asked Earl if he wanted to go back inside, but Tom laughed, asked what the kid could do inside with the women. "Let him stay outside with the men," Tom said. Earl watched Tom warily, but said he wanted to stay. Reese helped Earl up, and Tom told him to stay off the windmill, to behave himself. "Don't make me tell you again," he said. Reese looked at Earl, who nodded, and sat on the horse trough to watch.

The third time was the last. Reese had the mill's wheel in his lap, straightening the fletchings so as to best catch the wind. Tom had gone to his truck to refill his flask, and when he came back, he found Earl in the dirt, playing with his tape measure. Earl had it stretched all the way out to the very end, and was trying to get it rolled back up in the casing. But it wouldn't roll the right way, and the boy was getting panicked when he saw Tom coming back. He sprung to his feet as Tom approached, like a soldier at attention. Reese started to speak, but was too slow. Something in Tom snapped—that thing, that small insufficiently developed thing that held Tom's anger in check broke clean in two. Tom didn't say a word—he just looked at Earl, picked him up with one sweep of his arms, and dunked the boy's head under the water of the horse trough.

"What the hell did I tell you?" Tom yelled as he forced Earl's head under the water. Earl was fighting and kicking, trying desperately to take a breath when Tom would let him up for a second before submerging him again. "What the hell did I tell you?" He pulled Earl up out of the water, and looked straight in the boy's eyes. "This is what happens when you don't listen," he said, and then thrust his head back under. Tom thrust Earl's head into the trough over and over again, his voice a roar, each word punctuated by another dunk. *This. Is. What. Happens.*"

Reese jumped up, letting the wheel clatter to the ground, feeling his knee groan beneath him. He stumbled but recovered fast, and grabbed onto Tom's arm, trying to match the volume of his yelling, trying to make Tom stop for a second and notice that Reese was there at all.

Tom didn't stop, but he did notice—he let loose of Earl with the arm Reese was pulling on, and shoved Reese back away from the trough. Reese fell, bouncing off the tower of the nearly-complete mill, and falling to one side, hitting the ground with his hip and his hand, jamming his wrist. As he fell, Reese could hear Earl gasping for breath—big, choking sounds of gulping air. Tom pointed at Reese, furious, and said, "If you can't control this little bastard, then I will. And when I do, you'd damn well better not get in my way." And that wasn't all. Reese could read something else in Tom's eyes, in the way he was standing, the way his breaths came hard and deep, in the way Reese was reminded of that night years before at the Pool Room. *Don't do it, Reese. Don't make me hurt you, too.*

Tom looked at Earl and sneered. He threw the boy back into the trough and let go, walking off to his truck and taking a long pull of whiskey as he did. Earl, drenched and scared, peered out over the lip of the trough. Reese caught his eye and nodded toward the house, and Earl jumped out and ran back across the yard as fast as he could. Glorrie and Clara had been standing on the porch, watching it all—Clara had her palm over her mouth in shock, and Glorrie was shaking her head, her hand on her hip.

Reese had thought about going over to talk with Tom, but he didn't. Reese didn't want to, and besides, Tom didn't look like he wanted the company. Reese gathered up his tools and the wheel and what hardware was left, took it all into the barn, and sat in his chair. He'd stayed there for hours, trying to shake off the shame he felt in his chest. Tom drove off, the day had fallen into night, and Glorrie brought Reese out his dinner. She sat on his desk, crossed her legs, and told him what she wanted.

"I want us to put Tom down."

Reese looked up. Glorrie's eye gleamed green in the dim light of the barn like a cat's. "You want us to what?"

"You can't deny it needs to be done," she said. "After today. After all this time. You can't deny it."

"The hell I can't," Reese said. "Tom's not a horse who's come up lame, Glorrie. He's not something you can just do away with like an animal."

"You're wrong."

"I'm not wrong," Reese said. "It's not right, and you know it. You should be ashamed for considering such a thing."

"I should be ashamed? It isn't right? Is it right that he hits me?" Glorrie said calmly, as though she were reading from a script. She waited for an answer. "Is it?" she repeated.

"Of course not," Reese said.

"Is it right, what he did to Earl today?"

"No. But that still— "

"Is it right that he told you straight out he'd do it again?"

"He didn't."

"He did."

"He didn't mean it that way."

"He meant it exactly that way," Glorrie said, shaking her head, looking up at the sky, laughing bitterly. "I know the man better than you ever will because he's always on his best behavior around you. Don't you know that? Your opinion means more to him than nearly anything. And so you above all others see the best of Tom Horseman, and yet you still hate him."

"I don't hate him."

"You should," Glorrie said. "And you would, if you knew all the things he'd done to me. Not to mention the things he's talked about doing to Clara, when he's really drunk, because he knows she helped me, because he knows she knows what he's done. And the things I promise you he will do again to Earl. And someday, to James, if we don't do something."

"What's he talked about doing to Clara?"

Glorrie shook her head. "Does it matter? You know what he's capable of, Reese. You know what he's willing to do. You think that's somehow limited to me? That I'm the only one he doesn't mind hurting? All I'm saying is I want him to stop it, all of it, once and for all. I don't know any other way."

"We can't," Reese said.

"Why can't we?" Glorrie asked.

"Because we're better than him!" Reese said, his anger rising, his voice getting away from him for a moment. And then, more softly. "We have to be."

Glorrie smiled. "No," she said, glancing carefully back to the house and then catching Reese's gaze again. "We're not better. You know that. We all have our secrets." She reached down and caressed Reese's jaw. Her voice was pillow-soft, just like when she'd invite him into her bed. "Both you and I, we have our little shames. We're no better than him. Clara? She's better. Earl and the baby, they're innocents. But you and I are fallen, Reese. We've done what we've done, and we've learned to live with it. Learned to put it out of our minds and convince ourselves we can keep going with our heads up high. And that's why we can do it. Why we're the ones who *have* to do it. That's why we can kill him."

*Kill him.* The words rang in Reese's head like a cracked bell. "I'm not proud of what we did together, Glorrie," Reese whispered, "but we did it, and it's over. And my God, that's not killing a man."

Glorrie shrugged. "Mortal sin is mortal sin, if you want to bring God into it. It's all the same. And besides, that's not all I'm talking about."

"What then?"

"The thrasher, silly," Glorrie said flatly. "Or have you gotten so good at denial you've actually forgotten that you helped Tom get away with murder?"

Reese's head snapped. "It wasn't murder."

"It wasn't?" Glorrie asked. "Don't try to fleece me, Reese, because I know better. Tom told me himself. Years ago, Tom got drunk, and instead of getting angry like usual, he got very, very frightened. So I asked him what was wrong, tried to find out what was bothering him, what it was that would keep him up all night sometimes, reading the Bible and drinking. Turns out it was the thrasher. He told me everything. How the stranger killed that boy you worked with, how you tried to jump him but fell, how he got so mad he made his way up there and just threw him in. Said you watched him do it. Horrible way to die." Glorrie paused here, staring off into space, like she was considering something, and then dismissing it. "Anyway, he told me about how you both concocted that story, how the sheriff probably would have gotten to you if it hadn't been for the mine going up the way it did. So you see, Reese, I know you can help someone kill a man, because you've already done it once before."

"How long have you known? Before the war?"

"Is that a subtle way of asking whether I knew before you and I were together? Yes." Glorrie smiled. "It didn't bother me, Reese, it really didn't. You didn't have much of a choice. That man had killed a friend of yours in cold blood. I knew it when I married Tom, and I knew it when I was with you. It was simple justice. Just like this."

"This isn't simple," Reese said.

"But it's justice."

Reese clenched his pipe between his teeth, and rubbed his thumb into the palm of the other hand. "I can't, Glorrie, I'm sorry, but I just can't. I've spent my life regretting that day. I won't do it again."

Glorrie's smile drained away, and her voice lost its purr. "You're all I have left, Reese. All I have left." Her eyes were suddenly wet. "It's getting worse, can't you see? Tom's getting worse. There was a time when he would have rather died than let you see him the way he was today. But this afternoon, out by that damned windmill, he nearly drowned our nephew for no good reason but that he was drunk. And when he gets drunk, he gets angry, and he's always drunk now, Reese. He's always drunk and he's going to kill somebody. It may be Earl, it may be Clara, it may be your son, but it's probably going to be me. It's going to be me. It's more than just hitting and pushing. More than him throwing bottles, more than him forcing himself on me when he comes home in the middle of the night stinking of liquor and sweat and God knows what. I've lived through that. But lately, he says things. Tells me I'm worthless, that I'm fat and I'm ugly, that I don't deserve to live in his house, that I don't deserve him. Says he'd be better off single again, and how if he could just find his shotgun, he would be. I hid his guns under the house months ago. It's a matter of time. Don't you see? Killing him is the only way I'm going to see another birthday."

Reese sat forward in his chair, put his elbows on his knees, and rubbed his temples. "Jesus, Glorrie," he said.

Glorrie stole another look towards the house, and then leaned over and kissed the top of Reese's head. "I know you tried to talk to him that one time during the Centennial. I appreciate it, even if it did mean things got worse there for a while. I appreciate the gesture, Reese, the risk you took for me."

"You knew?" Reese asked, his voice dead.

"Yes," she said, wiping her eyes. "I wanted to thank you. I don't know why you never told Clara about it, since I know she's been on you for years to do something, anything, but—"

"Because I got my hat handed to me," Reese said. "I stood up to Tom, stood my strongest, and he put me on the floor like he was dropping a sack of feed. I did my best, and I did nothing."

"He told me about it. That night, he came home and told me. He was so angry, beyond anything I'd seen before. He beat me up for telling you about my problems, for making him look bad in your eyes. Hit me so hard against the side of my head I couldn't see, and then when I fell down, he kicked me in the ribs. I think he broke one or two—they were sore for weeks. And then, the next morning, he rode in that damned float and threw candy to the children, waving and smiling. That son of a bitch."

"So it was worse than nothing, what I did."

"No," she said. "Don't think of it that way. It was worth it to me, whatever Tom ended up doing. Because that night? I wasn't alone. I wasn't by myself, even if it was just me getting knocked around. I loved that you did it, Reese, I loved that you did it for me. It helped me make it through."

Reese took his pipe from his mouth and sat in the gloom of the barn, feeling claustrophobic, suddenly, like the air was pressing in on him. The owl up in the rafters shuddered. It was normally a sound that soothed him. He shook his head. "God dammit, Glorrie, what you're asking—"

"He killed my baby." Glorrie's voice was as flat as the thin line of her mouth.

"What?"

"My baby. Why do you think I don't have children?"

Reese felt like getting up and walking around, maybe walking off the dizziness he was suddenly feeling, but didn't. "Because—"

he started, "Clara told me it runs in your family."

"Clara and I are two of three girls, Reese. Clara just had a son at forty. Bea had Earl. And I was pregnant until Tom kicked me in the stomach one night." Glorrie's face was like painted stone, the blush on her cheeks standing in stark contrast to the pallor of skin. "I dreamed it was going to be a boy," she said. "I was early in my pregnancy. Clara helped me that time. Got me to Doc's, stayed with me through it. Doc Pistorius said that depending on how the miscarriage went, I might have trouble getting pregnant again, and he was right. I never could. Clara and I decided not to tell you. We thought it was for the best."

"When?"

Glorrie looked at Reese, something defiant in her gaze. "Not too long after Tom came back from the war."

Reese let this sink in. "How long after?"

"Right after."

"How long?" Reese asked again.

"A few months," Glorrie said.

Reese's knee itched him. He took a long draw on his pipe, exhaled, and watched the cherry smoke curl up around Glorrie's head. "So was it—" Reese didn't get a chance to finish the question.

"No telling," Glorrie said. "No telling."

Reese could tell she was waiting for him to look at her, watching him like a hunter pausing to see if the buck drops. He said nothing.

"That was my last card, Reese," Glorrie finally said. "I've nothing left to play. It's all out on the table, now. What we have to do. Why we don't have a choice. The only thing keeping him from killing Earl today was you, and that won't work again. Do we all live in fear of him now? Do we wait until he kills again, or do we stop him?"

"I don't—" Reese didn't finish. He thought he could feel a hole in his chest, then, a black thing pulling at him from all sides, threatening to swallow him up. He could feel it just below his breastbone, a pit sucking away his breath. It grew in him, tingling out to his shoulders, his fingertips, his forehead. Reese didn't know what to do. He felt like throwing his pipe across the room, but was afraid he'd start a fire. He wanted to yell, but he was afraid Clara would hear. He wanted to drive to Tom's house, dunk the son-of-a-bitch's head under water, but he knew he couldn't. He clenched his fist, looked at it, how small it was.

"You're my last hope," Glorrie pleaded. "You've never let me down before. Don't start now."

"Jesus, Glorrie," Reese said, his resignation mingling with the pipe smoke. He rubbed at his eyes.

"We can do it, Reese," she said softly, getting down on her knees, her hands on his knees, forcing him to look into her eyes. "We can do it," she whispered.

Reese sat back and crossed his arms over his chest. His face was burning, the hole in his chest pulsing. He reached up and scratched his ear. "How?"

Glorrie took a deep breath, and her soft smile returned. "Like I said, he drinks all the time," she said. "I know where he keeps his bottles. All I need is something to put in his whiskey. Something to make him go quietly, in a drunk, and end it."

"Like what?"

"I don't know. Weed killer? Pesticide? Would any of that work?"

Reese looked around. His eyes settled on the high shelf against the wall, on the opaque brown bottles covered in dust. He broke away from Glorrie, went to the shelf, and took one down. He took off the cap, angled the bottle to check the powder inside. It was the color of bone. *God is sleeping*, Reese thought. "Here," he said. "It's all I can do. All I'm going to do."

"What is it?"

"Arsenic. My mother used it to kill weeds."

"Strong stuff for weeds," Glorrie said.

"I guess."

"Okay," Glorrie said, examining the bottle. "Do you know how much to put in?"

209

"No," Reese frowned. "I've never poisoned a man before."

Glorrie cocked her head, admonishing. "Don't be like that, Reese," she said, "please. It's hard enough, doing it, but—"

"Is it?" Reese asked.

Glorrie stepped back. "Yes," she said, her words clipped. "Yes, it is."

"Listen to me," Reese said, his voice stern. "We won't talk about this. I don't want to know about it. I don't want to know when you do it, or how it happens. You know the pact we made about the thrasher? This is the same thing. We don't talk about it. Not with Clara or anyone else. I owe him that, at least. Tom's made his mistakes all right, but he deserves to be remembered for the good he did, not the bad." Reese paused, looked away, and muttered, "We all do."

"He's done a lot more bad than good, Reese, you have to admit."

"He fought for our country."

"Because you and Sheriff Dawes forced him to."

"He buried a baseball in the dirt over Stupak's grave after he was killed, did you know that? He didn't have to. It was a nice gesture. Stupak would have loved it."

"The fact you have to reach back in time that far should tell you something, Reese."

"He was your husband. Can't you think of a damn thing?"

"Not right now," Glorrie admitted. "Not right now."

Reese shook his head. "Tom wanted to be a better man than he was. That's got to count for something." He scowled at himself when he realized that he was already speaking about Tom in the past tense.

"If you say so." Glorrie's voice was cross, but she sighed, closed her eyes, calmed herself. "Don't let this wear on you, Reese. This isn't the beginning of something bad. It's the end. You have to believe that."

Reese tapped his pipe. "Yeah, well," he said. He was breathing better, now. "I don't know what to believe."

"I knew you'd come through for me, Reese. I knew I could depend on you." She hugged Reese with her free arm, clutching the brown bottle to her breast, and kissed Reese softly on the cheek. Her lips were gentle, and she smelled of talc and rose water. "Thank you."

"For what?" Clara stood in the doorway, drying her hands on her apron.

Glorrie slipped the bottle into her dress pocket, and turned smoothly on one heel. "Reese said he'd help me fix my fence next weekend," she lied. "Is that all right with you? Reese said you didn't have plans, and I really need the fence to keep the dogs out of the yard. I'm so tired of cleaning up other people's messes. And Tom's no help around the house at all. I can't ask the man to do anything."

Clara gave a silent quick nod. She looked almost sad, but it was deeper than that, Reese thought. Like she was barely there.

"Thanks again, Reese," Glorrie said. She walked past Clara and out of the barn.

"Yeah," Reese said, staring at his wife. They stood like that, looking at each other. Reese had run out of things to say, even small, meaningless things. He opened his mouth, but before anything had a chance to come out, Clara stopped him.

"Don't," she said. And then she walked away, back to the house.

Reese stayed out in the barn for a while, and once he was sure Glorrie had gone home, he went inside. Most of the lights were already out. Reese checked on Earl first, made sure he was okay. Reese watched the boy sleep for a moment, considered that he was dry and quiet, then pulled the covers up over his shoulders. Satisfied, Reese went into his own room, which was lit pale blue by the autumn moon that stretched through the east window. He saw his son in the cradle by the bed, his tiny arms bent at the elbows, his ineffectual hands up in the air like he was surrendering. Reese yawned, rolled his head around, popped his neck. He took off his clothes and laid them on the dresser like Clara was always after him to do. He crawled into bed and lay next to his wife, but she pulled away from him, left him alone with his blanket, his secrets, and the moon outside.

Tom Horseman was found dead two weeks later, sitting up in his living room chair, a bottle of whiskey spilled on the floor and the *Mickey Mouse Club* blaring on the television. Doc Pistorius came out, and based on what Glorrie told him, said it was probably his heart, given out after a lot of hard living. This was good enough for the county coroner, too, and he signed the death certificate without a look at the body. Glorrie took it all very well, and folks around town said Tom would have been proud of her, the strength she showed. Those closer to Glorrie, those who knew about Tom's drinking, whispered that heart attack or not, it was the bottle that did him in. And Glorrie nodded sadly.

They planted Tom down at Mud Run, on a hillside that had seen so much November rain it looked like it was melting. Earl refused to see it at all, and played in the small, abandoned schoolhouse at the bottom of the hill during the service. Clara, who wordlessly stood next to her husband the whole time, carried the baby back down the hill as soon as the first shovel of wet dirt hit the casket with a hollow knock. Others filed away until only Reese and Glorrie remained.

"He always brought me lilacs on our anniversary," Glorrie said. Her voice was flat and quiet. "Never missed it once, except during the war, and even then, he sent me letters with a little lilac drawn on the envelope. They were the flowers he bought me for my wedding bouquet." She wiped at her nose with a white handkerchief. "You asked me if I could think of something. Well, there it is, Reese. There it is."

Glorrie left Reese alone at the grave, then. She touched Reese's arm as she went, a gesture meant in comfort, but that cut like a thrasher blade.

Reese stood there for some time—he didn't know how long. He looked down and felt the rain dampen his wool overcoat, the sharp chill in his knee, that hole in his chest that felt like it would never go away, what it was like to be all alone. The clouds spit down upon Reese, covering everything equally and overmuch, the pelting water dripping off the brim of his hat, running into his eyes and over his face. Even the rain felt unclean.

But the mud was the worst of it. Reese could feel the mud creeping into his shoes, even as he stood still. When he turned to leave, it was worse, the earth tugging at him with every step, pulling him down. It was inexorable. And in the end, Reese knew, the pulling would be enough that he'd end up here, beneath the sod, alone, with only a stone to mark he'd ever walked above.

# Chapter Twelve

*NOVEMBER 7, 1987. A SATURDAY.*

THE FARM WAS FULL OF GHOSTS. I looked around the old house
and all the land surrounding it. How could a person live here all his
life, die here, and not have some part of him linger? It made sense
to me that something would remain, and I felt like I wasn't alone. I
hadn't slept all night, having been bothered by the cut over my ear
and the nagging questions about what Mom had meant in her rant-
ing, or if there were answers at all. I wandered around the house for
a while that night, and finally found myself in Glorrie's bedroom.

Glorrie's room was full of pictures on the wall, most of them in
frames, a few just tacked up. One wall looked to be entirely made
up of her travels: a picture of her on a burro in the Grand Canyon,
one of her in the mountains of Colorado, many of her travels abroad.
She's smiling in all of them, waving in some. There was only one picture on the wall she wasn't in, and it was the picture I remembered
sitting on her mantle for so many years, the one of me and Dad and
Mom and Earl and Tom, on the day they said the windmill went up.
It was the only picture of Tom, the only one on the wall that had
been taken before he died. Made me want to snatch it down, keep
it for myself, this relic of a life passed. Glorrie would have wanted
me to have it, too—but right then, that bleary early morning, it
was still too soon. I sat on her bed and looked around me at all the
pictures. Glorrie's life had been something.

I went back into my bedroom and lay down. I still didn't know
what to make of Mom's fit, but we had gotten her cleaned up all
right, Earl and me working together to wash her cuts and put her
to bed. I'd wanted to take her to the hospital right then, but Earl
said she just needed to rest, that we'd call up Doc Pistorius in the
morning to check on her. I wasn't sure—we'd all gotten cut a little
in the process of getting her out of the barn. I asked Earl what was in
those bottles—some of them had to be old pesticide or God knows
what else. What if some of it got into our systems? He smiled and

told me to take the fact I wasn't dead yet as a good sign. I finally drifted off, but my rest was fitful; I dreamed of Mom's rage, of the glittering mud in the barn, of Glorrie and the memoirs she'd never had a chance to begin.

The next morning, Doc Pistorius was over before I was dressed. He examined us, looked at our various wounds, told us we'd done the right thing in calling him and that we were lucky that we hadn't gotten a good dose of whatever was in those bottles. He asked to see them, but Earl had already watered their contents into the floor of the barn. Doc asked what the powders looked like, but he couldn't tell us much. I shot a look to Earl, *I told you so*, and he shrugged back at me, grinning casually. Doc gave us each a shot—tetanus, just in case—and told us to keep an eye on Mom. And then he said we were going to have to decide what to do with her now that Glorrie was properly buried. He said it to both of us, but he was talking to me.

Mom was like a zombie all morning, shuffling around the house and muttering things we couldn't understand. It was heartbreaking. I wanted to talk about her with Earl, try to figure out what to do, but he insisted we wait until she was asleep. We sat around and watched our coffee grow cold as we waited for her to tire herself out. She finally did.

It was colder that day, and the skies were so gray they were nearly white. There was snow coming, no doubt. I could smell it in the air. Earl and I freshened our coffees and sat at the kitchen table to have it out.

"I want you to know I'll visit her whenever I can," Earl began. "And that you shouldn't worry about her."

I shook my head. "What are you talking about?"

"I'm talking about where Clara goes from here. I'm thinking the nursing home here in town. It's a good one, and it costs a little more, but I think we can handle it, especially with some of the money from Glorrie's will. That way, I can drop by and see her most days, and you can come see her pretty easily yourself."

"I still don't know," I said. "Part of me is thinking I should come back here. Come back and at least see Mom through all this, until she's gone too. And then I'll go." I smiled, mostly to myself. "And then there's the part of me that's still screaming run away, run away, run away."

Earl raised an eyebrow. "Honestly, Reese? Living your life ain't what I call running away. And I'm not just saying that."

I looked at him. "Maybe."

"Besides, you can't just up and leave your school like that, can you?"

I brushed aside his concern. "The administration wouldn't like it much, but they'd understand. And if they don't, to hell with them. Besides, NCHS hasn't been the right place for me since the divorce. It's really Carrie's place, not mine. This could be a good enough reason as any to get out."

"Well, I don't know about all that," Earl said, sipping his coffee. "Look, like I said, we're okay on money. But you can't just give up on your career. Not for Clara, not now especially. She's going to get worse, and soon. This is probably her last Christmas coming up. That's Doc's guess, not mine. He says people with this disease tend to slip away pretty quick."

"But that's maybe all the more reason for me to be here now, you know? I mean, what am I going back to? What's left up there for me? An ex-wife? A half-empty apartment? Honestly, all I've got is my students, and they'll find another teacher who'll take my place so fast it would make me cry to see it. I wouldn't be gaining anything by going back there."

"What are you gaining by staying? Time with Clara? She didn't even know we were here this morning, doesn't know who we are half the time. That's only going to get worse."

"Maybe I owe her," I said. "Maybe I need to be here not because I'll get something from it, but because she will."

Earl sat back and blew out a long, slow breath. "That's a great sentiment, Reese, but I know how hard it was for Glorrie here. I know the sort of things she had to do, and the sort of things she knew she'd have to do soon. Glorrie and I would talk about this sometimes. She knew there would come a day when she was going to have to help Clara just to feed herself, and that she'd have to help her use the bathroom, for Christ's sake. I know I don't want to do that—and I doubt you do either."

"She did it for me," I said.

"Not the same thing and you know it. Cleaning up a baby is one thing, cleaning up a grown woman is another. And the fact that it's your mom might make it tougher than you think."

"This is already tough," I said, but I had to admit the thought of cleaning up after Mom had been limited to wiping her face when she dribbled soup. "We could get a nurse for her. A live-in, even. We have the room, and it would still be cheaper than the nursing home, wouldn't it?"

"I don't know," Earl said. He looked like he was going to say something more, but he didn't. "I don't know."

"I don't want her to die in an unfamiliar place. Even if she doesn't recognize it at the end, she'll know it on some level, I think. She'll know me. Or at least, I'll think she does, and that will make it better, somehow."

Earl nodded. "So if you moved back here," he finally said, "what would you want to do? For money, I mean?"

"Don't worry," I laughed. "I've tried the farming thing. I'm not going to horn in on your territory again."

He nodded. "You'd keep teaching?"

"I don't know," I said. "I haven't thought about it. I'd be taking care of Mom pretty much full-time."

"Yeah," Earl said. "I guess." He took a long drink of his coffee. "You should really think about this, Reese. Don't quit your school up there until you're sure. Damn sure. It's not that I don't want you back here—now that Glorrie's gone, and Clara sort of is too, it might actually be good to see you again now and then." He seemed genuinely surprised that this was the case. "But be sure, you know?"

"Yeah."

"I'm serious. If nothing else, I don't want you back here if you don't want to be here. We've done gone through that, cousin." Earl smiled. "And that could be tougher on your Mom than anything else."

"Yeah," I said. "Well, this isn't set in stone. Just an idea."

"Just do what's right, Reese. Whatever that is."

I smiled. "Still thinking about it. I'll see what comes."

Earl got up and poured himself another cup of coffee—he offered me some, but I declined. "I suppose you'll be wanting to talk about the land, too, so long as we're talking."

"Not really," I said. "But I will if you want to."

Earl shook his head. "Not my thing," he said. "You're the one who wanted to give me an earful, the way I heard it."

"Donnie talks too much."

"He's a bartender," Earl said. "And this is Moweaqua."

I nodded. "Okay, so I was pissed when I first heard about it, but the truth is, what the hell am I going to do with it? Buy it all, I don't care. The money will help take care of Mom anyhow, no matter what I do."

Earl held up his hands. "Hang on there, hotshot. I'm not in a position to buy all the land. Even adding the bit of money from Glorrie, I can only buy maybe half of it. Glorrie said I could probably keep renting the other half until I could afford to buy the rest later, if I wanted."

"Man, I don't care about the details," I said.

"You're going to have to care. You're going to have to get power of attorney for your Mom, and work this out with me before next season. We'll have to hook up with one of the guys at Ayars' Bank and get them to help us hash this all out."

"All right," I said. "So we will."

Earl nodded. "Okay then."

"All right."

Earl looked at me for a moment, and then asked if he could fix me a sandwich. I said I wouldn't mind it, if he was making himself one, and then I popped open a couple of beers from the fridge. The two of us retired to the living room, put our feet up on the coffee table, and watched college football, just two gentlemen farmers on a bleak November Saturday.

It had snowed an inch or two already by that evening, but the Moweaqua-Lewiston game was still on, and so was my date with Amy. I grabbed my father's overcoat—or I guess it was mine now—as I left the house, pulled my gloves on once I was outside, and raised the collar up to cover my neck and the lower half of my ears. The snow was still falling, and I turned to face the lights of Moweaqua High School—no, Central A&M, I reminded myself—and started walking. The field was literally across the road from our farm's edge, and I could almost see the plays from our lawn, though I couldn't make out what the announcer was saying.

I walked down to the entrance on the south side of the field, where the ticket booth used to sit. It wasn't there anymore, but I could see a newer one sitting up under the announcer's booth all decked out in red and black, the colors of the new Central A&M Raiders. The game had already started, and no one was there to take tickets, so I walked in like I was supposed to be there. No one stopped me.

The game was pretty close. We were winning, but just barely. People said Moweaqua had a shot to go to State this year, if they could hold it together long enough, make few enough mistakes. It was supposed to be a good team, but an old one—most of the first string was comprised of seniors, kids who would be gone after this season. Still, if they had the stuff, this was the season that could win it all. Like my coach always told us, it's this season that really counts. All the crap about "there's always next season" was made up by losers, for losers. That's what we were told, and we believed it.

I looked on the field for number 22, but I couldn't see him. I tapped a guy I didn't know on the shoulder and asked him if number 22 had broken the record so far this game. He looked at me and asked me what record. I thanked him without answering, and walked straight up the left side of the field, under the metal bleachers and toward the concession stand. It was actually just a wooden shed with a counter and an extension cord run out to it, a place for school boosters to sell cups of hot chocolate, candy, and popcorn served in lunchsacks to help fund the school sports programs. They also sold coffee, which was what I was after.

I got up to the front and waited behind a kid who was buying a red licorice whip and a candy bar with a wet dollar bill. I recognized the woman running the counter, but couldn't place her. I considered turning around and forgetting about the coffee—that's how much I hate talking to people I'm supposed to remember but don't—but the kid was gone and the woman had already greeted me before I could.

"Reese," she said, and I realized I had seen her at the visitation. "Good to see you out and about. Come back to relive old memories?"

"I heard my old record was going to be beaten tonight," I said, "so I thought I'd come down and see it."

"Oh, I didn't know they still had records from that far back."

"They don't," I said, not wanting to explain. I ordered coffee.

She started pouring some into one of those small styrofoam cups. "You wouldn't happen to have anything bigger than that, would you?" I asked.

"Well," she looked around behind the counter. "I have some bigger plastic cups they use for sodas, but they'll get pretty hot with the coffee in there."

"I'll use a napkin," I said, smiling. I surprised myself with how easily I was talking with this person I couldn't place. It must have been the visitation and funeral, I decided. No wonder Gum is so smooth—years and years of practice.

She poured the coffee in the plastic cup and wrapped five or six napkins around it. "There you go, Reese. That's fifty cents."

I was bringing out my wallet when I heard a familiar voice behind me. It was a voice threw me back about twenty years, and seemed to fit perfectly this field, this weather, this night. "I think you promised me a cup too, sport." Amy.

I turned and smiled. "Sport?"

Amy winked. "Hey, it's better than hotshot, right?"

"This is true," I said, then turned back and raised a couple of fingers. "Make that two."

"Black, thanks, Barb," Amy said waving to the woman. The first name didn't help me at all. Amy turned to me, and leaned her head up against my shoulder. "I've been looking for you," she said. "It's damn cold out here."

Barb handed Amy her cup, and I paid for them and thanked her. Amy and I walked back toward the field, to see the game.

Amy took a sip, and winced a bit. "Shoot, it's hot."

"Yeah, be careful."

"Thanks," Amy blew on the coffee, and her breath steamed off the top, made little ripples in the dark brew. "So you wouldn't want to go someplace warmer, would you?" She was grinning.

"I could probably be talked into it," I said. "But I'd like to see your niece's boyfriend break my old record before we go."

"Kyle? You missed that a while ago. He had a thirty-yard run on the first play."

"Oh," I said. "I asked a guy in the bleachers, but he didn't seem to know what I was talking about."

"There was a lot of celebrating, but it wasn't much of a deal to anyone but Kyle and his friends. All the records got re-set after the consolidation."

"I know."

"Most people watching the game don't know the old stats anymore. A few years ago, maybe, but the school made such a point of ending all the old and bringing in all the new, they managed to get even the die-hards on their side. These seniors playing now are probably the last kids who'll know the old records."

"Doesn't that bother you, even a little?" I asked. "It's like we've been erased, like we were never here."

"It did," Amy said, looking down at the ground, "especially when they took down the class pictures that used to hang in the halls. I didn't like the idea of that. But it's not like they broke into our houses and burned our yearbooks."

"You still have your yearbook?"

"Don't you?"

I didn't answer, because I didn't know. It was probably still up in my room at the house. Amy looked at me like she expected an answer, but I feigned sudden interest in the game. Someone from Central A&M fumbled at one point, but then Lewiston threw an interception, so things sort of evened out.

"Not a bad game," I said.

"Pretty good," Amy said. "We've got a shot."

"Follow the team pretty closely, do you?" I teased.

"No," she said, looking up at me, "I just repeat what people say every year. It gets me by." She winked at me again, and I suddenly missed every day I'd ever spent without her.

"Well, if I've missed the big breaking of my record," I said, "you want to go for a drive or something?"

She cocked her head to one side and smiled. "I'd like that," she said.

"Good. Me too,"

"Let me just tell Cindy I'm going," she said, and waved at the bleachers far-off, pointed at herself, pointed at me, and then pointed away, towards the house.

"Cindy?"

"Come on, Cindy Frader? My best friend since elementary school?"

"Wow, is she still around?"

"Who isn't? She married Billy Hill, but kept her name. Big hubbub."

I squinted, but couldn't find anyone in the throngs of people. "Can you see her all the way over there?"

"No," she said, "but she sees us."

"How can you be sure?"

"Are you kidding?" Amy said. "She's been watching us through her binoculars since I came up behind you."

I laughed. "You ready?"

"Absolutely."

We walked across the culvert and crossed the street to the driveway. The truck was there waiting for us. I opened the passenger door and helped her in. As I walked behind the truck to the driver's side, Amy had not only unlocked my door for me, but she'd reached over and opened it too. It was a good sign.

"Thanks," I said as I got in and closed my door. "Where should we go?"

Amy shrugged. "I don't know. Take me anywhere."

I smiled. "That's a dangerous thing for a lady to say."

"I trust you," she said. "And I haven't been a lady in years."

We drove through Freddy's Freeze and each got a burger, shared some fries. Drove out west of town, out where the Flatbranch runs, by the old ballfield, over the one-lane bridges and gravel county roads, and back into town, up 51 to Main. Thought about stopping at the bowling alley, but it looked pretty crowded, so we passed. I wanted to just talk with her a bit, see if she was feeling the same things I was. We talked the whole time, but we finally ran out of places to go. We finally decided to head back to the barn, where we'd spent so much time as teenagers. She thought it would be fun to see it again. I told her it would be, but we'd have to watch out for the pile of muddy glass in the middle of the floor. I explained pretty much everything as we headed back, about what had happened the night before, about all the things she didn't already know. Amy was a good listener—she always had been. I asked her for advice about what she thought I should do, and she gave me the same answer she used to give me years before—that I already knew what I had to do. I just had to do it. Amy was always a big believer in that, in me. A lot more than I ever was.

We pulled into the driveway and made our way into the barn. I was feeling all of seventeen again, creeping quietly into the barn with Amy, and I think she felt it, too. I closed the barn doors to keep out the chill, and walked Amy around the debris still half-buried in mud. I pulled the light on over the workbench, flipped on the portable heater, and led Amy back to the Ford Galaxie 500, the huge, beautiful boat of a car I'd spent way too many hours trying to keep running. It was still a great car—I'd seen it lurking in the shadows the night before, and had been meaning to come out and take a look at it again. It was dusty, even under the tarp, but still in pretty good shape.

"God, I can't believe you still have this," Amy said laughing.

"I couldn't believe it either. I didn't know it was still in here." I opened the passenger door for her, and it creaked open on old hinges. "After you."

"You want me to get in this old thing?"

"Why not?"

"I don't know. Is there anything living in the front seat?"

I peered over. "No, all clear."

Amy laughed again. "Okay," she said, and got in, bouncing up and down a little on the bench backseat. "Hey, these seats are still pretty comfy."

"I know. Not bad, huh? Maybe I'll give fixing this old car another shot."

"Good luck getting it back to Bloomington-Normal." Amy said, and settled back in the seat. We sat in the half-lit interior of the Ford, particles of dust floating around us like angels. "Well, we're here," Amy finally said.

"Yeah," I said. "Brings back old memories all right."

"Except we'd be laying in some hay instead of your old car."

"Rolling in the hay," I shook my head. "What a cliché."

"This whole town's a cliché."

"I guess," I said. "But it's been good to be back, you know? At least for a while."

"I've missed you, Reese," Amy said softly. "I think about you sometimes, wonder how you're doing."

"Same here," I said. "You visiting this week really helped me out. Gave me a boost when I needed it. Tonight, too—it gave me something to look forward to all week."

"I looked forward to it, too." Amy paused for a moment, letting the conversation lapse and looking at me out of the corner of her eyes. "So," she finally said, "I heard you got married."

"Ah, now we're getting to the important stuff."

"There's no point in avoiding the question, since I already know the answer."

"Fair enough," I said, and nodded. "Yes, I did. And then I got divorced."

"Hey, me too. Big club, small world," she said. "When was yours finalized?"

"Not too long ago," I said. "Who was he?"

"You didn't know him. Jack's from St. Louis. He was an architect in Decatur for a while."

"What do you mean, for a while?"

"He got a better job offer in Missouri."

"And he didn't want you to go?"

"He asked me to, but he didn't mean it."

"Things were bad already?"

Amy nodded. "Bad enough. Things were never good, not really. I knew that when I married him."

"So why'd you do it?"

Amy looked up into the rafters, and shrugged. "I stopped believing in the perfect man. Stopped believing I'd find him, anyway. I always thought I'd have to give up one thing I valued—the men I dated were either smart but boring, or motivated but arrogant, or fun but totally unreliable."

"And Jack was?"

"Motivated but arrogant. I let myself believe it was a strength of character thing, a self-assurance, I guess. But it wasn't. Of all the things I wanted from a man, I'd put emotion—romance—up at the top. And it was the first thing I sold out when I accepted his ring. He was obsessed with his work and not much else. Still is, I imagine." She ran her fingers through her hair, and took a deep breath, and then smiled at me. "Not that I'm bitter."

"No," I shook my head, returned the smile. "So what was I?"

"What?"

"Fun but unreliable?"

"Yeah," she said. "You pretty much defined the category. Why, have you changed?"

"I think so," I said. "Can I call for a recount?"

Amy laughed, and thought about it for a moment. "Actually, to be fair, I don't know if you were unreliable, really. There just came a time when you weren't there anymore. You just sort of left."

"I guess I did," I said. "But if it means anything, I don't think I knew I was leaving. I don't think I was conscious of it, you know, until I found myself gone. Does that make sense?"

"No," she said. Her voice was flat, but still amused. "So what's your story, anyway?"

"My story?"

"Every divorcee has one."

"Oh, that. I don't know. Carrie and I...we just stopped loving each other. It wasn't really either of our faults."

"She left you, huh?"

"Is it that obvious?"

"No offense, Reese, but when you're the one breaking it off, you have all the reasons defined in your head. Whether they're true or not, the list is there, ready to just spill out when you need it."

"Yeah, she left me," I said. "But things weren't good between us."

"How so?"

I shook my head. "No spark left, I guess. We were out of things to talk about, we agreed on nothing anymore. We were just sort of living with each other, and only talking when we fought. I changed for her, and then resented it. She says she changed for me, too, but I never saw it, never really believed it. In the end, we wanted different things in life."

"Like?"

"Like she wanted an Escort, and I wanted my truck."

"She wanted a family."

"I guess."

Amy nodded. "No, I'm telling you. She wanted a family. That's why people buy cars like that. They're thinking about family, about trips to see the grandparents, about whether or not the carseat is going to be easy to get in and take out, whether the windows only roll down halfway in the back seat, that sort of thing."

"You know a lot about this."

"This, I know about," she said smiling. "When you've gone toe-to-toe with the old biological clock as long as I have, you get to know your enemy. He's very clever, that clock. Sneaky bastard."

"The clock's a he, huh?"

"When you're my age, Reese, all villains are."

"But you're not bitter."

"Definitely not."

We laughed. "You know what I miss most about being married?" I asked. "Or even just being with someone?"

"The sex?" Her smile was coy, and I noticed her breasts under her sweater. It was one hell of a sweater.

"That too," I grinned. "But honestly? Mostly I miss having someone tell me it's time to come to bed. I used to stay up all hours of the night, grading papers or reading or watching Letterman, and Carrie would come in, kiss me on the head, and tell me it was time to come to bed. I miss that. I miss having someone, you know?"

"Yeah," Amy said, her smile turned softer. "I do." We sat in silence for a few minutes, both thinking of what was, I guess, what had been. Amy pulled us both out of it. "So when are you going back home?"

"I don't know," I said without thinking. "I really don't. I've been thinking of staying and looking after Mom."

"Full-time?" Amy said, surprised.

"I guess."

"Do you know what that entails?"

"Not really," I said, "but she's my mother."

"Yeah, and this is your life. Are you kidding me? Do you want to spend the next bunch of years taking care of your Mom?"

"Earl says she'll go fast."

"He doesn't know that. No one does." Amy shook her head. "Christ, Reese, what about your job?"

"That's just it," I said. "I've sort of hit the reset button anyway. Carrie and I are over, and I'm just now trying to get things back in order. I haven't been able to do it so far, felt like I was just spinning my wheels, you know? But maybe I could do that more easily if I were living somewhere other than Bloomington-Normal. Maybe I could do that here."

She shook her head. "What the hell would you do here? You'd go crazy."

"Take care of Mom, first," I said. "Eventually I could get a job teaching here, or maybe up in Decatur. There's plenty of schools."

She scowled as if this were all preposterous. "Do you want to?"

"It would be all right. And I know people here, Amy."

"Who do you know? I mean, anymore?"

"The guys at Sweet's. Earl."

"Earl?"

"He and I are getting along now, more or less."

"Really?" she said. "So when comes the plague of frogs and the ritual killing of the firstborn son?"

"I'm serious," I said.

Amy threw up her hands in mock surrender. "Okay, whatever. But even if you and Earl are chummy now, I don't think that's a reason to move here. I mean, he's already got a life. And I'd really advise against moving back for the bunch at Sweet's. They're good guys, I guess, but jeez, you can find a bar full of guys with nothing better to do than drink just about anywhere."

"Yeah," I said. *And then, there's the possibility of you.* The words were on my tongue, ready to spill out of me and sweep her off her feet. But I said nothing.

Amy got up and sat on her knees, faced me, and took a deep breath. Her sweater was riding up in back, and I could see the pale skin of the side of her stomach. I remembered what it was like to touch her skin. "I worry about you."

"Do you?"

"Yeah," she said. "Old habit."

"I appreciate that."

"You should."

"I do."

She cocked her head, bit her lower lip, brushed some hair out of my eyes. "I think it comes down to this, Reese. What do you want?"

I was having trouble thinking. "That's a tough question."

"It's the only one that really matters. The one that determines everything else. So there it is. What do you want?"

"I want..." I began, and then stalled. "So many things."

"Name one," she said, and then said it again, leaning in close to me, nearly whispering. "Name one."

Before *you* was on my lips, Amy was. The kiss was crushing. Her hand cupped my head, her fingers stroking the back of my neck. I took her by the waist, my hands holding her sides and drawing her closer to me. She broke away momentarily, maybe to gauge my response, or maybe just to look at me. She was beautiful, glowing, and there was this playful, almost hungry smile in her eyes. She licked her lips.

"You," I managed to croak out.

"No kidding," she said breathlessly, and kissed me again. She straddled my lap, pushed herself into me as she pulled me closer to her, pulled her sweater over her head, and kissed me again. I undid her bra and felt the smooth map of her back, the warmth of her skin in the cold barn. I kissed my way down her neck to her breasts, nuzzled her there, savoring the sense of her stomach against my cheek. She giggled, pulled me up, took off my shirt, and then smiled and then kissed me again as we sank down into the backseat of my Ford, just like old times.

It's been said that reality can never live up to the fantasies that we imagine for ourselves, and while perhaps we didn't do everything I'd dreamt of in the past few years, it was enough. We made love in the back seat of my old car, and when we were done, I pulled an old picnic blanket from one of the shelves and then held her close to me as we dozed off there. I didn't dream at all, then; I just drifted away, comfortable for the first time in what seemed like forever.

When I woke up, I saw Amy up and standing by the heater, pulling her pants back on. "Cold?" I said, rubbing my eyes. From the light through the crack of the barn door, it looked to be early dawn. The snow had stopped, but about an inch or so of snow was still on the ground.

"Yeah," Amy said with a grin, "but I've gotta go, too."

"You're leaving?"

"Yeah," she said. "I'm supposed to show some houses this morning, and I've got to get home and change. Not to mention do something with my hair."

"Well, let me get some clothes back on and I'll drive you down to your car," I said, reaching for my shirt.

"Don't be silly," she said. She sat down in my father's chair to put on her shoes.

"I insist."

"Reese, it will take me less time to run over there than it will for us to get in your truck and drive."

"I know, but it's freezing, and it's like, what, six in the morning? I just want to make sure you get there all right."

"Freezing, I'll grant you, but this is Moweaqua. Six in the morning is just as safe as six in the afternoon."

"All the same."

She smiled. "Okay, okay. I give."

I drove her back to the Central A&M parking lot. The only car left sitting there was an old powder-blue Ford Escort. "Don't tell me," I said, getting out of the cab of the truck.

She was already out, fishing for her keys in her purse. "I told you I knew what I was talking about."

"How long have you had that?" I leaned against the truck grill, drawing what little warmth the engine offered.

"It's a '79."

"The year before I graduated from college," I said. The year she and I finally broke our on-and-off relationship finally off for good.

"Around there," Amy said quietly, gazing at the car. "But I'm going to trade up after Christmas. I've had it too long."

I wasn't sure what to say. "Listen, Amy, I..."

"Go home, Reese," Amy said. "And I don't mean back up to your mom's house."

"I don't know where home is anymore, Amy," I said. "But last night..."

"No," Amy cut me off, shaking her head. "Don't stay here for me." She whispered, the words hanging in the air like fog. "Don't you dare stay for me now."

"It feels like I just got here."

"Yeah," she said. "But I've been here. My whole life." She smiled, then, put her hand on mine and looked up into my eyes. "It was so good seeing you again. It was perfect, really. Now go be happy."

"But..."

"Go." She was firm but smiling.

My head was swimming. All I could think to do was agree. "Okay," I said. "You too."

"I will." She leaned over and gave me a lingering kiss on the lips. Had she let me, I would have leaned in as she drew back and kissed her again, held her tightly there in the cab of my truck, but she gave me no such chance. She simply transfixed me there, with her face close to mine, the warmth of her breath on my ear. And then she pulled away, before I could do anything. "We should do this again sometime," I called as she walked away.

She blew me a kiss and smiled, but said nothing more as she walked to her car. *No we shouldn't,* that kiss said, *and we couldn't. We could never do it again, Reese. Not in a million years.*

I stood there in the parking lot and watched her disappear off in the distance. Some blackbirds took wing from the top of the grain elevator, dark waves of shadow against the morning. I took a deep breath of the cold air to clear my head, but it didn't do much good. I was still standing there, just watching the road in the early morning gray, when Phil Bilyeu passed by on his tractor. He recognized me, smiled, waved, mouthed "morning" over the rumble of his engine. I waved back, and smiled. It was good to be recognized.

When I pulled my truck into the driveway, I noticed an odd, snow-covered lump on the planting bench over by Mom's garden. I trudged through the snow over to the garden, brushed the snow away, and found her gloves, her trowel, and a small pile of what looked to be shoeboxes, stacked there like a cairn. I opened one, and found a pair of ladies' shoes: brown leather flats, and well-worn, from the look of them. There were black flats in the second box, and cranberry pumps in the one on the bottom. And right next to the stack of boxes was a hole, partially filled in with fallen snow.

A chill rushed up my back, but it wasn't the cold. I dropped to my knees, grabbed the trowel, and began digging in the icy soil. It was tough going, but in just a minute or so, I had unearthed a man's shoe—a brown loafer with laces that had started to rot away. Dad's. The ones in the boxes were Glorrie's. I kept digging, and came up with my father's wingtips, Glorrie's Sunday heels, and, finally, the old boots I knew I'd left home years before. I placed my boots there on the ground and stared at them, these seeds of mine, my aunt's, and my father's. My mother had planted a garden of shoes, cultivated this fruitless soil, and waited for all of us who had gone before to stop our foolishness and just come home.

The weight of the cold hit me. My hands were numb, my legs were asleep from the knees down. I walked slowly toward the house, thinking about going to church later on with Mom and Earl, and calling the school to say I'd be out for some time while I sorted things out. My feet were frozen, my socks were wet, and these shoes, for now, were still above ground. I stepped in the snowy footprints someone had left for me, leading up to the house and back home again.

Printed in the United States
63438LVS00002B/52-141